DANGEROUS DENIAL

Amy Ray

BARKING RAIN PRESS

NOTE: If you purchased this book without a cover you should be aware that this book is stolen property. It was reported as "unsold and destroyed" to the publisher, and neither the author nor the publisher has received any payment for this "stripped book."

This is a work of fiction. Names, characters, places and events described herein are products of the author's imagination or are used fictitiously. Any resemblance to actual events, locations, organizations, or persons, living or dead, is entirely coincidental.

Dangerous Denial

Copyright © 2014 Amy Ray (www.writeramyray.com)

All rights reserved, including the right to reproduce this book, or portions thereof, in any form.

Edited by Narielle Living (www.narielleliving.com)

Barking Rain Press
PO Box 822674
Vancouver, WA 98682 USA
www.barkingrainpress.org

ISBN Trade Paperback: 1-935460-96-X
ISBN eBook: 1-935460-04-8
Library of Congress Control Number: 2014936335

First Edition: April 2014

Printed in the United States of America

9 7 8 1 9 3 5 4 6 0 9 6 1

Dedication

This book is dedicated with love to Henry and Barbara, my wonderful, supportive parents.

Coming Soon from Amy Ray

"All's Fair," short story in *Love Free or Die*
in the *New Hampshire Pulp Fiction* anthology series

WWW.WRITERAMYRAY.COM

Acknowledgements

Much gratitude goes to Barking Rain Press for the opportunity to have my work published. A huge thank you goes to my editor, Narielle Living, for guiding me through the process with her keen editing skills. And since books *are* judged by their covers, appreciation goes to Stephanie Flint for her creativity and expertise.

Feedback is crucial and I gratefully acknowledge the time and effort put in by Lisa Turcotte, Barbara Therriault, Brittiany Koren, and members of my writing group. Also important is the chance to network with other writing professionals at conferences sponsored by the New Hampshire Writers' Project and Grub Street Inc.

Finally, I would never forget to credit my fantastic family—especially my beloved husband and daughter—for encouragement and support during my journey to publication.

Amy Ray

Prologue

BK Hartshaw stared at the face of the man with the gun. She recognized him. *Lenny Mayhew.* They met less than an hour ago after she spotted someone peering around the stage curtains at the guests attending Max-Maid's magic-themed charity ball and auction. He convinced her that he was simply doing his job as the magician's assistant, surveying the crowd which just so happened to be a mix of Boston's most rich and powerful. She should have listened to her gut.

BK closed her eyes and did something she should do more often. She prayed. *Please, God, help me through this. Don't let me get shot. I don't want to die alone. All I have is Shelby. I need another chance with my family.*

She could picture the faces of her mother, stepfather, sister, and half-brother. She cupped her hands tightly and continued. *And about Max… I want another chance with him.* She tried to catch her breath. *I need time to fix things.* She opened her eyes and glared at Trevor before continuing. The coward was crouching behind Max, trying to hide. *Please, God, let me out of here so I can make sure Trevor didn't hurt Shelby. I need to know she's all right.*

Her interview with the psychic flashed through BK's mind. Madame Zona's first prediction when applying to give readings at the charity ball: "This event will be widely covered by the media."

BK had wanted to laugh in Madame Zona's face. She didn't believe in psychics and was hiring one purely for entertainment purposes. This "insight" reinforced her skepticism.

BK worked for a public relations firm, for goodness sakes; the main goal of the ball was to get publicity for Max-Maids and to raise money for Haven, a shelter for abused women and children. If the event didn't get coverage, she should resign from her job, effective immediately.

Madame Zona had been dressed for the part. She wore a flowing gauze dress in granola tones. She fingered BK's Montblanc pen that had been a gift from Shelby when she landed the job with Lindlay Associates.

"The one who gave you this pen…" She snapped the cap on and off with annoying repetition. "This person will be released from her prison the night of the ball."

Okay. That had gotten BK's attention.

Zona wiggled slightly in her seat and licked her lips. "I don't usually get names but this is coming through clearly." She looked directly into BK's eyes. "Heed this warning. Stay as far away from Trevor as possible."

BK's mouth had dropped open. She'd hired Madame Zona on the spot—for all the good it did her now.

A premonition about a gunman raiding the charity ball would have been more helpful, Madame Zona...

CHAPTER 1
1977

The clicking of someone's heels echoed in the hall. Lenny longed to be outside. He stared at the clock as the second hand swept around and around hypnotically.

"...and the money came from a totally different person than from where the protagonist thought. Who can tell me the source of the money?" The English teacher was droning on and on about the plot of *Great Expectations*.

Lenny didn't know what a protagonist was and he didn't particularly care. Mrs. Melman had great expectations of her own if she thought he would actually read this whole fat book. He noisily fanned the pages of his copy of the Dickens classic.

"Mr. Mayhew, please..." She glared. "Do you have the answer for me?"

Lenny shrugged and turned his attention to the girls seated in the rows around him. Felicia, Gail, and Fatty Patty were the only ones worth anything in this group. The rest were either snobs or kiss-ups. Gail Akers was easily the best looking girl in the class, perhaps in the whole school, with her long brown hair and chocolate brown eyes. *I could look into those eyes for the rest of my life if only she would let me.* Lenny ran his hand over his bumpy cheek. *I don't stand a chance with her.*

Class stretched on for an agonizing forty minutes, most of which he spent staring at Gail or doodling her name in his notebook. When the bell finally rang, he bolted toward the door, unaware of any of the material that had been covered in class.

Cool air hit his face as he stepped outside and walked quickly into the woods behind a water tower a few hundred yards from the school. Teachers fought to fence off the area at the beginning of each school year, but due to budget constraints the space remained wide open. Kids continued to gather there, sneaking cigarettes between classes or after the final bell rang.

"Hey, Gail." Lenny waved as she joined the group. She was wearing a brown and blue plaid skirt that rippled in the afternoon breeze. Lenny wished for a sudden gust of wind.

"Hi, Len." She gave him a friendly smile as she reached into her purse to find a pack of cigarettes. Lenny lit a match and held it out for her. "Can you believe how long Melman went on about that stupid book?" She paused to exhale a puff of smoke. "I thought I was going to fall asleep right there in the middle of class."

"Tell me about it. I heard that the test—"

"Hi, Bruno." Gail interrupted him and turned to face Lenny's friend who had walked up behind them. Six feet tall with thick dark hair and a muscular build, Edward Brukowski was well known to most of the kids at Lincoln High. An honors student and captain of the football team, he rebelled by hanging around with a group of kids that were nothing like him. They were more interested in hot rods and skipping school than doing homework.

Lenny glowered at Bruno.

"Gail..." Lenny tried to draw her attention back to him. "I was saying that I heard the English test next week is going to be over a hundred questions."

"Yeah." She didn't take her eyes off Bruno. "I heard that too."

Lenny kicked a rock half-buried in the ground. *Bruno's head*, he thought, as his foot hit the rock with one final thud. He tuned back into their conversation.

"You can come over to my house tonight to study. My mother has to work late so we'll have the whole place to ourselves," Gail was saying.

Bruno laughed. "Study on a Friday night? Are your grades that bad?"

A burst of unseasonably warm October wind blew dried leaves from the trees, sending them down like extra-large snowflakes. Lenny's eyes darted to Gail's skirt but it hadn't caught it quite right.

"I just thought I'd get a head start," Gail answered quietly.

"No thanks. I'm stoked for Ace's party tonight."

Lenny took a puff of his cigarette. Smoke escaped from his mouth as he spoke. "I'll study with you, Gail. God knows I can use the extra help. I can come over right after work."

"On second thought, I think I'll go to Ace's party."

A pain shot from Lenny's teeth to his ear. He unclenched his jaw. "I guess I'll go too." He mumbled under his breath, "I ain't got nothin' better to do now."

"Hey, Ace," Bruno called to his friend who was standing nearby. "What's the charge to get into the party tonight?"

Ace Simeon bent over and carefully stubbed out his cigarette on a rock. He slid the butt back into the pack and walked over to join them. "For you, Bruno, my friend, no charge. If you come, I'll get me a good turnout. The chicks follow you and the guys naturally follow the chicks. It works out nice for everybody."

Ace scratched his greasy head. "And Lenny, there'll be no charge for you neither. Just bring all your friends. They all do whatever you tell 'em to."

Lenny nodded but a sneer strained against his lips. He'd rather be alone with Gail.

"Not that you're bossy or nothing." Ace backed away, running into the edge of the cement pad under the water tower. "I just meant that you're a leader."

The Akers house was like Gail: a small beauty among the ordinary. There was no peeling paint or sagging stairs like the apartment houses that dwarfed it on either side. The yard was too small to accommodate a tree but two neatly trimmed shrubs stood guard on either side of the door.

Lenny lingered outside. He was going to pretend to be on his way to the party when she left so he could walk with her. His plan was ruined when two of her friends showed up. He darted around the side of the house before they spotted him and stood under an open window framed with stiffly starched ball-fringe curtains. *It must be her bedroom.* His pulse quickened.

He heard giggling. Hoping to catch a glimpse of an outfit change, he stood on his toes and peeked between the puffy balls at the bottom of the curtain.

Gail's small room was filled to capacity with a twin bed, piled high with a collection of stuffed animals, and a massive dresser. Gail was rubbing makeup over Felicia's face.

Felicia's forehead wrinkled. "Are you sure you can cover all my freckles with that? You don't seem to be putting very much on."

"It's my mother's. I can't use too much more." Gail poured out a few more drops onto her fingertip. "I hope she doesn't notice how much is missing." She held the bottle up to the light. "I'm not even supposed to be wearing makeup."

"You're sixteen." Felicia snorted. "She's got to let you grow up sometime."

Gail nodded as she passed over the hand mirror. "Okay, take a look. What do you think?"

"Cool! I can hardly see my freckles." Felicia admired herself, turning her head from side to side. "If only I could cover this red hair." She tugged at one of her loose auburn curls.

"Oh, Felicia, I love your hair. You're never satisfied." Patty shook her head. "I wish I had your color instead of this mousy old brown." She pulled a clump of her shoulder length hair over the lower half of her chubby face. "I'd feel adventurous if I had exotic red hair."

The three friends laughed. Lenny rolled his eyes. Patty had been a drama queen ever since first grade.

Gail finished applying bright red lipstick to Felicia's lips. "Here," she said handing her a tissue. "Kiss this."

MY RAY

"I hope this isn't the only thing I kiss tonight." The girls giggled some more. Lenny was enjoying this look into the secret lives of girls.

"You're next, Patty."

Patty waved her hand. "Don't bother wasting your mother's makeup on me. I'm only going to this party to keep you two out of trouble, and from the sound of things, I'm going to have my work cut out for me."

"Very funny." Felicia held up a pink floral scarf. "My mother would hate this outfit," she said with a smile. "You know how she hates me to wear pink."

"We know. She thinks it clashes with your hair." Gail laughed. "Come on, Patty. You'll look great with some makeup on."

Patty pursed her lips and pulled her baggy navy blue sweater down over her hips.

"Don't be stubborn. You're a pretty girl. Just let me put a little bit on." Gail dabbed some on the end of Patty's nose.

"I guess I don't have much of a choice, now do I?" Patty sighed as Gail went to work on her.

"This will complete the look." Felicia wrapped a black belt around Patty's waist.

"You look great," Gail said as they gathered around the full-length mirror.

Patty shrugged. "I look okay, I guess. Let's do Gail now." She turned to her friend but her eyes went right back to the mirror. "Enough about me."

Yeah, enough about you. Lenny's calf was getting a knot. He sat down and rubbed it. He'd seen enough anyway. All the fake compliments were enough to make him puke. With or without makeup, Gail was gorgeous. Nothing was going to help the other two.

He could still hear Gail. "I know how you feel, Patty. You two tell me I'm pretty but you're my best friends so you have to be nice."

"Oh, Gail, please…" Patty said.

"I don't feel pretty at all. You don't see any boys lining up at my door waiting to ask me on a date, do you?"

Lenny almost laughed and blew his cover. He was *literally* lined up at her door. Or her window. Close enough. If she only knew.

Gail continued, "Compared to some of the other girls in school who go out every Saturday night, I'm a hermit."

"That's not why they get all the dates and you know it. You're not that kind of girl," Patty said.

"I think there is one person who likes me," Gail said.

"Who?" Felicia was fast to ask. Lenny could picture her face all pinched up because some boy likes Gail instead of her. Hell, what guy wouldn't prefer Gail over her?

"Lenny Mayhew."

Lenny jumped up and looked in the window again.

"*Lenny Mayhew?*" He didn't care for Felicia's condescending tone.

"Yeah. I think he has a little crush on me. He's always staring at me in English class and once, I got a peek at his notebook and I could've sworn I saw my name doodled all over the page."

Felicia's eyebrows shot up. "Really? Are you interested in him?"

Lenny's cheeks burned and he was sure the girls would hear the drumming of his heart.

"Goodness, no. He isn't my type. But don't think I'm stuck-up or anything. It's not his looks, it's his moodiness that puts me off."

Great, Lenny thought. *She thinks I'm ugly and moody. Anything else you wanna throw in there?*

Felicia nodded. "He gives me a weird feeling every time I talk to him."

"So, it's not just me."

"I keep thinking he's going to snap at any minute."

"We should cut the guy a little slack, don't you think? From what I've heard, his life hasn't been easy," Patty said. "It's no secret that his father beat him right up until the day he died."

Lenny sank back to the ground. Everybody knew? He thought he'd hidden it well. He always had a believable excuse for the bruises, cuts, and burns. Now Gail was going to pity him. Being thought of as moody didn't seem so bad compared to that.

He stood up and brushed grass off his pants. He couldn't let this get him down. It would be like the old man winning all over again. He knew what he was going to do. He was going to turn into a combination of Mr. Nice Guy and Mr. Funny Guy, and win Gail over.

He'd start tonight. He thought about his first move as he followed the girls to the party.

Ace's parties had become routine since he had found a way to profit from them. Mr. and Mrs. Simeon looked the other way when their boys got a little wild, if they even noticed at all.

Lenny trailed behind the girls. They were lucky it was him instead of some criminal out to rob them. They had no idea they were being followed.

As he walked up the street, he could hear music filtering out from the detached garage.

"Do you have enough money to get in?" Patty said.

"Yes Mom," Felicia and Gail replied in unison.

"I can't believe Ace charges his friends to come to a party," Felicia said. "He even has the nerve to charge the girls."

"At least he has parties. Imagine how dead it would be around here without something to do on Friday nights. I mean, you can only see a movie so many times," Patty said, tripping on the broken cement sidewalk.

"Walk much?" Felicia reached out and gave her a push, causing Patty to stumble a few extra feet.

"Thanks a lot, Felicia."

Gail smoothed her red skirt and undid the top two buttons of her blouse as they walked up the driveway.

"This part of town gives me the creeps," Felicia said. They reached the end of the driveway and stared at the peeling duplex that housed Ace's family and his grandparents. Light was shining dimly through the Simeon's dirty garage windows. "It looks like a haunted house."

Lenny invoked Mr. Funny Guy. "Boo!"

The girls screamed. Then Felicia glared and Patty clutched her chest.

Gail laughed. "I guess you got us good."

"See you inside." He walked past them and went into the garage, ready to deploy Mr. Nice Guy.

Ace greeted the girls at the door of the musty garage. "Good evening, girls. You all look lovely tonight."

Patty was first in line. "How's the party shaping up? Are we too early?"

"Right on time, Patty-Pats. Right on time." Ace had an annoying habit of nicknaming people. The only name he didn't tamper with was Lenny's. Everyone else was fair game.

Patty frowned but didn't say anything.

"Now that you're here, the party will really get going." Ace put his hand up as Felicia tried to give him her money. "No charge."

Felicia tossed her hair back. "That's more like it."

He pointed. "Compliments of Mr. Lenny Mayhew."

Lenny waved from the corner. He and Bruno were standing by a barrel of rakes and shovels talking to a small circle of girls, all of who appeared to be hanging on their every word.

They walked up beside him, Patty lingering behind. "Thank you for paying our way in, Lenny," Gail said. "That was sweet of you."

"Anything for you, Gail." His face lit up.

Felicia cleared her throat and put one hand on her hip.

Lenny barely looked at her. "And your friends." His gaze returned to Gail almost immediately.

Gail was watching Bruno pull something from his pocket. She whispered into Lenny's ear, "Is that what I think it is?" She stared at the hand-rolled cigarette.

Lenny nodded. "Just act like you know what you're doing."

"Come on, girls, let's go get a snack," Patty said loudly. She leaned in close to her friends and whispered, "We'd better get out of here now. I don't want to get involved with this."

Gail spoke for Felicia. "You go on if you want. We're going to stay here for a while."

"Hanging around a cute boy isn't worth it if it gets you thrown in jail."

"Don't be so melodramatic. We'll catch up with you later," Felicia answered.

Patty turned and walked away.

"Want to try some?" Lenny held out the cigarette that had already been passed around the circle.

"Sure," Gail said, sounding confident, but her hand reached out haltingly to accept it. She didn't know the names of the other girls but she recognized them as seniors. None of them gave her a second glance at school but they were staring at her now. This was her chance to show them, and Bruno, that she was cool. She put it to her lips.

"You've got to inhale," Bruno said, laughing. As she'd seen the others do, Gail closed her eyes and inhaled deeply. She quickly passed it off to Felicia.

Patty came up behind them. "Are you two ready to come with me yet? Don't you think you've tried enough of that stuff?"

"No. Leave us alone," Felicia said, not even bothering to whisper.

"What's the matter, Patty? Are you their *mother* or something?" Lenny said.

Patty looked at her friends but they were pretending to be deep in conversation with each other. "Fine. It's your life."

Gail chewed on her thumbnail as she watched Patty walk away.

"She'll get over it," Felicia said.

"What are your plans after graduation?" Bruno asked.

Felicia spoke right up. "I'm going to beauty school to become a hairdresser. I might go out to Hollywood with Patty."

"Good plan," Bruno said. "What about you?"

Gail's face got hot. She couldn't tell anyone that she dreamed of going to college—it didn't have to be Ivy League or anything—a state school would do. She had wanted to study business ever since she joined DECA last year. At the first meeting, she didn't even know what DECA was. She only went because she heard Bruno belonged. He wasn't there that day, but she stayed anyway and learned about marketing, finance, and management.

But her dream wasn't going to happen. If she was accepted somewhere, her mother couldn't afford to pay the tuition. She'd try, no doubt, probably even sell the house, her only asset, if she had to. She always put Gail first but Gail wasn't going to let her. She had sacrificed enough since Gail's father died. Gail bit her lip. "I'll get a job, I guess. I'm just a junior so I have another year to decide."

"I guess that's what I'll do too. Maybe a full time job at the gas station. They love me there," Lenny said.

"Want to dance?" Bruno asked.

Gail's breath stalled. She tapped her index finger against her chest. "Me?"

He nodded. "Yeah, you."

She wished she could check her teeth for lipstick and pop a breath mint first. "Okay."

Bruno led her to the center of the garage where a few other couples were dancing to "You Light Up My Life" from a portable record player.

Lenny stormed out of the garage when Gail started dancing with Bruno. *It should be me pressed up tight against her.* He took a few breaths of the cool night air before he went back inside. He had to know what was going on.

They were still swaying back and forth to the slow beat. Gail had her eyes on Bruno's face, almost like she wanted him to kiss her.

Lenny dug a small white pill from his pocket and swallowed it dry.

Felicia came up from behind him. "Want to dance with me?"

Lenny's eyes narrowed. "You don't even like me."

"Why do you think that?"

He couldn't admit he heard it from her own mouth earlier while he was eavesdropping outside Gail's window. "Just a feelin' I get from you."

"Fine." Felicia walked off. "Maybe you're right."

Lenny watched as Bruno's arms tightened around Gail's waist and pulled her closer to him. He buried his face in her neck and ran his hands through her hair.

I can't let this go any further. Lenny sauntered up to the record player and stopped the music mid-song, replacing it with "Cold As Ice."

It did the trick. They separated and Bruno headed for the snack table.

Gail stomped over to Lenny. "Why'd you change the music while I was dancing?"

Lenny's tongue wasn't cooperating, his words were beginning to slur. "Never mind that." As he started to lose his balance, he grabbed Gail's arm. "How 'bout dancing with me now?"

"I don't want to." She shook him off. "Bruno will be right back." She pointed to a rickety card table where Bruno was talking to another girl. "Who's that?"

Lenny smiled. Thank God Bruno was a dog. "That's Ace's older sister, Stacy Ann. Graduated two years ago, I think."

Gail's shoulders drooped. "He was supposed to be getting me something to eat. I should have gone with him."

"I'll get you a snack." *Mr. Nice Guy to the rescue.* When he returned with a cup of punch and a handful of popcorn, Gail was rubbing her temples and had her eyes closed. "Whatsa matter with you?"

"I'm getting a headache," she said, reopening her eyes.

He let the popcorn spill through his fingers onto the floor. He reached in his pocket and pulled out another nondescript white pill. "Here." He held it out to her. "Take this and your headache will be gone before you know it."

"Is this some kind of aspirin?"

Lenny shrugged. "Sure. What else?"

She popped the pill into her mouth and took a swallow of punch.

"It'll work even better than aspirin."

"What? I can hardly hear you. It's getting so crowded in here." She fanned herself. "And hot." She gulped down the rest of the punch.

"Never mind." They stood for a few minutes watching the kids on the crowded dance floor. "Feeling better yet?"

"I guess so." She pinched the bridge of her nose. "Smoking that stuff must not agree with me. The room is spinning."

Lenny spun around in a complete circle. "Let's take advantage of the spin and dance."

"Sure, what the heck. It doesn't look like Bruno is going to come back any time soon."

Lenny enjoyed the usually stiff and reserved Gail as she danced like she had never danced before, bumping up against him to the beat of the music. People were watching them.

Lenny pulled her close whenever a slow song played and whispered in her ear, but when he followed her gaze he knew she was looking at Bruno. He was dancing nearby with Ace's sister.

Gail disentangled herself from Lenny. "I need some more punch."

Mr. Nice Guy was getting a workout tonight. When he returned, Bruno was talking to her. "I've been watching you. You're a great dancer."

"Thanks. I was waiting for you to come back and dance with me again." Gail's shyness had totally disappeared. Lenny had wanted that, just not with Bruno.

He grabbed her hand. "Then let's go."

"Wait," Lenny shouted. "I have your punch." They either didn't hear or didn't care.

A slow song started playing and Bruno bent down and kissed her on the lips.

Lenny's grip tightened around the punch. Red liquid rose to the brim of the flimsy paper cup and cascaded over the side.

Bruno winked as they walked past him on their way to the door. "She won't be needing that, Len. I'm walking her home." He mouthed, "Her mother's at work."

The door closed behind them. Lenny ignored the Bee Gees singing "How Deep Is Your Love" and the kids slow-dancing around him as he whipped the cup at the wall. The remaining punch splattered and dripped down toward the floor.

Chapter 2

Patty stared at Lenny, her mouth hanging open, as the punch ran down the concrete wall. "She was never going home with you anyway. She's had a crush on Bruno forever."

He spun around and glared. The ugly words flew at him like daggers, cutting through his heart with the truth. His face must have betrayed him because she apologized.

"I didn't realize you were that hung up on her." She reached over and touched his arm. "You'll find someone else."

"I don't want nobody but Gail." He grabbed Patty's wrist and jerked her toward the dance floor. "You're supposed to be the big actress, right? So, act like Gail." *I guess you're the closest I'm gonna get to the real thing.*

"Let me go!" She tried to twist out of his grasp. "I'm not going to pretend to be Gail. It's too weird."

"If You Leave Me Now" was playing. He held her tight as she tried to wiggle out of his embrace. "Stop it, *Gail*. Listen to the song. You can't leave now. You know you want me as much as I want you." He jammed his lips on hers. With his eyes closed, he was kissing Gail.

Patty tried to push him away but Lenny's arms were strong from working at the garage. She couldn't stop him and the kids around them were too high to notice. Even if someone did, they wouldn't dare cross him anyway. Lenny had worked his whole lifetime to earn the respect and, more importantly, the fear of his peers. When he knocked out Ace's front teeth, the message was sent. No one messes with Lenny Mayhew and gets away with it, not even his best friend. Ace's delusional parents had sent him the dental bill. Lenny had paid it, all right, using Ace's money. They never knew.

"Come on." Lenny dragged Patty outside to the dark area behind the house. She tripped on a twisted piece of metal and fell to the ground. Blood oozed from a gash on her knee.

"I'm sorry, Gail. Let me help." Lenny picked her up and carried her. "You gotta be more careful."

Patty hit him. "I'm not Gail! Stop calling me that."

He dropped her next to a scrub pine tangled with an old newspaper and pinned her down. "You are tonight."

She struggled to get up. "I don't know what you're on but you've lost your grip on reality. I'm *not* Gail. I'm Patty and I want to go home."

He put his hand over her mouth. "Quiet, Gail. You don't understand how much I love you. I just want to show you."

And he did.

Lenny spotted Gail as she re-entered the garage, holding the doorjamb for support. He didn't expect to see her back here. The party had begun to break up and the few remaining people were gathered together in little groups. Thick smoke hung in the air. Gail coughed as she made her way toward Lenny.

A wave of lascivious laughter rose from the group as Lenny pulled her close for a hug. He wondered if it was too soon to call her babe.

She backed off. "What are you doing?"

"Don't play shy," Felicia said. "Lenny told us *everything*." She raised her eyebrows.

Gail turned from Granny Smith green to Macintosh red as another wave of laughter rippled through the group. She faced Lenny, her voice rising as she talked. "How would you know? Were you spying on me?"

"I was there," Lenny said, squeezing her arm.

"You can't fool us," Felicia said. "You're no longer Miss Goody Gail. I never would've guessed you'd be with Lenny." Felicia looked at him. "No offense intended."

"I wasn't *with* Lenny. I don't know what you're talking about. I don't feel right." Gail rubbed her forehead. "Has anyone seen Bruno?"

"Isn't one guy a night enough for you?" Felicia's chin jutted out and her tone was dark and vicious.

Gail sounded confused. "What's going on, Felicia?"

The girl next to her coughed "slut" into her fist.

Felicia responded with a coughed "whore."

Lenny watched Gail's mouth open but no words came out. She couldn't see what was obvious to Lenny. Felicia was jealous. Whenever Melman handed back a test, the first thing Felicia did was crane her neck to check out Gail's grade. If Gail scored higher, Felicia looked like she wanted to kick a puppy. Gail's goodness blinded her to Felicia's true character.

"Don't pay no attention to them, Gail." Lenny touched her arm again. "There ain't no shame in what happened. It's all natural. The way things are supposed to be."

"Natural for a prostitute, maybe," the girl said as Felicia laughed. Lenny's vision distorted like he was looking in a fun house mirror. Felicia's head seemed long and skinny and the rest of her body, short and stout. Then she changed shape on him again. Those little pills were strong.

Gail pulled him aside. "Do you know where Bruno is? I need to talk to him."

"You don't have to go," Felicia called. "We're just joking."

"Sure, *Benedetta* Arnold," Gail spat back.

Lenny liked her feisty side. "Do you realize how beautiful you are? You were fantastic tonight. I'll never forget it." He leaned in to kiss her.

She jerked back. "You're crazy, Lenny. That wasn't aspirin you gave me, was it?" She pressed on her temples. "I bet you took some yourself." She looked directly into his eyes. "Nothing was *fantastic* between us tonight. I was with Bruno, not you."

Lenny turned away. *No. It had to be you.* Then, like a wave of ice cold water hitting his face, he remembered.

"At least tell me where I can find Patty."

He flung the words over his shoulder. "Check the lot out back."

"This is Stacy Ann Simeon. Patty was at my house for a party and I think she may have forgotten her sweater here," Ace's sister said into the phone as Lenny stood next to her. They were in Stacy Ann's powder-puff explosion bedroom. Everything was soft and textured, as if he had fallen into the middle of a dandelion that had gone to seed. "Her mother's getting her," Stacy Ann said, and handed the receiver to him before leaving the room.

"Hi, Stacy Ann," Patty said, her voice flat. "I don't think I left anything at your house."

Lenny cleared his throat. *Except your virginity.* "It's not Stacy Ann. It's Lenny," he said. "I want to talk to you about our, ahh, night."

He thought she might have hung up. Not a crackle of static broke the silence. "Patty?" He heard her shut a door. "You might as well talk to me or I'll just come over to your house."

"No! Don't come here. I don't want you anywhere near me."

"Hold on. I think you may have gotten the wrong idea about our little rondez…" He tried to pronounce a French word to make it sound classy but he couldn't remember how Bruno said it. "Ahh, you know what I mean. About us gettin' together last night."

Patty snorted. "It's pretty clear. You raped me." She spat the accusation like it was poison hemlock that she had to get out of her mouth fast.

He felt like throwing the phone but he tried to remain calm. "That ain't what happened. Don't be sayin' that."

"Why? That's *exactly* what it was. *Rape*."

His mouth went dry. "You're not goin' to the cops, are you?" He didn't need yet another visit from the police. They'd be all too happy to investigate Lenny again, especially if they could get something that might stick. So far, he'd been lucky. No, not lucky. Careful. Lenny was exceedingly careful whenever he did a job. Both he and Ace knew the importance of a good plan, thorough surveillance, and cautious execution.

But last night wasn't one of his typical break-ins. It was a drug-induced crime of stupidity. And jealousy. A bad combination.

If he had been in control of his faculties, he never would have given Patty a second glance. Well, maybe her curves. She had a little extra padding in all the right places and he liked it. A lot.

The bottom line was that she wasn't Gail. He'd never love her but he could have some fun with her while he was waiting for Bruno to break Gail's heart. "There's no need to go to the cops if we decide to go out again," he said. "On a real date this time."

"Are you *out of your mind*?"

"Why not?"

"Because you violated me. You make me sick. Literally. I went home and puked half the night thinking of your filthy hands touching me."

Lenny's spine stiffened. "You liked me well enough last night."

"You're *delusional*. And yes, I might report you to the police. You deserve to be behind bars."

That wasn't going to happen. Lenny kicked the wall, marring Stacy Ann's green and white oasis. "They won't believe you. I have eyewitnesses who will swear that you led me on. They all saw you making out with me on the dance floor."

"Who? Who would *lie* to the police?"

Who wouldn't lie to the police? He rattled off a list of names that included Ace and Stacy Ann and even a few kids who weren't at the party. "You know each and every one of them would lay their hand on a Bible and swear to my version."

A long silence passed. "Fine. I just want to forget about the whole disgusting thing anyway."

Picking at her cuticle, Gail waited at the water tower. She watched Bruno, wearing blue jeans and a jacket, walk in her direction from the bus. Ace and Lenny trailed behind him.

When they got close enough, she forced cheerfulness into her voice. "Hi guys! Great party, Ace."

Bruno ignored her and looked at Ace. "You had a good crowd. How much did you net?"

"Not much, Bruno, not much at all." Ace put on a mock look of despair while shaking his head slowly back and forth. "You know I only do it for fun."

"Sure you do, Ace." Bruno laughed. "By my calculations, you do quite well for yourself."

Ace fumbled in his pocket for a cigarette.

Gail stood immobile while listening to their trivial exchange. The tiny spark of hope she felt this morning was quickly snuffed out as Bruno avoided looking at her. She should have known when she felt that quiver in her stomach when he slammed the door behind him Friday night. He was escaping but she was desperate to believe otherwise, desperate enough to chase after him. But he didn't go back to the party like she thought he would. All she found was Patty, crying but unwilling to talk. She spent the weekend jumping from worrying about her friend to willing the phone to ring.

She started to step away but changed her mind. "Bruno, can I talk to you in private?"

"But I'm in the middle of talking to Ace."

"Go ahead, man." Ace popped the cigarette in between his lips.

"Then I guess so." Bruno seemed reluctant as he followed her to a quiet spot next to the tower. Newly painted graffiti boasted of the freshman class's win at a recent pep rally. "What is it?"

"I thought we should talk."

He kicked the leg of the tower. Rusty flakes fell to the ground. "I don't want to be late for class."

"You don't have anything to say about what happened Friday night?"

"What's there to say? It was great and we were great together—"

"Were?" Gail cut him off. "You're already talking about us in the past tense."

"Listen, Gail," he said, his tone like a parent about to start a lecture. "We're both seniors and we have our whole lives ahead of us. Right after graduation, I'm leaving for Cape Cod for the summer to work as a lifeguard and then I'm off to college. I can't get into a steady relationship. High school is our last chance to be free. Now isn't the right time."

"I told you I'm a junior." He didn't even listen to her.

"Whatever." He shook his head. "The point is still the same. Our plans would get messed up if we got involved now."

"What plans? I don't have any plans. Besides, there's plenty of time before graduation." She counted silently. "There's over eight months left. We could have lots of fun between now and then. We could go to your senior semi-formal, the spring picnic…" Her voice trailed off as Bruno crossed his arms on his chest.

"I didn't want to be blunt but we had a good time and that's all." He uncrossed his arms. "It's over. It never really began."

"Oh, I see." Gail looked down at her brown loafers. "Well, if that's the way you want it, we'll just be friends." Tears sprang to her eyes.

"I'm glad you understand." Bruno tilted her face toward him. "I didn't mean to hurt you. You were the one who made sure I knew your mother was out for the night. I just took you up on your offer. I thought you knew what you were doing."

She shrugged. "Sure, I knew. I just thought we had something special together and it might be fun to keep it going. No problem."

"See you around," he said, glancing back at her as he walked toward Ace.

Lenny had known Gail would confront Bruno and stayed within earshot, wanting to know how it was going to play out. If he knew Bruno, it wasn't going to go the way Gail was probably hoping. He was ready to rush in like a hero, Mr. Nice Guy, and pick up the pieces of her shattered dreams. As soon as Bruno walked away, he went to her. She was facing the tower, her shoulders shaking like she was crying. Lenny wanted to punch Bruno and hug him at the same time.

"Stupid, stupid, stupid," she muttered. "This is the last time I'll ever chase after a boy. From now on I'll follow Mom's advice."

"Is that the old one about the free cow's milk or somethin'?"

She spun around. "Oh, Lenny. It's you." Her body drooped again. "Yeah, exactly. My mother was right." She frowned. "Did you listen in on my private conversation?"

Lenny cleared his throat. "I couldn't help it." He pointed. "I was standin' right there."

She put her hands on her hips. "I think that stinks. But you've been doing a lot of shady things lately." Her red-rimmed eyes narrowed. "What exactly did you give me at the party? I've never felt so weird in my life. I wasn't able to sleep because it felt like I was on the Tilt-A-Whirl. I didn't even start to feel normal till Saturday night. My mother was convinced I caught the flu."

"I'll talk to you when you're not so upset about Bruno. You're just taking your anger out on me." Lenny stalked off. He'd had enough practice with that in his lifetime.

"What's your problem?" Gail shouted after him. "Because you're busted, you get mad? Well, forget you, Lenny Mayhew! Who needs you anyway? You're nothing but trouble."

CHAPTER 3

Giggles filled the school corridor which was lined with chipped blue tiles and beat-up lockers. Half the combination locks no longer functioned, thanks to Lenny and Ace. Now they could get in and out of any locker without leaving a trace, but during their training years they had used the smash and grab method. *Amateurs,* Lenny thought. *But you gotta learn somehow.*

The giggling continued behind Gail and him. "Is that her? The tramp?"

Gail whirled around. "What's so funny?"

"Nothing," one of the girls answered before darting into the nearest classroom.

Gail pressed her hand against her stomach. She looked like she was going to get sick. "Are you okay?" Lenny asked.

She nodded but her hand remained in place.

"I can put a stop to all this teasing if you want."

"How?"

Lenny grinned. "I have my ways. A few well placed words and you'll see how fast the busy-bodies shut their traps." If Gail really thought about it, she'd know Lenny was behind it all. No one in their right mind would taunt her with Lenny standing there unless they knew he sanctioned it. But since the night of the party, Gail hadn't been thinking clearly.

She sighed. "Go ahead. I'm sick of all the snide comments that follow me wherever I go. At first I thought I could ride it out by ignoring it but I've had it. Enough already."

"It has gotten out of hand." *I didn't think it would get this bad,* Lenny thought. *But it accomplished my goal. I'm the only one who stood by her. All her so-called girlfriends scattered like cockroaches. She had no choice but to turn to me.* Now looking into her eyes, lined with black circles and sorrow, he felt a twinge of regret for setting it in motion. Lucky for him, twinges pass fast.

"Felicia," Gail said. "It's so good to see a friendly face."

Lenny turned to his locker as Felicia started to brush past Gail. He wasn't going to stop them from talking but he wasn't about to miss anything either. He rearranged his books, touching some of them for the first time since they were issued to him in September.

"Hey, Felicia," she said. "What's your rush? Aren't you going to lunch?"

"Yeah, but I'm meeting some friends."

"Okay if I come?"

"I thought you had gym class now."

"I'll skip. I want to try to find Bruno. Maybe he'll be in the cafeteria."

"I doubt it. He wasn't in homeroom this morning. He's probably out sick."

"Well, I could do with some friendly conversation anyway. We've hardly seen each other these last few weeks outside of English class. I can't ever seem to catch up with you."

Felicia pulled her to the edge of the hall, next to Lenny's locker. He pulled out a comb and was about to run it through his closely cropped hair but he could tell they weren't paying any attention to him. He felt like he'd turned into a ghost that none of Gail's friends could see. Or maybe they were so used to him being at her side that they accepted his presence.

"Listen, Gail." Felicia picked at the book cover on her math text. "I think you'd be better off staying away from Bruno with all these rumors flying around about you and him. You need to distance yourself from the situation."

Thank you, Felicia, Lenny thought. He liked where she was going with this.

"I haven't been able to tell you what's been going on," Gail said.

Felicia put her hand up. "I know. It's kind of been on purpose."

"What do you mean? I haven't purposefully been keeping things from you."

Felicia rubbed her eye. "It's me. All the times you called and my mother told you I was out. Well...I wasn't."

"You've been avoiding me? I thought we were best friends. You, me, and Patty."

Felicia muttered, "We were."

"I don't understand."

"It's the rumors, I guess."

"So when the going gets rough, you abandon me? That's great. Just what I needed today." She turned and walked down the hall. Lenny slammed his locker door and was two steps behind.

"Gail, wait," Felicia called after them halfheartedly.

Gail didn't look back. Throwing her books into her locker, she grabbed her coat.

A Christmas carol drifted out from the principal's office as they escaped through the double front doors of the school.

Gail sat on a big rock near the entrance of the teacher's parking lot. Lenny sat down next to her. She didn't acknowledge him and he remained silent, listening to the tall pines creaking in the wind and watching the clouds change shape in the sky until she was ready to talk.

"I don't know how this happened. The rumors spread so fast. I wonder if Bruno started them. Mom says boys like to brag."

"You can't let this get you down," Lenny said. "Your real friends know the truth. They know what kind of person you are."

Gail snorted. "Real friends? What real friends? Felicia dumped me and I hardly ever talk to Patty anymore. She's become a hermit since the night of the party."

Lenny winced. "That probably ain't got nothin' to do with you."

"Didn't you hear Felicia in the hall? It has everything to do with me! She said so." She turned her face into the wind. "I wish I'd never gone to that stupid party."

Lenny put his arm around her. "You'll get through this. I'll help you."

Mrs. Melman's voice boomed in the open air. "Miss Akers! Mr. Mayhew! What do you think you're doing out here?"

Gail jumped up. "I was feeling sick to my stomach and I thought some fresh air would help."

"You do look pale." Mrs. Melman eyed her suspiciously. "Perhaps you should see the school nurse."

"I don't think that's necessary. I'm feeling much better now." Gail inhaled deeply as if to demonstrate.

"And what about you, Mr. Mayhew? Skipping class *again*?"

Lenny smoothed his jeans, shocked at how easy it was to explain the truth. "I was worried about Gail. I came out to check on her."

"Fine, then. Get yourself back to class." She pointed to the school. "Both of you."

Gail jumped up and started back toward the school.

"Wait." Mrs. Melman put her hand on Gail's shoulder. "You haven't been paying attention in class lately. You used to be one of my best students. You always completed your homework assignments and were ready for class but that doesn't seem to be the case anymore."

"It's just that—"

"Don't explain now." She glanced at her watch. "See me in my room after school."

"Yes, ma'am."

Walking down the long empty hall, it seemed strangely quiet now that the students and teachers had left the building. Shadows that went unnoticed when crowds filled the hall now stretched long across the floor. Gail reported to Mrs. Melman's classroom shortly after the last bell but the teacher wasn't at her desk.

"Lenny, what are you doing here?" Lenny was sitting all alone in the back row, doodling on the top of the desk.

"Week-long detention. A little spitball incident at lunch the other day." He smiled. "It's no big deal. She makes me sit here for about half an hour. Most of the time the old battle-ax ain't even in the room with me."

"I wonder how long I should wait for her." Gail glanced at the clock on the wall behind the teacher's desk. "I'll give her fifteen minutes and then I'm going home." She walked to the back of the room and took the seat next to Lenny. She stared out the window at the kids gathered below waiting for their buses. She could hear the happy shouts and general bustle.

"You look uptight. This must be your first detention."

She laughed. "It's not really detention, right? She only wants to talk."

"I guess not but Melman was right. You don't seem the same in class lately. You haven't been Little Miss Answers." Lenny sat straight up in his chair, waving his hand in the air.

"Very funny. I'm having a major life catastrophe and you're making fun of me."

"Oh, come on, it's just some stupid gossip. It ain't all that bad."

"You only know part of it." She picked up Lenny's stubby, tooth-marked pencil and fingered it.

Mrs. Melman walked into the room. "Miss Akers, why are you talking to Mr. Mayhew? He's on detention, not social hour."

"You told me to see you after school." Gail popped up and went to the front of the room. She didn't look back at Lenny.

"Oh, yes, I remember," Mrs. Melman said, sitting on the padded chair behind her desk. "It's been one of those days." She sighed while sorting through a pile of papers.

"I can come back tomorrow."

"That won't be necessary. This won't take long." She pushed the pile to one side. "Take a seat." Directing her voice toward Lenny she said, "You can go. I want to speak to Miss Akers alone."

Rarely did she use someone's first name. Gail could picture her at home addressing her husband. "Mr. Melman, clear the dishes. Time for bed, Mr. Melman. You have to get up early tomorrow morning." Everything with Mrs. Melman was a command, not a request.

"Yes, *ma'am*," Lenny said, as he gathered his jacket and shuffled out of the room.

Gail rolled the pencil in the palms of her hands. It clicked against the back of the ring that had been a gift from her father to her mother years ago.

"So, Miss Akers, why has your performance been slipping?"

"I've been having a personal problem."

Mrs. Melman cleared her throat. "I'll respect your privacy. I don't like to meddle in my students' personal lives so I won't ask any more questions but I feel it is only fair to warn you that if you don't change your habits, you'll flunk this class. Now it's up to you to decide what should be done. I suggest that you read the assigned chapter." She paused to look at her lesson plan. "Chapter twelve and complete all the homework questions." She looked Gail straight in the eye. "Do you understand me, Miss Akers?"

"Yes, ma'am."

"That's all. You may go." Mrs. Melman dismissed her abruptly and turned her attention back to the stack of homework papers.

"I'm taking my dinner break if that's okay with you," Lenny said. The rush of commuters low on gas was over. He and his boss had finished the last job of the day—a simple oil change that either one of them could've done with their eyes closed.

Lenny's boss wiped his hands then tossed the rag to Lenny. "You can knock off for the day. Go home and get some homework done for a change."

"Such a funny guy." Lenny put the rag in a bag to be washed before leaving. He stopped at the pay phone on the side of the building. Dropping a dime in the slot, he punched in the numbers he knew by heart but not because he ever called Gail's house before. He made it his business to know everything about her. If there were a class in Gail Akers, he'd get his first A plus.

She picked up on the fourth ring. "Hi, Gail. It's me. Lenny."

"This isn't a good time right now." Her voice quivered. "Can you call back later?"

"It's kinda important." A long pause followed while he waited for her to invite him over. She didn't. "I wanted to find out who's been badmouthing you. I need names if you want me to put a stop to it."

"I can't right now. Don't think I don't want your help because I do. It's just too much to face today." She began to cry.

"I'll be right over." He hung up before she could protest.

Lenny walked through the unlocked door a few minutes later, finding Gail still cradling the phone in her hand. He took it from her and put it back on the receiver before sitting next to her on the couch. "You said I only know part of what's going on with you. Tell me the whole story."

Her words spilled out as fast as her tears. "I'm pregnant. The father of the baby doesn't even want to date me, let alone marry me. I'm the laughingstock of Lincoln High and my best friends have deserted me because of it. And now, on top of everything else, I found out I'm probably going to flunk English. I've never flunked anything in my whole life. But what does it matter? I'll never be able to finish high school anyway. I don't know what to do."

Lenny was quiet for a moment while he decided how to use this bombshell to his advantage. He gently wiped the tears from her face with the red bandana he kept in his back pocket. "Let's start with the biggie. Does Bruno know you're pregnant?"

"No. I can't tell him. He hardly even looks at me. I'm nothing to him, just a girl he had a good time with." She took the bandana and blew her nose.

Lenny's fists unfurled. "Are you gonna keep the baby?"

"What choice do I have?"

"There are ways to get rid of it."

Gail buried her face in her hands. "No. I couldn't."

"Do you want me to talk to Bruno for you?"

She looked up. "Would you really talk to him for me?"

Jackpot! He wasn't going to pass up a chance to put his spin on things. "Sure," he said, careful to keep the excitement out of his voice.

She grabbed him and gave him a hug. "You're a lifesaver."

"Anything for you, Gail." He reluctantly pulled back from her embrace. "I'll go do it right now."

Chapter 4

Lenny whistled as he walked away from Gail's house. Pregnant. Not exactly how he'd planned it, but this could work to his advantage. He'd thought he would be consoling Gail about those nasty rumors he had started. He had easily manipulated the kids at school. They were as bad as their busybody parents and one carefully planted seed had grown and blossomed. He'd planned to defend her reputation and gain her confidence and hopefully, her love. But this pregnancy was the added bonus he needed to make her his forever.

He returned to the pay phone and fished another dime out of his pocket. He was afraid he wouldn't be able to carry it off if he saw Bruno face-to-face.

"I thought I sent you home an hour ago," his boss said, coming out of the garage with his keys in his hand to lock up.

"I came back to make a call." Lenny waited for his boss to drive away before dialing.

Ring.

Come on Bruno, answer the phone.

Ring.

He didn't even have to convince Gail to let him do the talking. Things were off to a good start. The situation was under his control.

Ring.

"Hello."

"Hey, Bruno, you lousy school skipper. How you feeling?"

"Hi, Len. I'm doing better. My temperature's back to normal."

"Glad to hear it."

"Haven't seen much of you since you got detention." He was one of the few allowed to tease Lenny. He was the only kid with whom Lenny had a mutual respect.

"Yeah, it stinks but it ain't gonna last much longer. Melman can't stand the sight of me. She'll probably let me off the hook early."

"That's great. What's the news from Lincoln High?"

"Nothing, really." Lenny tried to sound casual, carefully choosing his words. "Well, I guess I do have something to ask you." He paused. A sudden gust of wind rattled the glass walls of the phone booth. He pulled the accordion door shut.

"What?"

"It's about that girl, Gail Akers. You remember Gail, don'tcha?"

"Oh, yeah. Long hair, dark brown eyes. The quiet one—until you get her alone."

"That's the one." Lenny decided to go for it. "I got her knocked up. She told me today." He turned to face the road. Cars zipped by going much faster than the posted speed limit of thirty-five miles per hour.

After a shocked silence Bruno asked, "What are you going to do?"

"It ain't exactly what I planned but I guess I'll marry her. Problem is, I got a feeling she's still hung up on you."

"On me?"

"Yeah, you. Don't act as if you're surprised neither."

Bruno chuckled.

"She thinks there's something between the two of you." Lenny paused to clear his throat. "I'm talking about that night you walked her home. Shoot, the whole school's still talking about it."

"I didn't realize that you two were going steady but I'm telling you, I haven't done anything to encourage her since then. You've got to believe me."

"I know, I know." Lenny stuck his finger in his ear as a truck rumbled by. "Anyway, I need you to call her and tell her flat out that you don't want nothing more to do with her. If I go ahead and ask her to marry me, I want her to know there ain't no chance of you and her getting together."

"Are you sure this is what you want? Nothing against her but she does seem to get around."

Lenny bristled. "That ain't a problem. She ain't usually that way."

"Don't get defensive, man. I'm just thinking of you. I'm glad I'm not in your shoes. You're going to lose your freedom. You'll be tied down for the rest of your life. That's a long time with the same girl and a crying brat."

"I know what I'm doing."

"Hold on a minute."

Lenny heard Bruno's mother say, "Try to eat this."

"Okay, I'm back," Bruno said. "My mother brought me some homemade chicken soup."

Lenny heard him slurp a spoonful. His mother had never brought him soup in his life. He went to the table or he didn't eat. And forget homemade. She was the queen of the can opener.

"Getting back to your situation," Bruno said. "At least Gail's good looking. Too good looking for you."

They both laughed. Lenny didn't disagree. If they were planets, Gail would be the goddess Venus and he'd be the dog Pluto. "So you'll call her?"

"I already had to let her down once and, let me tell you, it wasn't easy with those puppy dog eyes looking up at me. Besides, what do you want me to say exactly?"

"Just what I said before. That you don't got no interest in having any kind of relationship with her now or in the future, especially since she's having a baby. But don't mention about me being the father. I don't want her to think I put you up to this."

"This easily could have been me instead of you. What if it's my baby? There's no doubt in your mind that it's yours?"

"The baby's mine. She's sure of it."

Bruno whistled. "There's a lot at stake. I could be walking down the aisle instead of going away to college. This is my only chance to break away from here, away from the run-down buildings, the bums, the minimum wage jobs. I can't throw away my scholarship. I worked too hard for it."

"Calm down, Bruno. Maybe your fever's back. You're rambling."

Bruno took a deep breath. "Give me her number."

Frigid February sleet pinged off the windows on Gail's wedding day. Gail agreed to take Lenny's mother up on her offer to get married at her house instead of at City Hall. "It will be more personal," Mrs. Mayhew had said in her quiet voice while twisting a dishtowel in her hands.

The home Gail shared with her mother was tiny but it was tidy and well-maintained. The only thing similar about the Mayhew house was the size. It was dingy and slowly falling apart. Cabinet doors were missing, there were holes in the wall, the wallpaper curled at the seams, and the carpet was as matted as Lenny's dog.

Gail was gazing blankly out the dirt-hazed window, sitting on her future mother-in-law's bed in a borrowed lace dress. Lenny sat next to her, blowing into his curled hands. "Sure is chilly in here. We should wait in the living room. The wood stove keeps it toasty."

Gail took his hand. "I need to talk to you. I'm not sure about today. The whole thing feels wrong without my mother here for the ceremony."

"Try calling her."

She shook her head. "She won't come. I don't want to hurt your feelings but she's been crying for days, pleading with me not to marry you."

"Bev ain't one to hide her feelings." He put his arm around her. "I don't care what she thinks of me. I only care about you and making you happy. Tell me exactly what she said. Maybe we can think of something to change her mind."

"Okay." Gail recounted one of their fights, sparing no details.

"Please, Gail," her mother had begged as they sat at the kitchen table. "I'll send you away and you can have the baby in secret and then give it up for adoption."

"I'm not going to do that."

She moved her chair closer to her daughter. "Or I'll raise it. I don't care what other people say."

Gail grimaced, knowing firsthand about the sting of words.

"We could move and tell everyone that your husband died." Her mother thought for a moment. "In a car accident. Yes. They'd believe that."

"No. I've made up my mind. I'm going to marry Lenny."

"He's no good, Gail. I don't care that he's the father of the baby."

Gail looked away without saying anything to correct her. She was never going to let her mother know she had a one night stand. It would kill her.

"Please, listen to me." She grabbed her daughter's shoulders and looked directly into her eyes. "Come to your senses before it's too late. He's not good enough for you." She tightened her grip as if she was going to shake her.

"Let go of me."

"I'm sorry, baby." She released Gail. "I'm just so frustrated. I don't understand why an intelligent girl like you would even consider marrying that loser."

"You haven't liked Lenny from the moment you met him. You never gave him a chance."

"He called me by my first name. All your friends call me Mrs. Akers. It's a sign of respect. And those filthy fingernails! When he went to shake my hand, I didn't even want to touch him."

"It's not his fault. He works with cars. Dirty nails come with the job."

Gail stormed off to her bedroom. "This is a waste of time." She plopped facedown on the bed. Reaching under herself, she pulled her stuffed animals out one by one, dropping them on the floor. When she found Oscar, her one-eyed bear, she held onto him, breathing in his comforting cinnamon toast scent.

"Gail, please listen to me." Her mother banged on the door. "Let me in. We need to finish our talk. I want to get this off my chest once and for all and then I won't say another word about it."

"Promise?"

"Yes. I promise. Can I come in now?"

"Okay."

Beverly opened the door and walked over to Gail's bed.

"Sit down if you want to," Gail said, rolling over.

Her mother took a deep breath. "You know I tried my best to get along with him. The first time he came over I spent half the day in the kitchen fixing him a big dinner and then he just stuck his nose up at it. Said he doesn't like vegetables." She rolled her eyes.

Gail started to object but Beverly continued.

"That wasn't even the worst of it. It's what he's been doing to you. In the month since he proposed he's been over here every day, even on Christmas, brainwashing you into thinking that you can't live without him, that you need him to save you." She frowned. "I've heard him so don't tell me it isn't true."

"He doesn't brainwash me, Mother."

"Then what do you call it? He's got you believing that if you don't marry him your life will be worthless, that everyone will scorn you for having an illegitimate baby. I told you I'd help you with that. No one would have to know."

"I'm not going away to have this baby and that's final."

"Fine. Then we can move and nobody would know that you haven't been married. You can wear Grandma Akers' wedding ring. I still have it somewhere around here." She started to get up, ready to tear the house apart.

"Sit down, Mother. You're the one who's a widow, not me. I'm not going to spend my life lying."

"But why rush into marriage? You hardly know this boy."

"I know him well enough to know that he loves me." Gail folded her arms across her chest.

"I'm not sure he even knows what love is. He's so phony. Who could tell? And all the 'Yes please, Beverly; no thank you, Beverly; let me get that door for you, Beverly' is an act."

"So because he acts polite, he's no good?"

Beverly ignored her. "And to top it off, he's as dumb as a stump. He's going nowhere. What's he going to do for the rest of his life? Work at that garage pumping gas? He won't be able to support you and the baby."

"The pay is pretty good at the garage and he does more than pump gas. He's a mechanic."

"But he doesn't even have his high school diploma."

"He's going to graduate in June."

"What about your education? You think I don't know you want to go to college but I do. I was going to make it work. Instead, he talked you into dropping out of school altogether."

"It's not about what you want, Mother. It's about what I want and what's best for my baby. I was going to quit anyway. I have to." She rubbed her stomach.

Beverly's eyes narrowed. "You see, he's brainwashed you into thinking that it was all your idea when really it was his."

Gail shook her head and turned onto her side. She was done. No matter what her mother said, her mind was made up. "Just go away and leave me alone."

Beverly started to open the door, hesitating as she held onto the doorknob. "Don't make a mistake that you'll regret for the rest of your life. You're a beautiful girl with a bright future ahead of you. Don't let that bum ruin it."

She paused, as if waiting for a response. When she didn't get one, she sighed. "Fine. If you go through with this, this…" she groped for the words, "…this fiasco of a wedding, don't expect me to sit there and watch it. I'll boycott my only daughter's wedding. Just think about that. And think of your father looking down on you. He wouldn't like this one bit. How does that make you feel?" She closed the door firmly behind her.

Gail whispered softly in the empty room. "Terrible. But I have to do it. And it's because of Daddy. My baby isn't going to miss out on having a father like I did."

Lenny gave her a squeeze. "Thanks for standin' up for me." He frowned. With the exception of his boss, adults had never taken to him. Starting with his father, his own flesh and blood, to his teachers, especially that old biddy Melman, and now his future mother-in-law. This seemed to be his status quo. "I think you were right. We're not gonna be able to change her mind. Her reasons for not liking me don't make no sense." He ticked off the reasons on his fingers. "I got dirty fingernails, I hate veggies, I'm a brainwasher, I'm dumb, and I try to be polite. She ain't rational. I don't think I could do anything at this point to change her opinion."

Gail nodded. "I guess not." She picked up her bridal bouquet, a single red rose with its stem wrapped in a ribbon. "When I was little, I dreamed of a big church wedding. My best friends would float down the aisle in clouds of pink. I'd follow in a puffy white princess gown." She touched her stomach. "That's out of the question now."

The phone rang. Lenny stretched to pick it up. "Maybe it's your mother," he said, handing it to her.

Gail grabbed it from him. The conversation had barely started when she smiled. "You don't know how happy I am to hear from you. I was feeling pretty lonely without anyone I love here to celebrate with us. Why don't you come over? The justice of the peace isn't here yet."

Lenny waited as Gail's smile melted. "The truth about what?"

He grabbed the phone from her hand. "Who is it?"

"Patty," Gail said, trying to take the phone back.

"She's got to go," he said, hanging it up.

Gail's face paled. "Why'd you do that?"

"What did she say to you?"

"She said, 'Trust me, Gail, *don't* marry him. He's bad. He'll only bring you pain. I need to tell you the truth.' I told you that today didn't feel right." Tears rolled down her face. "What's the truth, Lenny? What did she want to tell me?"

Lenny exhaled. *That was close.* He tried to make himself look sheepish. "There is something I should tell you."

Gail leaned in. "We should tell each other everything. Good communication is the key to a successful marriage. I read it in 'Good Housekeeping' at the doctor's office."

He turned away from her in case his face betrayed more than he wanted to tell. "Patty and I, uhh, got together the same night you and Bruno did."

"Patty? I can't believe it."

He turned back to face her. "She wanted to go out with me but I knew it wouldn't be fair to her since I knew I had feelings for you. I think she's jealous."

"That would explain why she's been so cold to me." Gail's hand was on her cheek. "It started right after the party."

The doorbell rang. Lenny's mother called to them. "The JP's here."

Saved by the bell, he thought. *The doorbell*. He jumped up and grabbed his bride by the hand. "To Hell with everyone else. Today is about you and me. Let's do this."

Chapter 5
1996

The sun shone brightly as BK Hartshaw swept the porch with a child-sized broom. She paused, looking up the beach to the rocks then down past the endless strip of sand to the south. Gulls squawked overhead, sandpipers skipped across the sand leaving a trail of tiny imprints, and waves crashed in the distance against the shore. Her older sister, Heather, was building a castle by the water's edge.

BK took a deep breath of the fresh salt air. "I love it here," she whispered to a gull sitting in the sand a few yards away. Outside their old apartment, the air used to choke her with exhaust fumes and city stench.

She was already beginning to feel that their weathered, wood-shingled cottage was home. It was located at the less desirable end of the beach, far from the mansions down by the country club but BK figured that the ocean was the same at either end.

"BK Hartshaw, aren't you listening to me? Stop daydreaming and pay attention."

Her spine stiffened. She'd heard that same sentence, or a close variation of it, daily last year from her fifth grade teacher. Junior high was going to be her fresh start. New school, new teachers, new BK with discipline and focus. Luckily she still had two months to cultivate those skills. "Sorry." She turned to face her mother who was standing on the other side of the screen door.

She smiled. "I asked you why you're not done sweeping but the answer is obvious."

"I'm almost finished."

Her mother stepped out onto the cement walk that encircled the cottage and inspected the pulls in her hose. "I need you to run to the store. This pair is shot even though I've only worn them a few times. What a waste of money."

"Can't Heather go? I haven't had a chance to play yet."

"If you finished your chores as fast as Heather, you'd have plenty of time."

BK opened her mouth to protest but her mother cut her off. "Don't say another word. Get moving." She snapped her fingers. "And wipe that defiant look off your face, young lady. Your father used to look at me like that." She went back inside.

Heather stepped onto the porch, tracking sand where BK had just swept. "Heather!"

"Oops." Heather stepped back and brushed off her feet. "I wanted to see if you were almost done so we could go for a dip. I think Mother's ridiculous for not letting us swim alone." Heather sat down on the steps and watched her sister sweep.

"When I'm done I have to go to the store."

Their mother came out of the house with her change purse. "It shouldn't take you long. You can swim later." Her voice had softened.

BK nodded and hurried through the rest of her work. Maybe her mother was onto something. It had only taken fifteen minutes once she set her mind to it. Then she jogged a half-mile to the store to save more time.

"Hello, BK." Mrs. Farnsby, one of the owners of the Seaside Five and Ten, greeted her from behind the counter. A fan was pointed at the cash register, barely rustling the air. "What can we do for you today?"

"I need to buy pantyhose for my mother."

Mrs. Farnsby, tall by way of her teased hairdo, went about finding the right size. "Here we are." She held up an orange plastic pouch. "These should fit. Will that be all for today?"

"Yes," BK said, placing the money on the counter.

"Well look who's here, little BK Heartbreaker."

BK turned around. "Hi, Mr. Farnsby."

"How's the prettiest girl in Seaside today?"

"Stop it, Ed, you're embarrassing the girl," Mrs. Farnsby said as BK blushed.

He tousled BK's hair. "She doesn't get embarrassed by the truth. Do you, BK?"

Mrs. Farnsby walked around the counter and whacked her husband on the arm. "BK, dear, would you like a piece of candy to give you energy for the walk home?"

"Not today. My mother didn't give me any extra money."

"It's on the house. Go ahead and pick any one you want."

BK lingered over the display of colorfully wrapped penny candy, agonizing over the decision. "Thank you," she said, choosing a grape lollipop. She picked up her bag and skipped out the door with the treat.

"We'll see you later," Mrs. Farnsby said.

Outside, BK bent over to tie her shoe. She could hear Mrs. Farnsby talking. "I feel bad for that one."

"Why do you say that?" Mr. Farnsby asked.

BK lingered to hear the answer.

"You've seen her mother in here with the other daughter, haven't you?"

"I guess so. The two blondes?"

"That's right. The mother's name is Jeanne. I've noticed she treats the two girls differently. She favors the one that looks like her."

"Maybe you're just imagining it."

No you're not, BK thought. She'd known it for years but didn't think it was obvious to everyone else.

"I don't think so. Lenora Wigg was in here yesterday. She's gotten close to Jeanne since they moved into her guest cottage. She told me that when Jeanne's husband found out she was pregnant with a second child, he started acting weird and then took up with another woman. Finally he ran off, two months before BK was born. Sounds like he was too young for all the responsibility. Lenora said she thinks Jeanne subconsciously blames BK for him leaving."

BK stood, dropping her bag on the ground.

"What was that?"

BK picked up her bag and ran all the way home. *It can't be true,* she thought, fighting back tears while trying to catch her breath. She sat on the sand-free front steps and unwrapped the lollipop. How could Lenora Wigg, or anyone else for that matter, know what her father had been thinking? She and Mrs. Farnsby got all their information from BK's mother—hardly an unbiased source. Pulling her pop from her mouth, she held it toward the sky and let the sunrays shine through it like stained glass. Her heartbeat had returned to normal so she went inside, putting the nonsense out of her head.

"Here you go." She tossed the bag onto the glossy page of the fashion magazine her mother was thumbing through.

Jeanne looked at her sternly. "What's the matter with you?" She didn't wait for an answer. "What have you got sticking out of your mouth?"

"Candy, but don't worry, Mrs. Farnsby gave it to me. I didn't use any of your money." She started toward her room to change into her bathing suit.

"You know I don't like you to eat candy. Your clothes are starting to get tight. I don't have the money right now to spend on new ones if you get any heavier."

BK detoured into her mother's room and studied herself in the mirror. *First I'm the reason my father left, now I'm getting heavier? Do I look heavy?* She pinched her stomach just above her shorts and shrugged. *I look the same as always.* This was enough concentrating for today. She was going swimming.

BK rolled over in bed and groggily opened her eyes. The pink curtains that veiled them from the curious eyes of tourists walking to the beach on the public path just outside their bedroom rustled slightly with the breeze. Sunshine spilled into the room around the edges and she could see a bird singing loudly from his perch on the electrical line. After a solid week of rain, it was a welcome sight.

She hung off the edge of her bunk bed and looked down at her sister, still curled in a ball, fast asleep. Sliding down quietly from her bunk, BK crept from the room and tiptoed down the hall, pausing to peek in through her mother's open door. The bed was already neatly made. The front door squeaked open as she started for the kitchen.

"Doughnuts." She clapped as her mother wiped her feet. "So that's where you went so early this morning."

"Give me a chance to get inside," Jeanne said as BK scooped the colorful box out of her hand.

BK stepped back. "How come you're wearing the same dress you wore to work last night? You never wear the same clothes two days in a row."

Jeanne's face flushed slightly. "You just mind your own beeswax Miss Beatrice Karen Hartshaw or you won't be eating any of those doughnuts for breakfast. You really don't need the calories anyway." She went to her bedroom and shut the door firmly behind her.

BK stared down the hall. "What'd I do to deserve the full name treatment?" She sighed and took the doughnuts to the kitchen, her mouth watering as she pulled back the lid. Jelly, toasted coconut, strawberry frosted…where to begin? Definitely jelly.

Jeanne came back wearing shorts and a T-shirt. "Couldn't wait, huh?"

"You know they're my favorite." She set her Boston cream down next to her half-eaten jelly and propped her chin up with her hand. "Mama?" No matter how hard she'd tried not to, she was still thinking of the things Mrs. Farnsby said yesterday. Did her mother really hold a grudge against her?

Jeanne measured water for the coffee maker. "What?"

"How come you gave Heather a better name than me? Beatrice Karen sounds like the name of some overweight nun or something. Heather Marie sounds like a ballerina." She scooped some custard filling out with her finger.

"Don't be ridiculous. Your name is perfectly fine."

"I don't like it. Heather never passes up the chance to introduce me as Beatrice either."

"She's just teasing you. I named you after my aunt. You remember her, don't you? She's very well off."

"I remember her. She's the one with the mustache." Her eyes had been fixed on the dark hair growing on the old lady's upper lip when they had met. "Stop staring," Jeanne had whispered in her ear while pinching her arm.

"You woke me up," Heather said as she walked into the kitchen. "What were you clapping for?"

"Mama bought doughnuts."

Jeanne frowned, looking pointedly at the chocolate-glazed in BK's hand. "But maybe I shouldn't have. Aren't you on your fourth one?"

"No. It's only my third. Why are you counting? If I'm not supposed to eat them, why'd you get them?" BK threw the last bite onto her plate.

Heather grabbed the box from in front of her sister and waved them under her nose as she sang. "Fatty, fatty, Beatrice Karen is a fatty."

"Shut up!" BK knocked the box out of Heather's grasp. Doughnuts rolled onto the table.

"You're getting wider and wider and wider." Heather opened her hands further each time she said wider.

As BK ran from the room, she heard Heather gloat. "Sen-si-tive."

"Give Mama a kiss." Jeanne pulled Heather toward her as they sat with the car motor running. "Have fun at the slumber party."

Heather turned to give BK a smug smile before skipping down the walk. BK had not been invited, a circumstance that had sparked two overly long debates. The first was an in-depth analysis of why she wasn't invited. Not outgoing enough? Younger than the other girls? Or, most likely in BK's opinion, that Heather had blackballed her. She no longer cared. The second centered around the fact that, according to her mother, she was too young to stay home alone while her mother went to work.

"Goodbye baby, be good." Her mother waved. "Climb in the front seat, BK. I don't want to look like your chauffeur."

BK giggled. "I don't think anybody would think a chauffeur was driving this old car." She straddled the seat and smoothly slid into position. They drove off leaving behind a small puff of black exhaust.

The sight of the country club and the promise that she could stay at work with her mother for her entire shift made BK forget all about the stupid slumber party. This would be the first time she was allowed inside the club since her mother started working there at the start of the summer season. Her eyes were wide as they drove up the hill that was surrounded by rolling green lawns on either side. Three columns soared from the ground to the roof of the building and black glossy shutters flanked the arched windows.

"Someday I'll be coming here as a member instead of as one of the hired help. I'll go that way." Jeanne pointed to the road that would take them to the front door of the club where a valet in a navy blue and gold uniform waited to park the members' cars. "There'll be no more back doors for me once that happens."

BK's eyebrows lifted as she looked at her mother. "And just how do you plan to pay the dues?"

"You'll see. And it won't take me long either. Maybe by the end of this summer."

BK wasn't convinced by her mother's matter-of-fact tone or her confident smile. "You always have some sort of plan. Remember when you tried to sell makeup, lugging that bright pink case around door-to-door? Or the bad-smelling cleaning stuff that ate the finish off the linoleum after you tried it a few times?"

Jeanne chuckled. "The landlord wasn't too thrilled with me, was he? I left about ten bottles behind when we moved out. I was afraid to pour it down the drain."

"We may not be rich but you sure do try hard."

Jeanne reached over and squeezed her hand. "It's nice you noticed."

"So what are you selling this time?"

"Nothing. I'm through with long shots. This time it's more of a sure thing."

When her mother didn't say anything else, BK turned her attention to the row of shrubs sculpted into animal shapes that extended around the back of the clubhouse. "I forgot how green everything gets since we moved. All I usually see is sand and more sand. The thick grass makes me feel like kicking off my shoes and running barefoot."

"Don't even think of it." Jeanne pulled the car into one of the employee parking spaces close to the edge of the golf course.

A man in plaid pants shielded his eyes from the glare of the sun as he lined up his next shot. Climbing out of the car, BK watched as the ball soared straight down the green.

"Come on, BK," her mother called from the service entrance. "You're going to make me late."

BK ran across the parking lot. Inside, rows of lockers lined the walls and two long benches cut through the middle of the room.

"I have to go talk to the chef about tonight's specials. Wait here for me." She disappeared through a large swinging door. BK remained in place, tucked next to the end of a row of lockers.

Two women wearing aprons over plain black dresses came through the back door. BK squinted as she read their name tags. Amanda, the taller one, dropped her cigarette on the floor and ground it out with the rubber sole of her shoe.

"Don't let Queen Bee see you doing that," said Kitty, the other waitress. She changed the pitch of her voice, jumped up on the end of the bench and looked down on Amanda. "You're at the Seaside Country Club, not at home or in some bar."

Amanda bowed her head. "I'm sorry, Ms. Hartshaw. I won't do it again."

BK willed herself to disappear.

Kitty hopped down. "Who does she think she is anyway?"

"I can tell you. She thinks she's a card carrying member here instead of one of the employees."

Kitty turned the dial on her lock. "At the rate she's going with that creep Georgopolous, she *will* be a member and then we won't have to take orders from her anymore."

Amanda sat down to tie her shoe. "If she's a member, she'll still be bossing us around."

"But at least it won't be day in and day out." Kitty hung her sweater on the hook inside her locker. "I've got to hand it to her though. I've never seen anyone throw herself at a member as fast as she has. And the surprising part is old Stan *is* interested." She turned to face her co-worker. "At least she's keeping him occupied so he's not complaining about everything to us anymore."

Amanda shook her head. "She doesn't stand a chance. With all the available rich old maids and widows around this place, he'll just use her until he's sick of her and then he'll toss her aside to marry one of the country club set."

"Probably. And it'll serve her right, the way she sticks her pointed little nose up in the air as if she's better than the rest of us." Kitty slammed her locker. "She's forgotten she's just a hostess. Nothing more, nothing less."

Amanda glanced at BK and lowered her voice but not low enough so that BK couldn't hear. "Betty in accounting told me that her name is really spelled 'J-e-a-n' on her social security card. She told Betty that she added the 'n-e' on the end because it looks more sophisticated."

Kitty snorted. "Figures."

They both jumped as Jeanne came through the door. She put her hands on BK's shoulders. "Have you met my youngest daughter?"

They choked out a greeting and hurried out of the locker area. BK wished her mother hadn't come back so fast. She wanted more info on this Stan they were talking about. At least she knew her mother's latest scheme.

"They're acting stranger than usual tonight. Rather rude, actually." Jeanne shook her head. "But don't mind them because I have a special treat for you. You can sit out at the hostess station with me tonight and watch everybody in their fancy clothes."

BK sat in her mother's overstuffed chair as Jeanne pulled two leather-bound menus from a shelf on the back of her podium. "Good evening, Mr. and Mrs. Fulton. Two for dinner tonight?" They nodded and Jeanne led them to a table before coming back and marking her book.

"Mama, can I go look around out there?" BK pointed toward the hall.

"No. Stay right here," she said, turning to greet the next customer.

As her mother walked away, BK got up and peeked out the door. She could see into the bar where a uniformed bartender was wiping glasses and hanging them on a rack overhead. A few men sat at the bar watching golf on a TV mounted on the wall.

Jeanne grabbed BK's arm and dragged her back. "I had to pull strings to have you here with me tonight and if any of the members complain, I could lose my job. You're not going to cause any problems, right?"

"No. I'm sorry. I'll behave."

A voice came from behind them. "Jeanne."

Her mother spun around and flashed her hostess' smile. It froze on her face. "S-Stanley. I thought you were out of town tonight." She stepped in front of BK. "I hope I didn't leave you standing there too long."

BK peeked around her mother. *This is Stan.*

He pulled out a fat cigar and ran it under his nose. "Who's the kid?"

"That's my, ahh, daughter," she mumbled, her eyes darting away from his face. "I couldn't leave her home alone tonight."

He put his hand on Jeanne's arm and drew her into the corner. He looked angry as the two of them whispered.

BK sat down, her leg jiggling while he was shown to his table. "Did you get in trouble because of me?" she asked once her mother returned.

"Believe it or not, BK, the world doesn't revolve around you." Jeanne rubbed her temples. "I'm sorry. It wasn't your fault. It was between him and me."

BK nodded. "I've never seen him before. Who is he?"

"He's your future stepfather, if I didn't just blow it."

Chapter 6

The cottage was so small if something was going on in one room, it sounded like it was happening next to you. BK couldn't concentrate on her book. She didn't have to move to have a front row seat; she could see the bathroom from where she was sitting on her bed.

"Where are you going?" Heather whined as she stood in front of the open bathroom door. Sand sparkled on her bare feet from her afternoon at the beach. "You said you were going to take us to the movies tonight."

"I have a date. We can go to the movies any old time." Jeanne picked up her makeup brush from the bathroom counter, sucked in the sides of her mouth and applied a rosy blush to her cheeks.

"No, we can't," Heather protested. "You only have one night off a week. This is our only chance."

"Stop bellyaching." Jeanne removed her robe and slipped on a low-cut black dress. She stepped back to admire herself in the mirror, patting her hair into place.

"It's not fair. It's not fair. It's not fair." Heather's protests got louder as she stomped her foot on the floor, speckling it with sand.

BK marked her page and set the book aside. She could tell this wasn't going to end well. Heather should know by now that when her mother was pursuing a goal, nothing would stand in her way. Hissy fits were a waste of time and energy.

Jeanne looked down at her disheveled daughter. "You need to take a bath before Mr. Georgopolous comes to pick me up." She turned the knobs in the bathtub to regulate the water before putting in the drain stop. "I don't want him to think I have dirty children. Go get some clean clothes and send your sister in here so I can see her."

Heather scowled but did as she was told.

"I have a date with the man you met at the club last week so we're not going to the movies tonight. He's coming here to meet you girls first," Jeanne said to BK.

BK wrinkled her nose. "He's not going to smoke his cigar in the house, is he?"

"If he wants to, he will. And I don't want to see any faces from you if he does."

Heather returned with a fresh outfit. "Why did you pick him to date? BK said he's kind of short and fat."

Jeanne glared. "Don't be disrespectful, BK. You know that's one thing I won't tolerate."

"But you make fun of Mrs. Wigg's clothes all the time. How's that any different?"

Jeanne's hand descended with a sharp crack on BK's cheek. "The other thing I won't tolerate is a fresh mouth."

Tears sprang to her eyes.

Jeanne put her hands on her hips, careful not to wrinkle her dress. "You shouldn't be so fast to judge others. You're not so skinny yourself." A knock at the front door interrupted her. "Oh my gosh, he's early! Quick, turn off the tub." She double-checked her makeup in the mirror before hurrying to the door.

BK let the water run over her hands from the mineral-encrusted faucet. She couldn't believe her mother hit her and she couldn't decide which hurt worse—the slap or her mother's words.

Stanley sat back on the couch like he owned it. He had his feet on the coffee table. BK knew it was strictly forbidden. Usually.

Jeanne put her hand on BK's back and propelled her toward Stanley. "You remember my youngest daughter, BK."

"What kind of name is that for a kid?"

"Her real name is Beatrice Karen but we call her BK."

"Oh." Stanley looked disinterested as he chewed on the end of his unlit cigar.

"And this is Heather." Jeanne rushed over to her side leaving BK standing uncomfortably in front of Stanley. She shifted from bare foot to bare foot.

"So is this all of them?" Stanley shifted on the couch to see around BK.

"Yes." Jeanne played with Heather's hair. "They're very well behaved. They're so quiet, I hardly even know they're around."

"Is that why you forgot to tell me about them?" Stanley seemed to enjoy watching Jeanne fidget.

She laughed nervously.

"Where's their father?"

"He left us years ago, before BK was born. We haven't seen or heard from him since."

BK's stomach tightened. She searched her mother's face for traces of blame but couldn't see any.

After setting his cigar on the table next to Jeanne's carefully arranged display of *People* and *Vogue*, Stanley reached for his drink and gulped it down. "Let's go."

Jeanne grabbed her black beaded purse. "Goodnight, girls." The screen door banged shut behind them.

"He's so creepy." Heather shivered. "I don't know how she can stand to kiss him."

"I heard someone at the club say he'd never marry her."

"Good. I couldn't stand it if he was our new father."

Jeanne and Lenora Wigg sat with their feet up on the porch rail, sipping coffee while Heather and BK sat nearby playing cards. BK was paying more attention to her mother than to the game.

Jeanne rotated her finger to catch the sunlight in the facets of her diamond. Lenora's eyes had bulged at the sight of the huge two-carat stone.

"Let me see it again." Lenora pulled Jeanne's hand in front of her.

"Isn't it beautiful? It's everything I've ever wanted in an engagement ring. It's even bigger than Suzanne Fulton's."

"I've never seen a diamond that big except in a picture of Liz Taylor."

BK closed her eyes, the sun making a bright diamond of her own on the inside of her eyelids. August had come fast, and so had her mother's engagement.

"It came as a complete surprise. He came to pick me up as usual, honking his horn out in front of the cottage and then leaning across the front seat to open the passenger door. I hate that," Jeanne said.

"Yeah. No class."

"Except for the fact that he's in a Cadillac that costs more than I make in a year."

"You've got a point."

"He took me to a restaurant for a late dessert and a nightcap. We always do the same thing since I get out of work so late. It's been feeling kind of stale lately and I'd been considering focusing my attention on this other single guy at the club, but then Stanley took a little box from his pocket last night."

"Rummy," Heather exclaimed.

BK looked at her cards. She held a pack in her hand that she hadn't noticed. She tossed them facedown so Heather wouldn't see.

"Quiet, girls," Lenora said. "Your mother's in the middle of an interesting story. Aren't you two excited about her engagement?"

Heather frowned. "I haven't had a chance to get used to the idea. I've only met the guy one time and that was a month ago."

"Give it time. Once you do I know you'll be as happy as I am," Jeanne said. "This isn't just my chance, it's yours, too. When we have money, our lives will completely change. No more scrimping and saving, no more used furniture, no more cheap hamburger. It'll be steak every night if we feel like it. We'll have more clothes than we can possibly wear and live in a house that's bigger than all our apartments combined. It'll be like a dream."

"Get back to your story," Lenora said.

"Okay. He took his time giving the box to me. He sipped his Scotch, leaned back in the booth and just watched me. All the while, I was dying to get my hands on it."

"The swine! Why'd he keep you in suspense?"

"He wanted to give a five minute speech first."

She groaned. "What on earth about?"

"He said how he's a successful businessman and successful businessmen do a lot of entertaining."

Heather shuffled and dealt the cards. "Are you going to pick them up, space cadet?"

"All right, already," BK said, her annoyance with her mother surfacing.

"Come on, girls," Lenora said, putting her finger to her lips. "So? What does that business stuff have to do with the ring?"

"My question exactly, although I didn't actually have the nerve to ask. He went on about how, since his housekeeper left last winter, he hasn't found anyone who can handle all the party planning and still run the house smoothly. And how he knew from the way I work at the club that I'm efficient and can handle people."

"Are you joking? It sounds like he wants to hire you."

"I'll tell you, the smile froze right on my face. I didn't know where he was going with it but then he pushed the candle from the middle of the table and grabbed my hand."

"Phew."

"Not so fast. He told me he ran a background check on me and that I was the right girl for the job."

Lenora frowned. "Did he actually call you a *girl*?"

"Uh-huh. Stanley's not up on the women's lib movement."

"I guess not."

"Well, I just yanked my hand back and asked him what kind of job he was talking about. That's when he finally said he wanted me to be his wife."

A gull squawked a long echoing cry overhead. *I couldn't have said it better myself,* BK thought. She wasn't sure how she felt about sharing her mother with Stanley.

Lenora continued prodding for information. "Then what's that business about a background check?"

"He said it was just a formality, that a man in his position has to protect himself."

"I see."

"It sounds like this is just another business deal to him but love and romance aren't what I'm looking for either. I married for love the first time and it got me nowhere. I've been stuck in dead-end jobs for years trying to support two kids on my own. Now I want money, position, and power, and Stanley Georgopolous can give that to me."

"Are you sure about this? Mr. Right may come along and you'll be stuck with Big Stan, the car man."

A crisp breeze blew off the water, clearing BK's mind. She knew the answer. Her mother loved money more than any man. Not more than her children, BK didn't think, but definitely more than a man.

"Stanley's my best bet. I have an investment in him. I've used every spare moment to charm him, clinging to his every word and laughing at all his awful jokes that are usually bigoted or degrading to women."

"Maybe that should be telling you something," Lenora said.

"I know he's no prince but I'm willing to do almost anything to make my dreams come true. There is a catch though."

Lenora rolled her eyes. "There always is. What is it?"

"His daughter will be coming for her annual visit next week. She has to approve of me."

Jeanne put on a pair of sunglasses. "Today is going to be the biggest test of our lives. Evangelina Georgopolous holds our future in her hands. Stanley took today off and arranged this picnic by his pool just so she could meet us. Make sure she likes you."

"How could she not?" Heather said, fanning herself with a piece of junk mail forgotten on the backseat. BK had been asked to unroll the car windows an hour before but she got distracted by a monarch butterfly and only opened them ten minutes ago.

Jeanne spoke firmly. "These are the ground rules. Absolutely no fighting, no talking back to me, and you're both to be extra nice to Evangelina. Understood?"

"Yes," the girls answered.

"And remember your manners. Say please and thank you even if you're talking to the maid."

"We've got it, already," Heather said.

Jeanne backed the car out of the driveway. "I don't know what I'm going to say to this girl. She has already traveled around the world with her mother and stepfather."

"We're not going to have anything in common," BK said, absently biting a hangnail.

"Let's brainstorm things we can talk about that might be of interest to her. I really don't know very much about her home life. Stanley's only mentioned his ex-wife once after having a few too many drinks. I gathered that the divorce was bitter."

"Animals," BK suggested.

"Fashion," Heather said.

"Maybe it won't be so hard after all," Jeanne said. As she steered the car up the crushed rock driveway, BK got her first close-up look at Stanley's house, although house wasn't an adequate description of his eight thousand square foot mansion. Set safely back from the edge of a steep cliff, Cliffside Manor overlooked the crashing waves of the Atlantic. A wall built from stones from the beach separated the property from the busy road that was often jammed with tourists looking at the grand oceanfront estates.

A butler rushed to the car to open Jeanne's door. "May I help you unload, Mrs. Hartshaw?"

Jeanne stepped from her old blue station wagon and handed him the keys. "The round one opens the back. There are a few bags we'll need by the pool."

"Very good, ma'am."

Even newly washed and waxed, the car looked dilapidated, given its surroundings. The butler, however, showed no surprise.

BK covered her mouth with one hand as she stared at the mansion. Her mother was right when she said, "Stanley does everything big—his yacht, his pool, his car dealership, his home, all huge." Their cottage seemed like a dollhouse in comparison.

Heather poked her ribs. "That butler guy told us to follow him. Aren't you coming?"

Stanley appeared at the door and gave Jeanne a quick kiss that missed her lips.

"Hello, Mr. Georgopolous." Heather smiled sweetly as BK fell in line behind her sister to give him a perfunctory kiss on the cheek. Stanley visibly stiffened as they approached. BK gulped a breath and held it to avoid the smell of his cigar-tainted breath.

"You girls go around back while I give your mother a tour of the house."

"Can I come too?" BK asked.

"Beatrice Karen Hartshaw," Jeanne said in a spurious southern accent. "Where are your manners? You'll wait for us outside as Mr. Georgopolous said."

"Yes'um." BK caught a nasty look from her mother who, although born in Georgia, had moved north as a child and had lost her accent long ago.

They followed the butler to the backyard. Sunlight reflecting off the pool temporarily blinded BK. She put her hand up to her forehead and squinted.

"What are you staring at, four-eyes?"

A heavyset girl, with her hairy arms crossed over her chest, was reclining on a striped lawn chair.

Heather approached the unfriendly girl and stood next to her. "You must be Vangie."

Evangelina mimicked Heather's bubbly tone. "I guess you must be Feather and KB. And for the record, my name is E-van-gel-ina." She carefully sounded out each syllable. "Not Vangie or Lina or any other stupid nickname you can come up with."

Heather shrugged. "I'm Heather and four-eyes is BK."

With a smirk, Evangelina pulled a chair over and invited her to sit down.

BK wandered over to the edge of the pool and was tempted to dangle her feet in the clear water. She dipped her fingers in and drew invisible pictures instead.

Two hands on her back suddenly propelled her forward. Her startled scream was silenced as water filled her mouth and she sank to the bottom of the pool. Panicking, she flailed her arms until she felt the side of the pool. She pulled herself up, coughing and spitting water. Evangelina and Heather were laughing.

"I see you're not much of a swimmer, four-eyes."

"What happened?" Jeanne's high-pitched voice rang from one of the open second story windows.

"The klutz fell in the pool," Heather yelled before BK could open her mouth.

"Go change into your suits in the pool house. I'll be right down. And be more careful, BK."

BK shook her head as she walked to a building dotted with life preservers and buoys. *This is going to be a real fun day,* she thought.

When BK emerged from the pool house a few minutes later wearing her favorite yellow swimsuit covered with daisies, she heard Jeanne groan. "What possessed you to bring that suit?" Jeanne wrinkled her nose and turned to Heather. "Can you believe she wore that faded old thing *here* of all places?"

"Leave it to you to wear that flower-power suit when you know Mama is trying to make a good impression. It's embarrassing enough when we're home and hardly anyone sees it."

"Nice suit," Evangelina said, obviously eavesdropping on their hushed conversation.

"Thanks, Vangie." BK stuck her tongue out when her mother looked in the other direction.

"I think it's nice." BK turned around to see a girl with straight black hair behind them.

"You would," Evangelina muttered under her breath before flashing the girl a fake smile. "This is Dad's neighbor, Shelby Fulton." She thrust her thumb in the direction of the house next door. "My father lets her come over to use the pool."

"You must be Tom and Suzanne Fulton's daughter," Jeanne gushed.

The girl nodded. "You know my parents?"

"From the club. I'm Mrs. Hartshaw." Jeanne took great delight in letting people think she was a member. "These are my daughters, Heather and BK."

Shelby gave them a shy smile as Heather and Evangelina went back to their chairs at the edge of the pool.

"Want to go for a swim?" BK asked.

"Sure." Shelby dove in, splashing water all over BK.

The two girls laughed as they started a splashing war, deliberately spraying water in Heather and Evangelina's direction.

"Cut it out," Heather screamed, brushing water droplets off her pink bathing suit.

The two conspirators grinned and managed to get them wet again.

Chapter 7

Trevor woke with a start, his father hovering over him as he lay in his bed. Lenny's face was a deep shade of red. Beads of sweat clung to his forehead and veins popped out like mud worms on his neck, straining against his pitted skin. His lips pulled tight across his teeth.

"You baby!"

"What'd I do?" Trevor asked, rubbing his eyes hard to stop his tears before they escaped and betrayed him. "I ain't no baby. I'm almost seven. Mommy said my birthday is just a few weeks away."

Lenny's screaming continued. "You wet the goddamn bed again. You sure don't act like no kid going into the second grade. Maybe we should send you to nursery school instead."

Clammy sweat began to cover Trevor's body as his father ripped back the bedding. The chill of the morning air sent a shiver up his spine. He instinctively pulled his knees up to his chest. He had already learned in his short lifetime that the best defense was to try to make his body a smaller target for the inevitable blows.

"I don't know what to do about you, boy. All curled up like the little turd that you are. Can't take your punishment without turning into a cry baby."

The acrid odor of urine drifted up to Trevor's nose. It replaced the morning smells with which other children were familiar: coffee brewing, eggs frying, bread toasting. The happy sounds of morning were missing too. No mommies clanging pots and pans, daddies shaving, or brothers and sisters playing. Trevor knew none of these.

"I ain't no cry baby. I don't cry or scream or nothing."

The louder Trevor cried out, the harder his father would hit. His screams used to pierce the household silence as he begged for him to stop or for someone to help.

No one ever came.

His mother stayed away until it was almost over. Now he knew it was best to keep quiet and hope that the beating wouldn't last too long.

"I ain't gonna have no boy of mine peeing his bed."

Lenny raised his hand, paused momentarily as Trevor inhaled sharply, then struck him on the side of his head.

The pain reminded him of the day Mrs. Gorman stepped on his foot. Mrs. Gorman worked at the office at his school and wore the highest heels he had ever seen. "I'm so sorry I hurt you," she had said, giving him a hug. "Such a brave boy not to cry. Come pick out a goody." She led him to her desk and opened the top drawer.

His eyes had lit up at the selection of candy. "This is as good as a store 'cept you don't need no money."

"Any money," she corrected. "Go ahead, take one."

But this time he knew there would be no apologies, no candies, no hugs, just more pain.

A barely audible moan escaped from Trevor with the second blow to his head. His father continued yelling and hitting him but he didn't listen because he was concentrating, trying to hear the faint footsteps heading toward him in the hallway. As the new day faded from view, he knew it would be all right. Mommy was coming. She would fix everything.

Just as his mother's face appeared in the doorway, the sun stopped shining and a darkness black as a night with a cloud-covered moon descended upon Trevor.

When he woke again, his mother was holding a washcloth wrapped around ice cubes on his face. There was a pounding in his head noisier than the drum beat in the Fourth of July parade last summer. He pictured all the people in the band playing their instruments while marching up the street. There were big animals throwing candy as children rushed to pick it off the ground. He knew that they weren't real animals, just grown-ups dressed in costumes. His father had told him that. Just like Santa Claus and the Easter Bunny.

"Trevor." He could hear his mother's voice but it sounded far away. "Wake up, Trevor."

He tried to focus on his mother's face. "You look all blurry and you have four eyes." As his vision cleared, he could see a big red bump on her face. Moaning, he held onto his throbbing head.

"Wait right here and I'll get you some aspirin. Don't make any noise because Daddy is reading his newspaper in the kitchen."

Trevor realized that he was on the couch, his father's space on the weekends. He had to move before he got in trouble. As he slowly sat up, the washcloth fell from the edge of the couch sending ice bouncing noisily across the linoleum floor. He froze, waiting for his father to burst through the archway that separated the living room from the kitchen. Nothing happened, so he carefully climbed off the couch and headed for a chair on the other side of the room. When dizziness overcame him, he fell to his knees and crawled across the cold floor.

"Why are you crawling around on the floor?" His mother's voice, as softly as she was speaking, hurt his head and he whimpered softly.

"Is that kid causing trouble again?" Lenny barked from the other room.

"No. Everything's okay," Gail called back in a singsong voice like she was trying to turn her words into a soothing lullaby.

Setting the aspirin on the end table, she picked Trevor up and placed him gently on the couch. "We need to be very quiet. Daddy has a hangover. Besides, you need to rest for a while." She handed him the glass of water and foul orange-flavored aspirin. "Take these. They'll help your head feel better."

He chewed the pills obediently and washed the taste away with the water. She took the empty glass from him, set it on the table, and sat next to him.

"Do you remember that Daddy got mad at you this morning because you wet the bed again?"

"Yes," Trevor answered, lowering his eyes.

"Quiet, remember?" She put her index finger to her lips.

"Right," he whispered.

"You're a big boy now." As his mother leaned in close to him, he could feel her warm breath on his face. "You have to grow up and stop wetting the bed. Then Daddy won't have to get mad at you anymore."

"I'll try." Although Trevor didn't know how since it happened while he was sleeping. He wasn't doing it on purpose. He reached up and felt the bump on his mother's head. "Did he hurt you too?"

She nodded. "I came in before he was done with you. He got a little mad at me but I'll be okay."

Trevor's fingers moved to the bumpy lines on her arm. "I'm glad he don't stick me with needles like he does to you. Don't it hurt?" Trevor never saw her try to stop him but she didn't seem happy about it either. He looked at his mother's eyes. They were framed with faint wrinkles. "You never cry."

"Never mind that. It's grown-up stuff." She pulled him onto her lap. "Just rest now."

A clock, sitting up high on a dark pine shelf, ticked loudly in the silent house. He watched its pendulum swing back and forth until he couldn't keep his eyes open any longer.

"How are you feeling?" his mother asked after some time had passed.

"A little better. My head don't hurt so much now."

"I'm glad." She bent down and kissed his forehead. "Now be a good boy. Go in the kitchen and give Daddy an apology."

"But he ain't going to take it."

"I know." Gail sighed. "But he expects one anyway. If he doesn't get it, you know what'll happen."

Trevor didn't protest any further. As he got up, his knees buckled. He was able to catch the arm of the couch before he fell.

"Daddy," he whispered from under the archway. He tried to get Lenny's attention without arousing any anger. "I'm sorry for wetting my bed last night."

Lenny looked up from his newspaper and swirled the coffee in his chipped motorcycle cup. Trevor knew the letters on the side spelled out Daddy's name. The motorcycle's back wheel was almost missing, flaking away like the paint on the walls around him. The dingy kitchen was lit only by a single exposed bulb suspended by wires in the center of the ceiling. Dominating the small room was a marred maple table that left only a narrow path from the side door to the archway into the living room. A sun-shaped magnet held Trevor's latest work of art onto the front of their wheezing refrigerator.

A smirk crossed Lenny's lips as he answered the apology. "You should be ashamed of yourself. Are you ashamed of yourself?"

"Y-yes."

"I can't hear you," he sang.

He spoke louder. "Yes."

"Good. I have the solution to your problem." He reached into his shirt pocket and pulled out a clothespin. "This will stop you from peeing the bed, won't it?" He laughed spitefully as he squeezed the clothespin open and let it snap shut.

Trevor's mouth dropped open. "But...but...that hurt me when you put it on my lips."

"And why did I have to do that to you?"

"'Cuz you wanted me to be quiet."

"And were you?"

"Yes."

"Then it worked, didn't it? Guess it'll do the job again. We'll find out tonight."

Trevor knew he should just turn around and retreat to the safety of the living room but the thought of going to bed with that pin pinching him was more than he could bear.

"No!" He yelled as loud as he could, watching with pleasure as his father held onto his head.

Gail put her hand over Trevor's mouth from behind. "Quiet! Are you going to do anything right today? All you had to do was apologize and leave the room."

"Shut up. Both of you," Lenny hissed. "My goddamn head is killing me."

Trevor looked up to see Gail close her eyes and rub the tangled mess on the back of her head.

He twisted away from his mother like a ninja. "You ain't gonna put that on me," he bellowed. "Mommy won't let you." He sprinted away before Lenny had a chance to get up from his chair.

Trevor could hear his father's footsteps thundering toward him just before the couch tipped forward, exposing him. Pillows fell onto the floor. His mother stood back, shaking.

"Leave me alone," Trevor shrieked. "I hate you. I hate you. I hate you." He could see his father's temple throbbing.

"You're gonna pay for this." Lenny grabbed him by the waist of his pajama pants and carried him, kicking and writhing, back into the kitchen.

"I'm gonna run away and never come back and then you'll never see me again."

"That's fine with me," Lenny spat as he deposited him on the floor with a thud. He swung his foot out but Trevor scurried under the table. Lenny's boot hit the table instead, cracking the old wooden leg.

"Damn it! Now look what you made me do. Get back here right now."

"No!"

Lenny squatted and grabbed one of his son's bare feet. He pulled his toes in opposite directions until one made a popping noise. Trevor dug his nails into the lower rung of a chair as his father played his sadistic version of tug-o-war.

"Stop! I'll come out."

"What on earth is going on in here?"

No one had heard Gail's mother knocking at the back door. Lenny immediately loosened his grip on Trevor's foot and he broke free, crawling over to his grandmother. "Gram," he said, latching onto her leg.

Lenny took a step back.

"What happened to you, sweetheart?" Beverly bent down and scooped up her grandson. She kissed the red mark on the side of his head.

"I peed the bed and—"

"He fell down and hit his head trying to get to the bathroom in time." Lenny forced a laugh. "Just now the little guy got himself stuck under the table and I had to try to pull him out. Ain't that right, boy?"

Trevor nodded in agreement.

"Is that so?" Beverly looked at Trevor and then stared at Lenny over the top of her glasses. "Where's my daughter?"

"She's gone out to the store to pick up some cigarettes." Lenny silenced Trevor with a look. "She probably won't be back for a while."

"Are you sure she's not here? The car's out front."

"She walked."

Beverly tried to peek around him into the living room. "You know what I think, Lenny? I think you've been doing your best to keep Gail and me apart. You used to let us talk even though you were always hovering, monitoring every word. But now you don't let me anywhere near her."

"If you think there's some kind of plot against you, you're crazy, Bev."

"Then how do you explain why I haven't seen her in weeks? I get an occasional phone call, if I'm lucky."

"Maybe she don't want to see you no more."

"Nonsense."

"What can I say?" He shrugged. "She's out."

"I find that very odd. She knew I was coming to pick up Trevor. She asked me a week ago if I would keep him so you two could go out tonight." She set Trevor down in a chair. "He's not even dressed yet. Does she even have a bag packed for him?"

"I'll check his room." Lenny disappeared for a few moments. When he returned, he tossed some clothes at Trevor. They hit him on the chest before dropping to the floor. "Go get dressed. Don't keep your *grandmaw* waiting."

Trevor grabbed the clothes and limped into the bathroom to change. "I'll be right back, Gram." He kept the door open so he could hear.

"It's all right, sweetie. Don't rush. I'll wait for you."

"Here." Lenny pushed a paper bag stuffed full of malodorous clothes into her arms. "That should be enough for him to wear. Go put it in your car and I'll send him out as soon as he's done."

"Tell Gail that I'm sorry I missed her and I want to talk to her." She spoke louder. "And tell her I love her."

"Sure thing." Lenny slammed the door behind her.

"I'm ready," Trevor exclaimed as he stepped outside into the bright sunlight. Beverly already had the car door open for him.

"You're a different boy once you're out of that house. Look at you. You're all smiles."

He reached over and touched her hand after he got settled in the passenger seat. "I'm happy to be with you, Gram."

"Would you like to stop for an ice cream cone before we go back to my house?"

"Yeah. Can I have two? I'm hungry now that my headache is better."

She glanced over at him as they pulled away from the curb. "Haven't you eaten lunch yet?"

"Nope. I ain't had nothing to eat all day."

"Don't say 'ain't.' You don't want to sound like your father, do you?" Trevor looked out the window and shook his head slightly. "Didn't you have breakfast?"

"Nope."

She bit her lip. "We can't let this go on any longer. I'm going to have to do something drastic. Things are not getting any better even though I had a secret talk with your mom last week." She glanced at Trevor. "But don't say anything to your father. He'll get mad."

Trevor shook his head. "I won't."

"Your father's full of fast talk and explanations but I don't believe half of what he says. You have too many bumps and bruises. It's not normal." She reached over and tickled his ribs. "If you're so accident prone, I'd know it. I take care of you enough. How many times have I heard your father say how clumsy you are? How you fell off a swing at the park, how you burned yourself on a cigarette, how you tripped on a toy, how you were in a fight with a neighborhood kid? The list of excuses is endless but I don't buy it. You act like a normal little boy when you're with me. A few minor accidents here and there, but nothing like you're supposedly having at home."

A tear rolled down Trevor's cheek. "I ain't supposed to talk about it. Daddy said *never*."

Beverly squeezed his arm. "I don't expect you to stand up against Lenny when you're petrified of him. It doesn't take a genius to guess that he threatens you to keep your mouth shut."

She glanced over at Trevor as she drove into the parking lot of the diner where she worked. "Why are you taking your shoe off, honey?"

"My foot's sore."

She pulled into a parking space.

"Let me see." She carefully removed his grimy sock.

"Ouch," he said, wincing.

"Oh my God. Your father did this." She looked at Trevor's swollen purple toe. "This is the last straw."

Trevor shrugged. He knew enough to keep his mouth shut.

Chapter 8

Early Monday morning Beverly readied herself and Trevor for a trip to the Child Welfare Office. As she laid out her best dress, she rehearsed what she wanted to say.

"I don't know why I'm so nervous. One look at you will convince them that your father is abusive."

Trevor snapped imitation LEGOs together as he waited. He had a bad feeling about what his grandmother was about to do today. He knew his father was not going to like it and if his father wasn't happy, no one else would be either.

It was already uncomfortably warm at nine o'clock as they walked to one of the tallest buildings in Philadelphia. A pigeon-lined statue stood guard at the top of the cement steps. Temperatures were predicted to soar today even though summer was still a couple of weeks away.

"We get to go in there?" Trevor bolted up the stairs and laughed while he waited at the top for her. "I beat you even with my sore toe."

"You're too fast for this old lady," she said as she climbed the last step.

A blast of stale air puffed in their faces as they pulled open the glass door and entered. The heat outside hadn't yet permeated the interior of the fortress-like building.

Trevor pointed to the directory mounted next to the elevator. "Fifth floor." He punched the button and the elevator doors slid open immediately. "It was waiting for us."

Upstairs, he could see a flurry of activity through the open door. Phones were ringing, people were typing, and a woman was filing manila folders in one of the many cabinets that lined the walls of the office.

The woman looked up from her filing. "Can I help you?"

"Yes." Beverly spoke softly. "I want to report the abuse of my grandson." She touched the top of Trevor's head as he clung to the flowing material of her dress.

She looked down at Trevor's face, then back at Beverly. "You can see Miss Peck over there." She pointed to a young woman with long wavy hair. Miss Peck removed her small round glasses and massaged a deep red dent across the bridge of her nose as they approached her desk.

"How may I help you?" she inquired.

"I want to report my son-in-law for abusing my grandson."

"Have a seat Mrs..." She lifted her eyebrows and gestured to the chair opposite her desk.

"Akers. Beverly Akers." She opened her purse and removed a few crayons and a small book of paper to occupy Trevor. Taking them, he sat on the floor cross-legged.

Miss Peck walked around her desk and bent down to talk to him. "Hello there. Aren't you a big boy? What's your name?"

"Trevor," he answered shyly.

"It's very nice to meet you, Trevor. That's a big boo-boo on your face. Does it hurt?"

He didn't stop drawing. "Naw. Not as much as my toe."

She examined his injuries before returning to her cluttered desk. From under a wilted spider plant she removed a form and inserted it into her typewriter.

"Before we get started I want to know if his father will find out that it was me that made the complaint."

Miss Peck aligned the paper. "He doesn't have to. We can keep your name anonymous."

"Will you hold the things I say against my daughter? She isn't the one who hurts Trevor. She's just as much a victim of that horrible husband of hers as her son is."

"If she isn't abusing her son, she'll have nothing to worry about."

Twenty minutes later Miss Peck was still typing.

"Are you sure his father caused the bruises and they weren't the result of some normal childhood accident?"

Beverly glared at her. "I'm absolutely positive. That man is a monster. I'm sickened to think of what my grandson has endured at his hands."

"Please, Mrs. Akers," she said, her fingers still resting on the typewriter keys. "Understand that I'm a neutral party and I'm obligated to ask these questions. It isn't because I don't believe you."

"It just seems so obvious to me."

"Then make it obvious to me too. Give me an example of abuse that you've personally witnessed."

Beverly looked up at the ceiling as she thought. "Lenny's always so careful around me. He tries to make them seem like the perfect family but there was an incident last summer when Gail, Lenny, Trevor, and I went for a visit to my cousin's beach house in New Jersey for the weekend. The trouble started when we stopped at a dime store to buy a sand toy for Trevor." She looked at him. "Do you remember that day Trevor?"

He nodded. He could picture the wavy heat rising from the pavement as his grandmother recounted it for Miss Peck.

"*We're here,*" *Gail had said, taking a deep breath of the salt air. "It smells so good."*

They piled out of Beverly's Dodge, each dressed with their swimsuits under their clothes.

"How come we're stopping here? I can't even see the beach," Trevor asked as they walked toward the store.

"We're gonna buy you a toy for the beach, little man." Lenny ruffled Trevor's hair as he flashed a sugary smile at the man behind the counter. "You can get anything you like."

"Really?" Trevor's eyes sparkled as he ran down the toy aisle. "I want this!" He grabbed a bag of sand toys tied together in a net bag and waved it in the air.

Lenny looked at the price tag. "You've got to be kidding me. This costs too much."

"But you said I could get anything I wanted."

Beverly looked at Lenny. "Let's not keep your father waiting. I'm sure he's tired after driving so long. How about this?" She held up a sand toy shaped like an octopus.

"Naw. I don't like that."

Lenny's voice changed to a growl. "Then pick something else."

Gail headed for the other side of the store. She seemed to be looking at the display of paperbacks but she didn't pick any up to read the descriptions. The metal rack squeaked as she slowly turned it.

Trevor reluctantly set down the bundle of toys and looked further down the aisle. He grabbed a kite from a cardboard box. "I want this."

A breeze blew through the store, rustling the display of floats that hung from the ceiling.

"I told you to get something to play with in the sand. That ain't no good."

Trevor tossed it down on the shelf.

"Pick that up or the man will come over and get you. He don't like no brats making messes in his store."

The man at the cash register coughed and looked away.

"No. It's not fair. You won't let me pick out what I want like you said I could."

"Pick it up."

Beverly reached over and placed the kite back into the colorful display box.

"Now look what you done. Your old granny had to pick up after you. You should be ashamed of yourself."

Two boys rounded the corner and stood next to Trevor as they looked at the toys.

"See? Them boys are picking out toys without being bad."

Trevor blushed. He picked up the octopus sand toy. "I guess I'll get this."

"You said you didn't want that." He grabbed Trevor's wrist and squeezed it until he dropped the toy on the floor. "Come on. We're leaving." Pulling him roughly to the front of the store, the two boys stared with their mouths agape.

"You said I could have a toy," Trevor wailed.

"You can't have nothing now. You spoiled it. You ruined our day at the beach." He yanked him out the door while twisting his arm. Gail ran after them.

Lenny started the car as soon as Beverly climbed into the back seat. Trevor was crying and a large welt was forming on his cheek.

She handed the octopus to Trevor. "I bought this for you, honey."

"He ain't having that." Lenny reached around and snatched the toy as they pulled out of the parking lot, tires squealing. He threw it out the open window. It bounced off the tar and landed in the sandy shoulder on the side of the road.

Miss Peck handed a tissue to Beverly. "Was Trevor's arm broken?"

She dabbed the tears from the corner of her eyes. "No. It was bruised but not broken, thank goodness." Trevor could feel their eyes on him as he scribbled black circles over the picture of a house he had drawn.

"Is that enough to convince you, Miss Peck?"

"It's a start."

"What's going to happen now?"

"A full investigation."

"How long will that take? I want Trevor out of that house today. I'll take care of him…and my daughter."

"It won't happen today, Mrs. Akers," she said, shaking her head. "Investigations take time."

Trevor got an uneasy tickle deep in his belly. He'd love to move in with his grandmother but he knew his father would never let his mother go. Not without a huge fight. He felt bad when the almost new, still pointy lemon yellow crayon snapped in half between his fingers.

"But—"

Miss Peck put her hand up and stopped his grandmother from protesting. "I understand your frustration but we can't march in and remove a child from his parents simply on the basis of one complaint. As I said before, a thorough investigation will have to take place first, and then there has to be enough evidence to be able to remove the child from the home. The law is very clear about that."

Desperation crept into Beverly's voice. "I thought this would put an end to the situation once and for all."

"I'll do my best." Miss Peck stood up and extended her hand. "I'll be in touch."

The September sun was paradoxically bright the morning Lenny drove Trevor to Masterson Brothers Funeral Home. Birds had the nerve to be singing and flowers were boldly blooming even though his mother was dead.

Dead.

Trevor tried to deny it but his heart remained empty and he knew it was true.

He was never going to hug her again. She'd never kiss his boo-boo, sing him a song, run after him in the dirt-covered yard, or build a tower with him ever again.

His tears were gone, all used up. He was numb. How could life be so unfair? God left him with his father, a man he hated and who hated him, and took the only person they both loved. That love was the only thing he had in common with his father.

Lenny pulled into the parking lot of the auto parts store next to the funeral parlor. "I need to pick up something for my boss." He pulled a bag from behind the seat and handed it to Trevor. "Bring this outfit for your mother to Masterson's."

Trevor trembled. "I have to go in there…alone?"

Lenny reached past him and opened the door. "Don't be such a *baby*."

"Can't you come with me? Please?"

Lenny's mouth was turning down at the corners. Trevor knew how his father felt about begging but he was desperate. "I ain't going in there till the wake."

Trevor stared at him, willing him to change his mind. Sometimes his psychic powers worked to ward off a whooping and sometimes not. It never hurt to try.

"I can't," Lenny said. "The place smells like carnations. I probably got some allergy or something. They make me feel like I'm gonna puke."

As soon as Trevor heard the word carnations, he knew his father wasn't going. He'd heard the story of the carnations before, a long time ago, from his mother. She had picked up a carnation, dyed green for St. Patrick's Day, from a bucket in the grocery store. She inhaled the flowery scent and held it out for Trevor to sniff.

"It smells good," he'd said. "Can I have one?"

His mother had shaken her head. "Your father hates carnations." She placed the flower back into the shamrock-colored water. "Your grandfather worked at a restaurant and wore a carnation in his lapel for work. Sometimes he'd come home drunk and beat your father. With every smack, your father smelled the scent of the carnation and since then, the smell makes him sick to his stomach."

Trevor gripped the bag of his mother's clothes tightly as he squeezed through the hedge between the parking lots. On the other side, he opened the bag and drew in the scent that lingered on the fabric. Looking up, he spotted something so familiar, so comforting, it was as if his mother had put it there to console him. His grandmother's car. He peered through the hedge to make sure his father had disappeared into the auto parts store before running to the big wooden doors of the funeral parlor and tugging them open.

He hadn't seen his grandmother in weeks, since the investigation began. Lenny had exploded after the first home visit from Miss Peck. When she left, his phony smile collapsed. He dialed the phone and yelled at Gram, using words that would have gotten Trevor expelled from school. He banished Gram from their lives. Forever.

So much for keeping her name confidential. Miss Peck obviously didn't know the meaning of anonymous. He was a kid and even he knew what it meant.

Inside the funeral home, Trevor walked down a long hall wallpapered with light blue and cream stripes. He heard voices coming from a room on the left. He recognized his Grandmother's voice and waited outside the door for them to finish talking.

"Gail is dead," Beverly said flatly. "It can't be."

"You…you…you see," a man stammered. "Your daughter was picked up from the hospital and brought here yesterday. I thought you knew."

"No one notified me, Malcolm. I found out when your secretary called me about bringing a dress for Gail to wear. She called Gail *the deceased*." She burst into tears.

Trevor peeked through the door. Gram held her head in her hands. "This is too much to take," she said. He wanted to give her a hug but he didn't dare interrupt an adult conversation. His father had plenty of rules and this was in the top ten. No interrupting. Ever.

Malcolm reached into his pocket for a tissue. "One of the tools of my trade," he said, handing it to her. "Beverly, my dear, I…I…I had no idea that you were estranged from your daughter. In all the years I've known you, you've always seemed so close to her."

"If only I could've seen her one last time," she sobbed. "I didn't even get a chance to tell her how much I love her. How am I going to go on without her?"

"I'm so sorry you had to find out this way. Please accept my deepest sympathies."

Beverly blew her nose. "What was the cause of death?"

He hesitated. "An accidental drug overdose."

Beverly pounded her fist. "Damn that Lenny Mayhew. It's his fault. He got her started on drugs. They should arrest the bastard."

Trevor blinked. His grandmother said drugs, not medicine. His father always said he was giving mommy her medicine. His teacher said drugs were bad and there were ads on TV that warned you to say no to drugs. Why didn't his mother say no? Then his father's face flashed through his mind. No one said no to his father.

"I'm sure the shock of your daughter's death is overwhelming. Perhaps you'll feel better if you go home and rest."

Beverly ignored him. "What if Lenny *intentionally* gave her too much and made it look like an accident? I never believed that he truly loved Gail. He wasn't capable of loving anyone, not his wife, his son, or himself. He could've done it. He could've *killed* her."

Trevor knew her theory was wrong. His father wouldn't have hurt his mother on purpose. *He saves all that for me*, Trevor thought. *She only got it if she tried to help me.*

"What's that bitch doing here?" Lenny's voice echoed through the hushed funeral parlor.

Trevor jumped. He hadn't heard the swish of the doors when his father entered.

Beverly rushed out into the hall. "Trevor!" Her face lit up like a sunrise.

Trevor dropped the bag and flew into her open arms.

Malcolm went over to Lenny. "I'm afraid I'm the cause of this confusion Mr. Mayhew. I asked Beverly to bring a dress for your wife to wear. The hospital sent over worn-out blue jeans and a T-shirt." He wrinkled his nose. "I'm sure you wouldn't want your beloved wife to wear them throughout eternity."

Lenny glared at Beverly, his son clinging like a vine on her trunk. "Gail don't need no clothes from the likes of you, old woman. What my wife wears is my own damn business and you don't got no right getting involved at all. I picked something out myself." He scooped up the bag and threw it against Malcolm's concave chest.

The bag bounced off the thin funeral home director and fell back onto the floor. Malcolm picked it up. "If I had known that there was…ahh…a misunderstanding between you and Mr. Mayhew, we never would have called you about the dress, Beverly."

"I don't want her at either the wake or the funeral. Understand, Masterson?"

Malcolm nodded, his face pinched.

"She don't deserve to see Gail again after what she done to us."

Beverly put Trevor down on the floor. "You can't do this to me. Please, Lenny. My daughter is dead. I have to see her one last time."

He sneered. "You shoulda thought of that before you went and told all them vicious lies." He addressed Malcolm. "She reported her own daughter to the Child Welfare Office."

"That's not true." Tears sprang to her eyes. "Did Gail think I reported *her*?"

"She did. And she hated you for it." The corners of Lenny's mouth twitched with a smile. "She died wondering why her own mother turned her over to the authorities. Maybe she overdosed on purpose."

Trevor knew that was a lie. He wanted to wash his father's mouth out with soap from the garage like he'd done to Trevor when he lied about having his homework done so he could watch TV. His mother would never, ever in a gazillion million trillion years kill herself and leave him. She *wouldn't*. He knew from her kisses. He knew from her hugs.

Beverly held her hand over her mouth. "Don't you *dare* say that." She crumpled against the wall. Malcolm rushed to her side and helped her to one of the crushed velvet chairs that were spaced in even intervals along the length of the wall. "I only wanted to help Trevor. I thought I was doing the right thing."

Trevor went to her and held her hand.

"Turning against your family is never the right thing," Lenny said.

"You turned against me. I'm family," Beverly countered. "You did everything in your power to keep them away from me. I'd call, you'd hang up as soon as you heard my voice; I'd write a letter, it would come back with return to sender scribbled on it; I'd knock at the door, you wouldn't let me in. I heard you yelling threats at Trevor, telling him what would happen if he opened the door. You've been a thorn in my side ever since the day you married my daughter."

Lenny shrugged. "You sealed your own fate."

"I didn't know what else to do. I was only trying to help the ones I love."

Lenny walked over to her, bending down to look in her face. "And how did that work out for ya? Tell him how the investigation came out."

Beverly didn't say anything.

"Fine. I'll tell him." He straightened up and looked at Malcolm. "They said the complaint had no grounds. If I'm rememberin' the words right it said no abuse had taken place in the Mayhew household. I'm innocent."

"You talked your way out of it. You're a convincing liar who's had plenty of practice. And that ninny, Miss Peck, let you get away with it." Her face turned to stone. "You can't keep me from coming to the funeral."

"Like hell I can't."

CHAPTER 9
1985

Summer heat in the late afternoon made the funeral even more unbearable. Lenny's head kept turning, looking left and right and left again.

He's watching for Gram, Trevor thought. Trevor had already spotted her but then, he was an expert at playing the I Spy With My Little Eye game with Gram. He always found everything fast.

Beverly was standing well behind Lenny, safely out of his sight. A thick veil covered her face. Her dress looked two sizes too big and like it was stuffed with pillows. She kept lifting the veil and dabbing her face with a hankie. He longed to go to her side, to hold her hand, and let her tell him that everything would be all right. He needed her yet there wasn't any chance that his father would allow it.

A small group was gathered at the edge of his mother's grave. He recognized few of the mourners. They were his father's friends: rough, dirty men and skinny, hollow-eyed women. His other grandmother was there but he didn't know her, even though she lived within walking distance. She'd never even sent him a card on his birthday.

Trevor was the only child in attendance and he stood next to his father, rocking back and forth on his feet, trying not to fidget. His hand kept moving to the Windsor knot at his neck.

A slight breeze rustled the weeping willow that served as Beverly's shroud as the minister began. "Our Father, who art in heaven…"

Dark clouds started rolling in, blocking out the sun, toward the end of the service. When it was over, Lenny walked off with his friends leaving Trevor behind.

Trevor looked after him, grateful to have been forgotten. He knew his way home. He'd rather walk than be in the truck with his father anyway. He went to his grandmother. She had her eyes closed, her head bowed in prayer.

"Please, God, help me set my grief aside and concentrate on Trevor. He's the only one who matters now. I have to figure out how to get him away from Lenny."

"Hey, Gram," Trevor said, touching her shoulder. She didn't jump like he expected. She was still, like she was half-dead from willing herself to join her daughter.

"It should be me in that casket. I'm old, not young like Gail was. You need your mother."

Tears came now for both of them. When they finally stopped, the only people left in the cemetery besides them were two gravediggers. They were busily shoveling dirt into Gail's grave. "I can't bear to watch," Beverly said. She looked up to the sky, gazing at the dark storm clouds blowing in their direction. "The wind is picking up. It'll rain soon. That should break this oppressive heat."

Trevor couldn't keep his eyes off the men. When they were done, he watched them walk off, out of sight. He thought what it would be like to be trapped in a coffin. The sweat that was already beading on his skin multiplied, making him slick. "Let's get out of here, Gram," he said.

"I want to see the gravestone first." The rain began, lightly dropping from the sky as they walked slowly across the cemetery. Trevor held onto his grandmother's arm, afraid she'd collapse.

She bent and read the marker aloud. "Gail Christine Mayhew. Wife and Mother. Born March 26, 1961. Died September 3, 1985." Beverly punctuated the ending with a small sob.

His mother's whole life was summed up in four lines on a cold, gray, flat piece of stone.

"Only twenty-four years old." Beverly shook her head. "She barely got out of her teens."

Sitting down, Trevor traced the words with his fingers. A new supply of tears began to flow, mixing with the rain that ran in rivulets over the loose dirt that covered his mother, and washed down to the dirt path that separated the rows of graves.

"Gail." Beverly choked out some words between sobs. "I wish you were here so I could tell you all things I wanted to say before." Her black veil stuck to the side of her face. "I only wanted what was best for you. I loved you more than you'll ever know."

Thunder rolled in the distance. It echoed in Trevor's empty heart.

After a long silence, she continued. "This isn't easy to say, even now. I know I failed you as a mother." She put her hand to her chest and drew a labored breath. "After your father died, I was all alone. I had to work long hours to support us. You've got to know that I truly tried my best. I'm sorry it wasn't good enough. Maybe if I had been home with you more, things would've been different."

"Don't say that, Gram. I bet you were a great mother. Mom loved you. I know that."

Beverly squeezed his shoulders.

As the storm got closer, Beverly touched the stone. "I swear to you that I'll make a difference in Trevor's life. I won't let him be hurt anymore. I'm going to stop Lenny. I give you my word."

A clap of thunder preceded a jagged bolt of lightning in the sky as Trevor stood up to leave, the storm raging around him.

A shiver ran up Trevor's spine. Pulling his thin coat around him, he held on tight to a gigantic turkey-shaped cookie he'd gotten at his class's Thanksgiving Day party. Thick, colorful frosting was spread over the white sugar cookie.

He was waiting outside the front door of the school for his grandmother to pick him up. They pretended that he was in therapy and that his grandmother drove him to the appointments. Lenny had no idea what they were up to.

Beverly had typed a note of permission and Trevor had slipped it to his father to sign. Lenny never read any paperwork from school so Trevor just said that it was a permission slip and he got the signature. He didn't even have to lie, really.

His "therapy" was really a weekly visit to the Child Welfare Office. Trevor didn't care if he had to see that creepy Miss Peck as long as he was with Gram and away from his father. Heck, he wouldn't complain if he had to get a weekly haircut as long as he was away from his father. And anyone who knew him could vouch for the fact that he did not enjoy how the barber waved his pointy scissors so close to Trevor's eyes.

He smiled and waved his turkey cookie when his grandmother drove toward him. "Look at this," he said, showing her the cookie. He had waited to take the first bite so she could see it. It was gone by the time they reached Miss Peck's office.

"Mrs. Akers," Miss Peck said, the corners of her mouth straining downward. "There's nothing new on the case. I've told you, I'll call you if there's any change in status."

"But what about the pictures I dropped off last week?" Her hand felt for the bulge in her purse. Trevor knew her camera was loaded with film, ready to record any new cuts or bruises on him. She said that even if Miss Peck saw his injuries in person, she may not accurately record them into the file. A picture was better.

"I reviewed them but I still see nothing to compel me to reopen the case."

"Are you blind? His arm was covered with bruises."

"I'm getting tired of your combative attitude." Miss Peck exhaled her coffee-laced breath with a puff. "What bothers me the most is the way you keep coming in here and harassing me every time you have an afternoon off from your job."

Beverly took a deep breath. "This shouldn't be about me. You should be thinking of what's best for Trevor."

"I am."

"If you were, you'd take him out of that house and place him with me."

"In your opinion."

Beverly directed her words at Trevor. "You'd like to live with me, wouldn't you?"

Trevor nodded. How many times did he have to answer this question before Miss Peck got it?

"Plus, it would get me out of your hair," Beverly said to Miss Peck.

"Lenny warned me you'd try to manipulate me."

Beverly's eyes narrowed as she leaned back in her chair. "Lenny? You're on a first name basis?"

"Daddy don't call her by her first name. He calls her Miss Peck-on-the-cheek."

Miss Peck's cheeks reddened. "It doesn't matter if he has a silly nickname for me."

Trevor looked at his grandmother. "And they hug a lot."

Miss Peck's voice went higher, like she was an opera singer warming up. "Many people hug when they greet each other. It's a polite form of communication. Maybe if you tried to communicate with him, Mrs. Akers, you could reach a compromise."

"Lenny only communicates with his fists. But it sounds like he's found another way to communicate with you, *Miss* Peck."

Her back stiffened. "What are you implying? I've been with this office for five years and I've never had so much as a single complaint."

"Maybe you've never gotten cozy with a child abuser before."

"Stop it right now." She stood and leaned over her desk toward Beverly. "I called him by his first name because I've had to go out and investigate him so often. Your constant interference has made my supervisor so nervous that I have to go do a home inspection just about every other week. It's quite understandable that I'd get to know him."

"Oh, it's understandable, all right. I understand everything clearly now." Beverly grabbed Trevor by the hand and stormed out of the building.

When Miss Peck dropped by for a surprise home inspection on her way to work, Lenny found out the truth about "therapy." She seemed so...happy when it became clear to her that Beverly had been taking Trevor to the Child Welfare Office without Lenny's knowledge.

Trevor's father, on the other hand, had been anything but happy. As soon as she left, his veins inflated like balloons, his face turned apple-red, and he came at Trevor.

Trevor fell to the floor and wound himself into the tightest ball possible, tucking his head inward.

Lenny began kicking. And ranting. "You don't know what *abuse* is, boy. You shoulda grown up in my father's house. He makes me look like a pussycat when it comes to punishing a kid."

Trevor didn't make any mistakes. No crying, no noises whatsoever.

When he was done, Lenny said, "Go to your room. There ain't gonna be no school for you today."

Trevor stayed there while his father went to work. He didn't have a choice, really, since his father installed a silver sliding lock on the outside of the door. His stomach rumbled but Trevor had gotten good at ignoring hunger since his mother died. But when he had to pee he knew he was in trouble. He searched the room for something to go in but his father had removed all his toys and left only the bureau and bed. The closet held a few pieces of clothing and a spare blanket. When he finally decided to climb on the windowsill and pee through the screen, it was too late. He wet his pants.

Trevor changed his clothes, stashed the wet ones in the corner of the closet then paced until his father came home for lunch.

As soon as he walked into the room, Lenny's nose wrinkled and he frowned. He knew. "How many times are you going to do this?" Grabbing Trevor by the arm, he hauled him to the couch and stripped him naked. "My father did this to me one time when I used his razor to shave Ace's head. I learned my lesson so it should work with you." He pulled him to the door and opened it.

Trevor shivered. "What are you gonna do?"

"You want to act like a puppy that ain't been housebroken? Fine! But I'm gonna tie you outside like the bad dog you are."

"No! Please don't! I swear I won't pee my pants no more."

"Too late. You done it. Now you pay for it." Lenny grabbed rope from a nail in the cellar stairwell and pushed Trevor out the door.

Trevor had learned a trick when things got at their worst. He left the punishment behind and retreated inward to his own fantasyland. As Lenny pulled the rope tight, Trevor was already deciding who he'd be playing with in his head. Scooby and the gang (he liked Shaggy especially), Tweety, Snoopy (but Lucy was banned because of her bad attitude), Ronald McDonald (who always brought lunch), or the guy from Schoolhouse Rock who sang "Conjunction Junction" (he couldn't get enough of that song).

Lenny set down a bowl of water and threw the welcome mat over him once he made sure Trevor wouldn't be able to escape. "See, I'm nicer than my old man. He didn't give me no water or mat."

Trevor watched him walk away and then crawled under the stairs. Digging down in the dirt, he tried to make a little hole to hide in, using the mat as a manhole cover.

What seem like hours later, he heard a voice. "Oh my God," Beverly gasped.

The sound of his grandmother's voice warmed his heart even though the rest of his body was numb. He crawled out of his hole.

"Trevor," she cried as she crawled to him and hugged his icy body close to hers. His hands and feet had turned a bluish color. She tore off her coat and wrapped it around him. "What are you doing out here? If I hadn't been looking closely, I might not have noticed you."

"Gram, look." He pointed to her car. Pulled slightly to the side of the road, the motor was running and cars swerved around the open driver's door as a man approached it.

"Hey! Stop!" she shouted as the man climbed in and attempted to drive off. The car stalled a few feet down the road. He tried in vain to restart it before jumping out and running off.

"I'll take care of it later. We've got to get your blood moving." She struggled to untie the knots that bound him to the railing. "There. Got it." She picked him up and gently rubbed his cold body. "Where's your father?"

"He left," he answered faintly. He felt so tired.

She carried him up the steps and tried the door, twisting the knob back and forth frantically. It was locked. "I have to get you inside where it's warm. My car's old heater barely blows a warm breeze so it won't be of much help."

"Mommy used to ride in your car with you."

"Yes, honey, she did."

"I wish she was here now."

"Me too." She ran her free hand along the top of the doorjamb while still holding onto Trevor. "Is there a key hidden outside?"

He shrugged. "I dunno."

Forming a fist, she punched out one of the windows in the door, sending glass fragments flying onto the kitchen floor. Trevor could feel the heat of the kitchen radiating through the hole. Reaching in, she unlocked the door and raced to the bathroom.

"Hold on, Trevor. Gram will have you nice and warm in a few minutes," she said, filling the tub. Pushing the coat free, she set him in tepid water.

He noticed blood trickling from the cuts on her hand. "Did you get hurt, Gram?"

"I'm fine. Don't worry about me." She kissed the top of his head. "What a good boy you are. After all you've been through and all you care about is your Gram."

He reached up and touched her cheek. "I'm sure glad you came."

"Me too." She picked a tiny piece of glass from her skin. "Why did your father do this to you?"

"I peed my pants again so he stuck me out there naked." Tears welled up in his eyes. "I crawled under the stairs to hide." He stared down into the water.

"What a bas—I mean, what a bad thing for him to do."

"But I done something wrong." A tear rolled down his cheek.

Beverly gently tilted his head, forcing him to look at her. "You have nothing to be ashamed of, Trevor. You had an accident, that's all. Nobody's perfect, not even grown-ups and especially not your father. Every person on this planet has accidents. There's no shame in that."

"Daddy says there is."

"And since when do you believe him over your Gram? Who loves you the most?" She added warmer water to the tub.

Trevor cracked a smile. "You do."

"I love to see that smile. With that missing tooth, you look like a friendly jack-o'-lantern."

He giggled. "Look, I ain't blue no more." He held out his hand and lifted his feet out of the water before splashing her.

She laughed. "I guess you're feeling better."

Wrapping him in a threadbare towel, she carried him to the living room. Dishes filled with half-eaten food were on every table. Knocking a pile of dirty clothes off a chair, she sat down. "How long were you outside?"

"Since he came home for lunch. It seemed like a long, long time."

Beverly glanced at the clock. Tears filled her eyes. "I don't understand how a father could be so cruel to his son." She hugged him tight. "Especially when the boy is you. You're special. You know that, don't you?"

"I know I am to you." Trevor smiled. "When can I come live with you, Gram?"

"I'd love to pack you up and take you with me right now."

"Did Miss Peck-your-eyes-out say it's okay?"

"Good name for her. Much better than Miss Peck-on-the-cheek." She frowned. "But no matter what we call her, I don't think she's going to help us."

"But you took all them pictures of me with my black-and-blues." He rhythmically kicked the chair wondering what else they could do.

"I guess she doesn't have a heart. Or a brain. But she doesn't matter anymore. I have a plan that won't fail this time. I just have to take care of a few things and then you and I will be together forever. Just don't say anything to your father."

"I won't." He closed his eyes and nuzzled his face into her neck.

A plan. His grandmother had been nervous and unsure dealing with Miss Peck-your-eyes-out but now she sounded like the old Gram and he liked it.

"Who broke my damn window?" Lenny screamed as he burst through the kitchen door.

Beverly was holding Trevor in the living room, only having left him alone long enough to move her car to the side of the road. "I broke your window, Lenny."

"I thought so. I saw your car." He stared at her from under the archway. "You're paying for it."

"You're worried about the stupid glass? What about your son? Aren't you concerned in the least bit about what you did to him?" She hugged Trevor tighter.

Trevor knew enough to keep his mouth shut.

Lenny put on his polite son-in-law act. "I know I made a horrible mistake and that's why I come back here to untie the little fella." He walked over and patted Trevor's head.

Trevor's body stiffened.

"I said to myself, 'He was a bad boy but enough is enough.' I figure he learned his lesson."

"There's nothing he could do that's bad enough to warrant the kind of degrading, dangerous punishment you dole out."

"I guess it was a little harsh to put him outside in the cold. I won't do nothing like that no more." He hung his head in mock shame as the clock began to chime.

"I'm glad you realize what you did was wrong."

Trevor worked hard to contain a smile that threatened to burst across his face. His grandmother was only letting Lenny think she bought his line. They had a plan and Lenny had no idea what they were plotting. His grandmother was going to the bank to withdraw her life savings. She had been saving money in a retirement fund for herself and, although she said it wasn't that much, it was enough to start a new life away from here. Trevor liked the thought of that. A new life.

"I'm glad we was able to work this out without running to the Child Welfare Office," Lenny said.

"I'm through going to them. We don't need them anymore."

CHAPTER 10
1996

Shelby's closet was crammed so full that BK could barely move the hangers. "Are you sure you don't mind if I borrow one of your dresses?"

"Go ahead. Pick any one you like. I want Heather's eyes to pop out of her head when she sees that you're not in one of her castoffs."

She grinned. "It will bug the heck out of her."

"So how come Stanley's springing for a party at the country club? I didn't think anyone could pry money out of his wallet."

BK pictured her mother with a crowbar working on Stanley's wallet. "He spends plenty when he wants to impress someone, especially if he thinks he can do business with them."

"It didn't take dear, sweet Vangie long to approve your mother."

"My mother's lucky Evangelina and Heather hit it off. They have such a good time tormenting me. I don't think she would've gotten the stamp of approval without Heather. If it were me deciding, there'd be no relationship. Evangelina isn't the one who'll be stuck living here as a family." But as usual, BK had no say in the matter.

Shelby picked up her alarm clock and set it back down with a thud. "It's been fifteen minutes. Maybe I should make a suggestion. I know just the one that would look perfect on you." She reached past BK and pulled out a plain white dress. "Simple. Elegant. So you." She held it under BK's chin and spun her around to look in the mirror.

"You're right. It's perfect."

"You'll make Heather green with envy."

"You're sure you don't mind if I wear it?"

"Would I wait around for you to decide if I minded?" She laughed as she lifted her thick hair off her neck and fanned herself. "I'm hot. Want to go next door for a swim?"

"I guess so." BK sighed. "I'll be glad when they're done putting your pool in so we won't have to go over there anymore."

"It's not going to be as big as Stanley's."

"It'll still be better. No ugly statues."

"What do you mean? He doesn't have any statues."

"Then what do you call Evangelina and Heather? Aren't they cemented onto those lounge chairs all day? They never seem to move."

Shelby laughed. "I know a way to fix those two."

A few minutes later they had squeezed through an opening in the hedge that separated the Fulton and Georgopolous properties.

"Are we really going through with this? I don't want to get into trouble before the party tomorrow night. I'd die if I had to miss it especially now that I have the perfect dress." She may not want Stanley as her new father but she didn't want to be Cinderella, staying home the night of the ball, missing all the fun. She was certain no fairy godmother would materialize to undo a grounding.

"Don't back out on me now." Shelby wagged a finger at her. "They'll never figure out what we've done, and even if they do, I'll tell them it was all my idea. They won't dare do a thing to me since Stanley is still trying to convince my father to buy the new company cars from him."

"Well…"

"Think of all the times Heather and Evangelina pushed you into the pool, dumped you off your float, made fun of your bathing suit, put salt in your soda, called you names and generally made your life miserable."

"Okay. You convinced me. Do you have the stuff?"

Shelby reached into her pocket, pulled out a box of candy-coated gum squares and shook it. She had already replaced a piece with a mint-flavored laxative. Opening the box, she dumped them out into her hand. "See? You don't even notice that they're not all exactly the same size unless you look real close." She carefully put them back into the box.

"Are you sure nothing terrible will happen, other than the obvious?"

Shelby dropped the box back into her pocket. "I pulled this on my creepy roommate at school last year and old Bitsy was fine." She smiled as she remembered. "You won't tell another living soul, right?"

BK stuck out her pinkie, swearing not to tell.

"Look who's coming," Heather said loudly as they crossed the lawn. "It's my stupid sister and her stupid friend."

Evangelina poked her. "I told you not to call Shelby names. My father will kill me if she goes crying back to her parents that we were mean to her. It could ruin his deal."

Heather frowned and rolled over.

"Don't mind us." Shelby stripped off her cover-up and tossed it on the empty chair next to Evangelina, making sure that the box of gum fell out of the pocket.

Evangelina grabbed it and helped herself to three pieces. "Want some?" She tossed the box onto Heather's back. "Our friend Shelby was nice enough to bring us a treat."

Heather emptied the box. "Thanks, Shelby." She tossed it on the ground as she chewed with her mouth open.

BK jumped in the water without remorse.

"Are you sure you're feeling well enough to stay through the whole party, Heather? I can arrange to have someone drive you home after dinner," Jeanne said as they climbed the stairs to the ballroom.

"I'll go home with you if you want," BK offered. Guilt had gnawed at her throughout the night as Heather tossed and turned in the bottom bunk, suffering from the trick she and Shelby had pulled.

"No. I'll stay. It was probably just one of those twenty-four hour things. I can't miss your engagement party."

"If you're sure, dear." The lights flickered as they entered the ballroom. Jeanne called to one of the waitresses. "It's so hot in here. What's going on?"

"The power's been going off and on all day," she explained. "I heard on the radio that it has to do with a drain on the power supply because of all the air conditioners running. We were without power for almost two hours."

Jeanne turned to BK. "Go down to the kitchen and make sure there aren't any problems with the food. The guests will be arriving any minute now."

BK ran into Shelby and her parents at the top of the stairs. "You're the first ones here."

Mrs. Fulton smiled. "Shelby insisted on getting here early. She said, 'It's BK's big night. We can't be late.' It's nice that you've become such good friends this summer."

BK smiled as Shelby's parents went into the ballroom. "I'm going down to the kitchen. Want to come?"

Shelby grabbed BK's arm and steered her to the elevator. "Follow me."

"Are we allowed to use this?"

"It's fine. I've used it a million times. I love elevators." Shelby pressed the button. The door slid closed and they began to move.

Suddenly, it stopped with a jolt as the lights flickered off. An emergency light began to glow over the control panel.

"Oh, no. We're stuck." BK began to punch the buttons, her pulse racing. "Did you just say you love elevators?"

"Hold on." Shelby grabbed her hands. "Stay calm. I'll push the alarm. Someone will get us out in a few minutes."

"My mother's going to kill me. I should have taken the stairs."

"Too late for that now. Let's sit down and you can tell me if Heather had any unfortunate health problems. Or maybe it was Evangelina?"

BK couldn't move. She felt beads of sweat on her forehead. "What if they can't get to us and we run out of air and suffocate?"

Shelby grabbed her by the shoulders. "Snap out of it. There's plenty of air. We'll be fine. They'll get us out in no time." She tugged her arm and made BK sit. "Now tell me, did anything out of the ordinary happen to your sister?"

BK shook her head. "Yes. But I don't want to talk about it now."

A few minutes passed with only the sound of the alarm ringing and BK's uneven breathing before a voice echoed through the elevator shaft. "Can you hear me? Everybody all right in there?"

"We're okay," Shelby called.

"How many people are in there?"

"Two."

"When the electricity went out, the elevator jammed. They're trying to find the handyman. He'll be able to get you out so just hold on."

"We will," Shelby called back. She turned to BK. "Now will you relax? Tell me all about Heather."

BK inhaled deeply and exhaled. "I'm never going to do anything like that again. I felt too guilty," she said as they made themselves comfortable on the elevator floor. "I spent half the night worrying about her, but when we got up this morning she was her mean, grouchy self again."

"You've really got to loosen up. Pardon the pun." Shelby laughed as BK rolled her eyes. "It was only a prank and, you have to admit, she asked for it."

"I guess you're right."

Shelby made a face as her stomach growled loudly. "I hope dinner isn't going to be late. I'm starved."

"I don't know how you stay so thin. You eat constantly. I wish I could be so lucky."

"What are you talking about? We're just about the same size. You're wearing my dress, for Pete's sake."

"That's not what my mother said. She said it's too tight."

"No offense, but your mother's a freak."

The girls jumped up as the elevator started moving. They dashed into the open arms of Mrs. Fulton as soon as the door slid open. BK didn't dare look at her mother or Stanley.

"Are you girls okay?" Mrs. Fulton cried. "I was so worried."

"We were only in there a few minutes, Mother."

"One hour and twelve minutes to be exact. Long enough as far as I'm concerned."

"It didn't seem that long," BK said.

Shelby laughed. "That's because you were busy hyperventilating."

Jeanne's eyes were blazing. "What were you doing riding in that elevator anyway, BK?"

BK saw the Fultons exchange a look behind Jeanne's back.

Shelby didn't give BK a chance to answer. "I'm afraid it was my fault, Mrs. Hartshaw. I wanted to ride in the elevator so BK went with me."

"Oh," Jeanne grunted, the rage still frozen on her face.

Stanley patted the top of BK's head like an obedient dog that had followed its master's orders. "That's a good girl."

"I'm just glad they're all right," Suzanne said, looking pointedly at Jeanne. "That's all that really matters. Let's get back to your party."

They piled into the back of Stanley's limousine just after two in the morning, still excited and wide-awake from the party. A long line of luxury cars, mostly American models in deference to Stanley's allegiance to Detroit, still extended down the driveway of the club. None of the guests had started to leave until well after midnight, with most staying to dance to the old standards played by the band Stanley had booked from Boston. BK moved in close to Heather to make room for her mother.

"Stop squishing me, moron." Heather pushed BK, slamming her into Jeanne's arm. Jeanne halted their activity with one look.

BK pulled out a piece of cake she had stashed in her purse. As she took a bite, greasy blue frosting stuck to her lips and white crumbs sprinkled down onto a paper napkin she had spread in her lap.

Jeanne reached over and snatched it from her hand. "You don't need another piece of cake, young lady. I'm putting you on a diet starting right now so you'll look good for the wedding."

BK's mouth watered for another bite but Jeanne threw it out the window with a flourish. *Shelby was right. My mother is a freak. Who throws out perfectly good cake?*

Jeanne wiped crumbs from her hand. "I have a job for you, Heather. I want you to keep BK from eating sweets from now until the wedding."

Heather looked at BK with a smirk. "How am I supposed to do that with all the junk she eats? Am I supposed to follow her to that old five and ten store and throw my body across the candy counter when she buys some?"

"Do whatever is necessary." She looked at BK. "I hope you won't give your sister a hard time."

BK struggled to swallow. The cake felt like it had turned to cement in her mouth. *Fine*, she thought, *if this is the way they want it, I'll do it*. She was going to show them and diet like no one had ever dieted before.

Chapter 11
1985

Sick feelings of dread slowly traveled up his throat, poisoning him, as Trevor watched for his grandmother. He only dreaded the risk they were taking today, not what they were actually doing.

He didn't stop looking out the front window of his peeling house. Any minute now, Gram would drive by and park the old brown Dodge a block away.

He loved that car. The rusty frame held memories of his mother and reminded him of sunny days and dripping ice cream cones.

"Watch out, Gail, it's going to get all over the car," his grandmother had said, thrusting a paper napkin in his mother's direction while trying to get her own ice cream cone under control.

Trevor had gotten his in a cup.

"Trevor was the smart one. I can't keep up with this." His mother's eyes had twinkled as she flicked her long brown hair over her shoulder. A sticky white stream ran down to her elbow in the summer heat leaving behind chocolate bit freckles. It was one of the last times he could remember hearing her laugh.

The school counselor told Trevor that things would get better in time, that he'd miss her less, that his memories would carry him through. The counselor didn't know what she was talking about. He was never going to go a day without missing her.

He wiped his nose on the back of his hand. He had to focus on today. Today he was running away, away from his father, away from these trash-strewn streets littered with loss and pain and sadness.

He watched a man stagger in the distance, almost falling over. His clothes hung loosely off his scrawny frame and the nearly empty bottle clutched in his hand fell to the sidewalk, the shattering glass piercing the quiet of the morning. The shards joined the weeds tangled with gum wrappers and cigarette butts.

Trevor looked at the grandfather clock. Time was dragging, each second feeling like an hour.

The Dodge finally drove by. He left his house as quietly as possible, not pulling the door shut to avoid the click. He didn't want to wake his father. As he walked to the corner, he glanced left and right, then checked behind him. He made sure no one was around to witness what was about to happen, his escape from a house of torture.

"Calm down, calm down," he repeated slowly, hoping the words would convince his stomach to stop churning like the torn newspaper page that was blowing and flipping against the curb.

When Trevor got close enough, his grandmother stretched to open the passenger door. "That's quite a shiner you've got."

"Yeah." He ran his fingers under his left eye. A purple bruise also encircled his wrist like a hospital identification bracelet.

They sped down the street, the car seeming to pick up its own momentum. They soon passed his elementary school. "Do you think we're safe yet?"

She patted his thigh and winked. "I think we're in the clear."

He shifted uncomfortably in his seat and swallowed hard. Bile traveled up his throat.

"Are you all right, sweetie?" She pulled the car over and killed the engine.

After he opened the door, the feeling passed.

"Nerves," she said.

He closed the door and glanced behind them. A dented white pickup was driving toward them, his father's pickup. "Go! He's coming!"

When she turned the key, the car stalled. She pumped the gas pedal and tried to restart. "Come on, baby, don't do this to me now."

The pickup veered in front of them and skidded to a stop.

Trevor slumped down in the seat as his father approached wielding a baseball bat. "Don't let him hurt me."

His grandmother covered his eyes as the bat connected with the window, creating a glass spider web. "What the hell are you doing with my son? Did you think I wouldn't notice him actin' so weird this morning? He was in such a hurry, he didn't even close the damn door."

"You'll never see him again, Lenny," she shrieked. "Not as long as I'm alive."

"Go get in the truck, Trevor." His father walked behind the car swinging the bat again. "You're not going nowhere with her."

Trevor froze as his father reached for the door handle.

His grandmother tried the key and this time, the engine turned over. "Thank you, Jesus," she whispered. She put the car into reverse and stomped on the gas pedal.

"Let me have my boy," he yelled as she made a U-turn and sped off.

The Dodge couldn't keep its lead on his father's souped-up truck, now approaching them on the wrong side of the road. "Jump out, Trevor," he yelled. "Do it!"

"Don't even think about it," Gram said, veering onto a side street. The car shimmied as the back end slid into the other lane. Dust rose in a cloud from under the tires.

The truck missed the turn.

Trevor had a white-knuckle grip on the door with one hand and the dashboard with the other.

"It's going to be all right. I know what I'm doing." But before she finished speaking, the truck was in view.

"When he gets hold of me, he's going to kill me."

"I promise he won't be anywhere near you ever again."

Their heads snapped back as the pickup rammed them from behind.

"What was that?" Gram gasped at the sound of the car's tailpipe bouncing off the pavement.

The truck pulled up beside them again. "That hunk of junk is falling apart just like you, old woman. You'll never outrun me."

She didn't respond to his taunt. She was watching an approaching bread truck as its driver took a sip of coffee. He was looking down at his cup as she leaned on the horn.

The honking and swerving came too late.

"Don't look back," she yelled to Trevor over the sound of crunching metal.

"Do you like it?" Beverly asked hesitantly after unlocking the door to their new apartment. They were on the top floor of an old house that had been converted into individual apartments. "This house must have been quite elegant in its time but these days most people can't afford such huge places so they cut them up into apartments. I've never dreamed of living in a mansion anyway."

"It's okay, I guess." Trevor stared at his new home. "Boston is different, that's all." The apartment was nicer than his old house. The cabinets were white with wood trim and the counter was bright red. He could see a blue plaid couch in the living room facing a decent sized TV. For all the nice stuff, it was missing something important—memories of his mother. He couldn't look at a scratch on the wall and remember the day his mother had tried to move the bureau without help. There weren't any wavy pencil lines on the cellar wall where she marked Trevor's growth.

"I think your mother would like it here," his grandmother said, as if reading his mind. "Once it's scrubbed clean, it'll suit me just fine." Beverly set a box of cleaning supplies down on the floor, tossed her purse on the table, and then scooped Trevor up and twirled him around. "For calling a real estate office picked out of an old copy of the yellow pages and renting the place sight unseen, I'd say we did real well. Even the furniture looks pretty decent."

Trevor's brow wrinkled.

"What's got you looking so grim now?"

"I was just wondering if we were gonna get in trouble for what we done."

"No," Beverly said. "You're a child. You won't get into any trouble and I did what I had to do."

Trevor wasn't so sure. What she had done was technically considered kidnapping, even if she was his grandmother. And the chase with his father had ended in that horrible crash. Gram told him not to look but he did. The bread truck hit his father's truck head on.

"I tried every legal way to get you out of a dangerous situation and all I have to show for it is a mountain of forms, typed in triplicate. I had to resort to desperate measures. I gave my word on your mother's grave that there'd be no more abuse in your life as long as I have a breath left in my body."

Trevor jumped. "Did you hear something? I think somebody's coming up the stairs."

Beverly looked out the window. "It's only the tenants from the second floor." She touched his shoulder. "Relax. No one's here."

"But if they come, they might put you in jail."

"They'll have to find me first and I'm going to do my best to keep that from happening. Let me worry about that." She collapsed into one of the chipped kitchen chairs and pulled out a folded newspaper from her purse. She flipped through it. "There's nothing in here. I don't understand it," she said, rubbing her fingers together, smearing the ink that stained the tips.

Trevor stopped looking in the broom closet that was going to make a great place to transform into Superman or, at the very least, a killer spot for hide-and-go-seek. He went over to her. "What are you talking about, Gram?"

"There hasn't been anything in the paper since the report of your father's accident. Nothing about you being missing."

Trevor looked at the familiar banner of the Philadelphia newspaper that his mother and father used to read. His grandmother had found a newsstand nearby that carried it even though they were far from home.

"Do you think my father's dead?" He sat down next to his grandmother. His voice was a whisper. "I wished he was dead over and over. A million times at least." He still wished it but now that it might be true, it gave him a swirly feeling in his stomach.

"You can't wish someone dead. It doesn't work. Plus there hasn't been any obituary. He can't be dead but I don't understand why he doesn't have everyone on the lookout for us." She was quiet for a moment. "Maybe he's in a coma."

Trevor chewed on his fingernail. "What do you think will happen if he wakes up and finds us? Will they make me go back and live with him again?"

"I won't let that happen." She slid him off her lap. "Stop thinking about it and go pick out your room."

He pointed to himself. "I get to pick?"

"Sure, honey." She smiled. "Go ahead while I get the last box out of the Dodge."

"You mean the new car." They had driven the Dodge to a large parking lot and abandoned it. When closing its squeaky door for the last time, Trevor had felt a pang of regret but he knew they couldn't risk keeping it. The boxy, nondescript vehicle that sat on the street below didn't have a personality. What it did have was plenty of room in the trunk for all the stuff they needed for their new life.

As soon as Trevor heard Beverly return, he yelled, "Come see! Hurry!"

"You've got to remember I'm an old lady. I can't move that fast," she said from the doorway. "When your mother was your age, I was twenty years younger and boy, can I feel the difference."

Trevor was in the blue bedroom, jumping on the bed like a trampoline. "I like this room. Can it be mine? This bed is the most bouncy."

Beverly smiled "If you want it, it's all yours."

"I'm gonna like it here." He hopped off the bed.

"I'm glad to hear it. Why don't you go to the kitchen and find the box of your stuff so you can unpack?"

As he ran off humming the theme song from a Saturday morning cartoon, he could hear her say, "I think I'm going to like it here too."

Beverly straightened the collar of Trevor's shirt. "Remember to agree with everything I say even if it's a lie."

Trevor nodded.

She frowned. "This is a terrible lesson to be teaching you but you understand we're in special circumstances, right?"

"Yes, Gram. I get it." They were going to his new school to get him registered under his new name.

The school secretary, dressed in a navy and white snowflake sweater, shook her head when his grandmother tried out the story on her. "You don't have his records from his last school? Tell me again why you don't have them."

Beverly spoke in the tone of voice she reserved for the elderly. "I left without getting them because my daughter recently died and the last thing on my mind was getting Trevor's records."

"I'm sorry to hear about your loss but I really need those records." The secretary picked up a pen. "What school did you say he went to? I'll have to call and see if they'll forward them even though that's not the normal procedure. I'm sure they're aware of your special circumstances."

"Can't you just put him in class without them? He's only in second grade."

The secretary looked at her strangely. "Is there some reason that you don't want me to get the records?"

Beverly leaned forward as if she was about to tell a big secret. "To be honest with you, he wasn't really doing that well in school. I think it would be best for him to start with a clean slate."

Trevor tried to look dumb but the secretary wasn't looking at him. Her focus was on his grandmother.

"I'd really like to help you, but I can't. You'll have to talk to the principal."

They were shown to a sparse office filled with metal: metal desk, metal bookcase, metal filing cabinets. Soon after, a short man with a comb-over joined them. "My secretary told me about your problem," he said, sitting down. "But I'm afraid we can't bend the rules for you. If we do it for one, we'll have to do it for all."

"I see." Beverly had come prepared in case the lie didn't work. She folded three hundred dollar bills in half and slid them across his blotter. Without looking up he had deftly reached out, scooped them up, and tucked the money in his pocket.

From that moment on, Trevor Leonard Mayhew was officially Trevor Stevens of Boston, Massachusetts.

"No! Get away from me. You're bad! I hate you! Leave me alone."

Trevor was jolted awake by his own screams. Breathing hard, he looked around and was surprised his father wasn't standing over his bed.

His grandmother ran to his bedside and took his hand. "It's all right, honey." She tried to soothe him. "It's Gram."

Drenched in sweat, he struggled to sit up. His pajamas were stuck to his skin. "Is he here?"

"I'm the only one here besides you. Your father is far, far away and doesn't know where to find us. Don't worry." She brushed his bangs off his forehead. "I'll always protect you. He won't ever hurt you again."

He realized he was safe in his blue bedroom and took a deep breath. The nightmares had begun when they confirmed that Lenny was still alive. There had been a short article in the paper. There was no mention that Trevor had been kidnapped, just that the accident victim had been released from the hospital and police were looking for witnesses. And now the nightmares were a regular part of his nights. "But he knows I wanted to go away with you and he'll be so mad that he'll whoop me good. He already thinks I'm a big baby 'cuz I'm scared of him."

"You're not a baby. It's normal to be afraid of someone who hurts you."

"Are you sure he don't know where we are?"

"I'm positive. If he knew, he would've already come here. Wouldn't he? But it's been two months since we moved and we haven't seen hide nor hair of him, have we?"

Trevor giggled and wrinkled his nose. "Hide nor hair?"

She tickled his ribs. "Okay, so your old grandmother talks funny. You don't have to make fun of me in the middle of the night." She got him into a fresh pair of pajamas, straightened out the bed and tucked him back in snugly. "How's that?"

"Good."

"I thought up a game we can play to make you feel better. We'll start tomorrow."

A little smile spread across his lips. "I love you, Gram."

She bent and kissed his forehead and turned off the lights. "I love you too. Goodnight."

Chapter 12

Beverly yelled the code word from the kitchen. "Stop!" Engrossed in his favorite game show, Trevor jumped in his seat before springing into action. "Hurry. I'm timing you."

Trevor knew if he didn't match or beat his previous time, he'd have to do it all over again. They had been playing this game for years, the game his grandmother thought up to make him feel safe from Lenny if he found them in Boston.

Turning off the television, he slid his notebook under the sofa so there wouldn't be any evidence that he was home. He ran to his hiding place, the broom closet, and latched the gate hook that his grandmother had installed inside.

Peering out through a small hole at the center of a knot in the wooden door, he tried to see what she was doing. "Don't you think I'm getting a little old for these silly drills, Gram? I'm a teenager now, in case you forgot."

"It never hurts to be prepared for an emergency. You never thought these drills were silly when you were younger."

"But I barely fit into this stupid hiding place." His head was pressed tightly against the shelf that held the floor washing bucket and spray starch and if he tried to squat down, his knees banged against the door. The only time he gave his father any thought was when he was crammed in this hiding spot. Trevor wouldn't want to see Lenny again but he was no longer the monster in his nightmares. "If Lenny hasn't found us by now, he probably never will. Can I come out?"

She ignored him. "You know you're not supposed to be making any noise."

"I'm missing my show and now I'll never know if the nice old lady from Sacramento wins the bonus round. You always pick the worst time for a drill."

"I have to know that you won't ignore the code word just because you're busy. But you passed. You can come out."

"Thank goodness." Trevor unlatched the door and rolled his eyes. "I thought you were going to leave me in there till supper time." He gave her a peck on the cheek before going back into the living room.

She called after him as she went back to cutting up a butternut squash for dinner. "I know you're getting older but I still think of you as a little boy. I guess having to shop for your clothes in the men's department should give me a clue, huh?"

"Yeah. That or the fact that I'm a foot taller than you, shorty."

She went into the living room, grabbed him and gave him a string of sloppy kisses on his cheek like she used to when he was younger.

"What'd you do that for?" He wiped the kisses off with his hand and laughed.

"Just because."

"You're something else, Gram." He grinned before he went back to watching TV.

"I don't know why you watch that trash. It isn't educational at all. Don't you have any homework to do?"

"No. We're having that big spelling bee tomorrow. Remember? The teachers didn't give us very much so we could brush up on our vocabulary lists. I'm already finished."

"Do you want me to quiz you after supper?" She straightened the pillows on the couch before returning to the kitchen.

"Sure, but I think I've got them down already." Trevor loved it when she had a night off from DeNunzio's Restaurant where she had been a waitress since they moved to Boston. She worked long hours to support them on a small salary plus tips augmented only by what he earned from his paper route.

But Trevor didn't feel poor. They were no worse off than their neighbors and they didn't all have what he had, a house filled with love. As he listened to the rattle of the vegetable peeler and felt the familiar sag of the couch, he couldn't remember a time in his life when he'd been happier.

"How'd you do?" Beverly stood up as Trevor burst through the kitchen door and threw his books on the table. "Tell me! I can't stand the suspense any longer. I've been watching for the bus for an hour."

"What are you doing home? You're supposed to be at work."

"I asked Mr. DeNunzio to let me out early. So?"

His lips twitched as he tried to hold back a smile. "I won. First place."

She clapped. "Congratulations! I knew you could do it."

Trevor picked her up and swung her around. "You're even more excited than me." He knew she'd been dreaming about the grand prize ever since she first heard about the contest. This win took him one step closer to a full scholarship to a fancy private school. He had to win it or they'd never be able to afford the tuition but he was more realistic than his grandmother about his chances.

"Did you win anything today?"

He opened his algebra book and carefully removed a blue satin ribbon with *First* written in gold letters. "Pretty nice, huh?"

"We'll hang it over the table so all your friends will see it when they walk through the door." She held it up against the wall.

"The final round is in two weeks." Two weeks of non-stop cramming. He wasn't sure it was worth it. If by some long shot he won, he'd have to make new friends. How could he replace the guys he'd known since elementary school? Plus, only rich kids went there. He'd stick out as the charity case. But he had to try his best for Gram. All she could talk about was how the scholarship would open up a whole new world for him. He didn't think there was anything wrong with the old one but she gave up her whole world to save him. The least he could do was try his best for her sake.

"Two weeks to study. Where's it going to be held? Can I go and watch this time?"

He pulled out a folded piece of paper. "It's going to be at the Beecham School auditorium and parents are invited." He handed it to her. "Here are the details."

Beverly's brow furrowed as she read the small print. "Will you need to wear a suit? It doesn't say if there's a dress code. I want you to look as good as all those rich kids but your only suit must be too short for you by now. I've already let the hems down as far as they'll go."

"Don't worry about it. I'm sure I can wear regular school clothes. It's only a spelling bee, not a fashion show."

"I don't want you to feel self-conscious."

"Me?" He chuckled. "You know I don't care about that kind of stuff. My friends like me for me, not for what I wear."

She smiled. "You've always had a good head on your shoulders. But I'm still going to try to scrape enough money together to get you a new suit. Or at least one that fits from the thrift shop."

Trevor shrugged. "Whatever makes you happy, Gram. I just want to see you sitting in the audience."

"This calls for a celebration. I'm going to treat you to an ice cream sundae after supper."

A warm breeze was softly blowing as they set out that evening to walk three blocks to the ice cream parlor. His grandmother had sold the car right after they had gotten settled since she worked nearby and Trevor always took the bus. A grocery store was two blocks away so they didn't need a car.

"There's nothing like springtime in New England after a long cold winter. I don't miss the snow or the gray skies." Beverly took a deep breath and closed her eyes. "It's as if the world is ready to start fresh all over again." She reached out to hold onto the peeling railing.

"Want some help?" Trevor held her arm as they descended the stairs. Her fall last month had scared him. If something happened to her, he'd be all alone.

"I'm still feeling a little stiff," she said as he led her to the sidewalk. "When I look at you, I feel young, no different than I did when I was your age. But when I look at myself in the mirror, I can't believe that the old lady staring back is me."

"You're not *that* old, Gram."

She chuckled and slipped her hand around his waist once they reached the crosswalk.

"Ah-hem." Trevor cleared his throat. "Not in *public*." He spoke in a low tone, his eyes wide as he motioned to her arm. "You know I don't mind this stuff at home but if any of my friends saw us, I'd never hear the end of it."

"Okay, okay." She dropped her arm to her side. "Can I at least *talk* to you in public?"

He laughed as they waited for traffic to pass. "Don't give me a hard time."

"I'll let you off the hook. What word won the contest for you?"

"Hyperbole."

"Hyper…what?" She waited halfway through the crosswalk until she was sure a fast moving red Explorer was going to stop.

He spelled it out for her as he helped her to the other side of the road. "It means to exaggerate to make a point, like the saying he's as strong as an ox. The other kid spelled it with a 'y' on the end."

"I'm not too good at spelling. Never have been. I don't know where you got your intelligence. Your mother was a pretty good student but she wasn't in your league. And you certainly didn't get your brains from Lenny."

"Thank goodness for that." He held the door open for her. He hoped he didn't get anything from Lenny. All he remembered about him was violence and hatred.

"Wherever it came from, you're awfully smart."

Trevor shook his head and pretended to concentrate on the list of ice cream flavors.

"I know you'll prove me right." She put her arm around him and gave him a squeeze. "I'm so proud of you."

"Don't get mushy on me, Gram." He shook her arm off but couldn't hide his smile.

"Are you too nervous to eat, honey?" Beverly asked, looking at Trevor's full bowl of oatmeal. "You haven't even eaten all the brown sugar I sprinkled on it. That's your favorite part."

He answered without looking up from the list he was reviewing. "I don't think I'm as nervous as you are. I just don't feel hungry this morning, that's all."

"Don't think about the grand prize." She gulped her coffee. "Just concentrate on the words."

"That's what I'm doing." He picked up his breakfast dishes and set them on the shelf next to the sink.

"I know, but the thought of that prize must be putting pressure on you. That school churns out businessmen, doctors, lawyers, judges—"

"And regular people too. It's not a magical school." He picked up his paper. "Besides, even if I win the scholarship, how are we going to afford the uniforms and books? I can get a job but I don't think I would earn enough."

"I'll work double shifts or find a second job if I have to. We'll find a way."

"I'm not going to make you do that."

"You couldn't stop me if you wanted to."

They arrived at the school an hour early to look around. Trevor's new suit screamed thrift shop once he was surrounded by manicured lawns and stately brick buildings. He watched the kids in their uniforms walking in groups and wondered if he'd be able to fit in. He fiddled with the satin lining sticking out of one of his sleeves, trying to push it back up.

His grandmother had a way of reading his mind. "This is the place for you, Trevor. You belong here."

Trevor found the auditorium. The well-oiled paneling reflected the twinkling light from a massive chandelier and the floor was covered with plush carpeting. Beverly unfolded a theater-style seat and sank into the thick padding. She winked and wished him good luck.

Trevor went backstage to a room full of hopeful contestants. He usually didn't get nervous, not even for tests or when speaking in front of a group. Living all those years with Lenny had taught him that there were far worse things that you could come up against. Even so, as they were ushered onto the stage and he looked out at his grandmother's hopeful face, his mouth felt dry and he had to fight the urge to run outside.

"The first word is orthodontics. Cynthia, we'll begin with you." The headmaster of the school was standing behind a podium with a pile of cards stacked in front of him. He wore a navy sports coat with the school emblem on the pocket.

A girl with red hair stepped forward and successfully spelled the word.

Three hours later there were only two contestants left on the stage, Trevor and a boy in a bow tie.

"Spell xenophobia." The headmaster of the school wiped his brow with a white handkerchief. Programs flapped noisily as audience members used them as makeshift fans.

Bow tie boy asked for the definition. A good sign.

"A fear or hatred of strangers or foreigners or of anything foreign or strange."

"Z-E-N-O-P-H-O-B-I-A," the boy spelled confidently into the microphone.

"I'm sorry. That's incorrect." The boy slumped back into his chair, his fingers yanking at his collar.

"Before I can declare you as the winner, Trevor, you must first spell xenophobia correctly."

Beverly covered her eyes as Trevor began.

"X-E-N-O-P-H-O-B-I-A."

"Congratulations, Trevor! That's correct."

The headmaster looked out at the audience. "Will Trevor's parents join us on stage?"

Beverly made her way onstage. "I wish your mother could see this," she whispered in Trevor's ear as they posed for the photographer. "She'd be bursting with pride, just like I am." She squeezed him tight as he held his trophy high.

Chapter 13

Lenny picked up the newspaper while waiting to order his breakfast. *The waitresses at this joint are fine looking and the grub ain't too bad either*, he thought. He inspected the figure of a harried waitress who was balancing four plates of fried eggs while listening to a customer yell out his order.

"I'll be over in a minute to take your order, sir," she said as she rushed past him.

Lenny impatiently thumbed through the paper. None of the places pictured looked familiar. He crumpled the pages back and mumbled, "Oh great, some foreign newspaper." Last week he had been stuck with *The Wall Street Journal*, which didn't even have pictures. Just his luck.

"Psst, psst." He signaled the wilted waitress. "Get me a local paper over here, pronto."

"I'll be right with you," she called back across the crowded restaurant with her teeth clenched behind an artificial smile.

Lenny didn't like waiting. He snapped his fingers. "Hey, I want the paper *now*."

The waitress bit her bottom lip. "Well, this morning you're going have to wait your turn like everybody else," she muttered as she slowly walked behind the counter, unloaded her tray of dirty dishes and poured herself a tall glass of iced tea before handing him *The Village Gazette*, a free local paper that featured school news, obituaries, and community events.

"Gee, thanks for nothing. I wanted a real paper, not this bird cage liner."

She shrugged. "It's the only one not being read by someone else right now."

"If I wanted to read about the local school brats, I woulda picked it up myself when I walked through the door." A pile of the free newspapers sat on the wide windowsill to the left of the entrance. He tossed it aside.

"Do you want to order?" She wiped her brow with a napkin from the stainless steel dispenser on the counter.

"Of course I want to order, doll. That's what I come here for."

She tapped her pencil on her order pad. "So, what'll it be?"

He studied the menu as though he had never seen it before. Then, as usual, he looked at the chalkboard hanging behind the counter and ordered the special.

Another waitress rolled her eyes and twisted her mouth as she walked by. Lenny's waitress grinned as she turned to clip the order onto the rack. "I ain't blind you know," he said to them.

While he waited for his breakfast to be cooked, Lenny reluctantly flipped through the local paper, grumbling the whole time. Turning the page, the grainy picture hit him like a pan of cold water. "I can't believe it… Trevor and the old lady." He read the caption under their picture, his lips moving silently.

Local Boy Wins Second Place. Billy Thornton, an eighth grade student at West Junior High, recently traveled to Boston to compete in the Albert Beecham High School annual spelling bee. Above, he congratulates first place winner Trevor Stevens as Jim and Nancy Thornton and Beverly Stevens look on. First prize is a full scholarship valued at seventy-five thousand dollars; second prize, a five hundred dollar savings bond.

The waitress came over to him. "Were you talking to me?"

Lenny didn't look up. *So, they changed their last name to Stevens.* His mind clicked. *Seventy-five thousand bucks. I wonder if they'll hand over cash to the old lady.* He reread the caption.

"Lookie here. My kid's going to a fancy pants private school. His old granny must have done pretty good for herself in Bean Town." He thrust the paper at the waitress but she walked by without stopping.

"That's nice," she said.

He rubbed the ring that Gail had slipped on his finger all those years ago. *Trevor don't deserve that money. He should have died instead of Gail. Maybe it's time he did.*

"Excuse me," the waitress exclaimed. "Are you going to move that paper so I can put your breakfast down?" Glancing at her boss standing at the grill flipping pancakes, she added "honey" as an afterthought. She looked at him over her shoulder. He didn't seem to have heard her.

Lenny ignored her. He picked up the newspaper and hurried toward the door.

"Hey, where are you going?" she called, still holding his plate. "You haven't paid for your breakfast!"

A sudden storm had cleared the children from the sidewalks; all the hopscotch and ball games were packed up for the evening. The day had started out deceptively warm and sunny. Lenny never would have predicted this storm. He pulled up the collar of his jacket to keep his neck dry but the rain didn't annoy him, he welcomed it. Empty streets meant no witnesses and fewer problems.

Lenny looked up at the house where his son lived. The first floor was dark. No one home there. The second and third floors had lights shining from the windows. His former mother-in-law's apartment was the top one so he knew Trevor was home safe and sound. Now he just had to wait for Beverly to come home from work and the fun could begin.

Figuring out her schedule had been easy. A few stakeouts and he had her routine down. He could've been a police detective or a private eye if he'd decided to stay on the other side of the law. But how profitable would that be? He made decent money at the garage but his gambling money came from his side jobs with Ace.

Lenny hid in an unruly hedge of lilac bushes that lined the street. He peeked out when he heard footsteps approaching. Beverly was walking toward him, carrying a white Styrofoam take-out container. He retreated into the leaves before she could spot him.

She glanced sideways. "Is someone there?" She fished for her keys in her purse and dropped them into her pocket.

He liked playing with her so he rustled the bushes again. She was easy to spook.

She picked up her pace. "Who's there?"

His answer was a soft whistle.

"I don't have any money. So if you're waiting to mug someone, forget about me." She started to run to the stairs that led up to her apartment.

Lenny jumped out and grabbed her from behind, jerking her head back. Her scream was drowned out by the sound of the rain gushing from the storm gutter. He covered her mouth with his hand. "Shhh," he hissed in her ear.

She stabbed his skin with her fingernails as she tried to pry his hand off her mouth but years of working on cars, working with those hands, had made them tough.

She arched her spine as he pressed a knife to her back. "Don't make a move or I'll slice you in two," Lenny said, jabbing the knife harder into her flesh to make his point. One hair further and he'd cut into the old broad.

Beverly's head tilted up toward the door of her apartment. Before he could stop her, she popped the tab on the take-out container and threw the contents over her shoulder. Steaming lasagna hit Lenny's face.

"You bitch," he yelped, letting go of her mouth to wipe his eyes.

With sauce still stinging his corneas, he managed a single blow to her Adam's apple, knocking the wind out of her. Gasping for breath she broke away, scrambling up five of the steps.

He rubbed his eyes again and put the knife in its shaft. "Where you going, *Grandmaw*?" Lunging at her, he caught her by the ankles. "This will teach you to throw hot food at me."

Her face cracked against the edge of the stairs before he pulled her back to the cement walk, her face bouncing off each step.

Blood gushed from her nose. "Help!"

"You don't seem glad to see your long lost son-in-law." He grabbed her feet and dragged her on her stomach to the back yard. Rocks scraped her skin and the skirt of her uniform bunched around her waist. She reached out and grabbed a half-dead azalea but the brittle limb broke off in her hand. "You're a tough old bird but you ain't gonna get away from me." He stopped behind a dilapidated storage shed. Wedged between the shed and a tall fence, he figured they were hidden from view.

"Help!" The rain pounded loudly on the tin roof of the shed overpowering her thin voice.

"Stop fighting already, old woman." Lenny stuck his foot on the back of her neck. "I hear you done pretty good for yourself up here."

She snorted mud from her nostrils. "If you call living paycheck to paycheck good. Why did you come find us after all these years?"

Lenny wanted to mess with her mind. "I wanted to see my boy. I want him back with me where he belongs."

"Ha! If you had really wanted him back, you would've come long before now."

He pressed his foot harder on her neck. She reached back and tried to push his ankle off.

"You ain't never gonna move my weight off you."

"You never even sent the police after us."

Removing his foot, he pounced on her back. He pulled her head up by the hair and ran the knife under her chin. "How could I? You left me for dead when you kidnapped my son. I was out of it for over a month in the hospital and when I come to, I had bigger problems to deal with, thanks to you." He withdrew the knife. "I want the scholarship money the brat won. Seventy-five grand won't make a dent in what you owe me but it'll be a start."

She spit on the ground. He wasn't sure if she was spitting in defiance or to expel blood. "I told Gail you were dumb," she said. "They don't give out *cash*. They give a tuition credit."

He reached into his back pocket and pulled out his favorite bandana. No matter how often it was washed, the familiar scent of gas and motor oil clung to its fibers. "This'll shut you up." He stuffed it in her mouth.

She gagged.

With his free hand, Lenny dumped out the contents of her purse. She hadn't been bluffing before. She really didn't have much money. "This is all you made in tips tonight? You must suck at your job, Bev." He rolled her over, plunged his hand into the pocket of her uniform and pulled out her keys. Yanking her up by the arm, he forced her to her feet. A muffled moan escaped from her lips.

"Oh, poor *Grandmaw*. You're getting so damn old."

She tried to cry for help through the bandana as she hit him.

He barely felt her feeble blows. He had been conditioned by the master. "Quiet." Hooking his arm around her throat, he pushed her forward with his body. She stumbled along silently. "We're going to your apartment. Don't try nothing smart. Understand?" He tightened his arm and jabbed the knife into her back.

A frightened grunt was his only answer.

"Good. And don't make no sudden moves to try to attract attention. I don't want to meet up with none of your nosy neighbors."

Still, she struggled to break free. He slid the knife into her lower back, piercing her skin fiber by fiber. "One more move like that, Grandmaw, and I'll cut out your shriveled old heart, throw it on the sidewalk, and stomp on it. Then I'll go find your precious little Trevor and do the same to him."

Beverly stopped struggling.

As they walked up the stairs she deliberately stumbled on the second floor landing, trying to attract the attention of the old people who lived there. No one came to their window.

He grabbed her tighter. "And you said *I'm* dumb…" He plunged the knife into her shoulder as she flailed wildly. The people in the apartment had their backs to her, watching their evening programs. They never moved an inch.

"Up to the top floor, Grandmaw."

As he pushed her up the stairs, she worked the bandana out of her mouth. It brushed against Lenny's arm as it fell. "You ain't making this easy," he snarled, immediately putting his hand over her mouth before she had a chance to yell.

As he inserted her key into the lock she bit his hand so deep it felt like teeth were going to hit bone. He yanked his hand back and instinctively sucked on the wound, the salty taste of his blood flooding his mouth.

Beverly yelled at the top of her lungs. "Stop! Stop! Stop!"

Lenny's knife plunged through her skin again and again until she blacked out.

Chapter 14
2000

Family meetings meant one thing—bad news. Stanley and Jeanne held family meetings in the living room, a room from which children were ordinarily banned since it was only used for entertaining.

Little Stan, BK's half-brother, was sitting on the hardwood floor playing with his cars and trucks. He was treated quite differently than his two older sisters. He was the preferred child. Stanley let him get away with murder and their mother never objected.

BK had a sinking feeling in the pit of her stomach. The last time they had been called in for a family meeting had been a week after the newlywed couple had returned from their Hawaiian honeymoon and she remembered exactly how that had gone.

"Good news, girls," her mother chirped, her skin tanned from the island sun. "Aunt Beatrice has offered to take you until Stanley and I have had a chance to settle in together as a couple."

"Take us?" BK questioned.

"You'll live with her for a while."

Heather pointed at Stanley. "It's because of him, isn't it? He doesn't want us around."

"That's no way to talk about your new father, Heather."

BK looked Stanley in the eye. "He's not my father." Stanley didn't blink.

"I guess your daughters aren't convenient to have around anymore," Heather cried. "But I won't go! We hardly even know Aunt Beatrice."

Stanley looked at Jeanne. "I thought you said you could handle them."

Her mother hopped out of her chair and hugged Heather. "It's only temporary. You'll be back before you know it."

BK had known that day would never arrive and she and Stanley were the only two who knew the real reason why.

The latest family meeting was called the night before they were due to return to Aunt Beatrice's after their customary two week Christmas visit at Cliffside Manor. BK saw something unmistakable in her mother's face but Heather bounced in and plunked herself down on a straight-backed chair, convinced that they were going to tell the girls that they could move back for good.

Her mother's eyes darted between the girls and Stanley. "We've decided the time has come for you to move out of your aunt's house. She's getting too old to handle teenagers."

BK had overheard her aunt complaining to Jeanne on the telephone about how much time the girls spent in the bathroom, on the phone, and watching TV. Aunt Beatrice had made it clear that she didn't need the checks Jeanne and Stanley sent her. Heather's smile widened but BK sat back and waited.

"Varoom." Little Stan drove his truck over Jeanne's leg, catching her designer hosiery in the back wheel.

"Oh, Stanny. Look what you've done to Mommy." She stuck her finger through the hole. "You're a very naughty boy."

Little Stan's face puckered up to cry. Stanley glared at his wife before snatching up his child to hold in his lap.

Jeanne continued. "We've decided to move you closer to home. We're going to send you to a boarding school where you can get the attention and supervision that you need."

BK looked at Heather. All the color had drained from her face. The room was quiet except for Little Stan's noises as he drove his truck over his father's protruding belly. Jeanne avoided eye contact with her daughters.

BK broke the silence. "Where?" No one answered. Jeanne seemed intent on studying the tree just outside the window. BK persisted. "Where are you sending us?"

Stanley intervened after shooting a look at his wife. "We've done some research and found the best three schools within a fifty mile radius. That way you'll be close enough to travel home for the holidays."

"Do we get to pick one of the three?" She looked again at her sister who still appeared too stunned to ask any questions.

"You have to apply and go on an interview but your mother has already filled out the applications for you. All you have to do is make a good impression."

Heather broke her silence. "No way. If I can't move home, I at least want to finish high school with my friends. I'm not going to a new school. You can't make me."

"Heather, stop this right now." Jeanne tried to silence her with the stern look that had always worked so well when they were younger.

Heather ignored her, yelling at Stanley as her little brother burst into tears. "It's all *your* fault. I hate you! I *hate* you! Everything was fine before you came along. I wish Mama never met you!" She ran from the room.

Stanley stood up with his crying son and escaped to the library, closing the door loudly behind him. BK could still hear her little brother wailing.

"Is that how you feel too? After all Stanley has given us?" Jeanne vented her anger on the only remaining target. "All those new clothes, a beautiful house, and now he's willing to pay for expensive private schooling for both of you. That's not something he has to do considering you're not even his *real* children. I can't believe my daughters would be so ungrateful."

"I do appreciate what he does for us, Mother." BK knew there was no changing her mind—and she didn't want to, anyway.

Jeanne's eyes narrowed. "I'm glad you feel that way because he *is* a generous man."

"To a fault."

Dressed in the school's navy blue uniform with her strawberry blonde hair pulled back in a ponytail, Bitsy Vanderburg sat on her unmade bed. "You don't really like it, do you? It's pretty tiny for two people." She looked down her thin, aristocratic nose as she tried to discourage BK from unpacking.

"I'm used to small rooms." BK smiled tentatively as she gave the room a second look. *Just not dirty ones*, she thought, taking note of the thick layer of dust that had settled on Bitsy's dresser. It was cluttered with jewel-tone perfume bottles and Clinique cosmetics. "Your name sounds familiar. Bitsy is an uncommon name but I know I've heard it somewhere before."

"I doubt we've met." Bitsy frowned as she looked at BK's dilapidated canvas suitcase, two paper grocery bags, and a vodka box picked up at the last minute from the liquor store.

"What happened to your roommate? Did she transfer?" BK inquired, not really caring one way or the other.

"No. She just changed rooms. You can do that if you talk to the dorm director. I can walk you down to her office if you want to see what other rooms are available."

BK sighed. "Listen, it wasn't my choice to come here but we're going to have to make the best of it. If it was up to me, I'd still be at my aunt's house going to school with all my friends."

"Public school, I suppose."

BK shrugged. "Don't get excited, I'll be back in a minute." When she returned from the bathroom, Bitsy was gone.

Gazing out the window on Bitsy's side of the room, she looked at the courtyard through a fine film of dirt. Watching groups of friends laughing together as they walked to class made her realize that she was completely on her own for the first time in her life. Even though Heather was across campus, she was an upperclassman and BK knew they wouldn't see each other much.

She turned and looked at her new room. She would have to make it feel like home. What choice did she have?

Bitsy stood in the doorway. "Am I in the right room?"

BK had hung posters, cleaned, and was in the process of making her bed.

Walking over to her desk, Bitsy set out a crumbly stick of incense and lit it before settling in to study.

BK covered her nose. "Would you mind putting that out? I don't like it."

Bitsy looked up from her history book. "I'll open the window."

A cold breeze blew the smoke at BK. "It doesn't help."

"Listen." She got up from her chair and stood about a foot away from BK's face. "We may as well get a few things straight since it looks like you're going to stay. This was my room first. It's first come, first served around here so that means I have seniority. I like incense and I'm going to burn it whenever I want. Got it?"

BK tried to shrink back but Bitsy just moved in closer. "And another thing, I don't want you cleaning my side of the room. I don't want you moving my stuff. Some of *my* things are valuable."

"I didn't touch anything of yours."

"Whatever." Bitsy waved her hand, just missing the end of BK's nose. "That's not the point. You walked in here and tried to take over." She squinted. "There's no way I'm going to let you. It was *my* room this morning and it's going to stay *my* room." She turned and went back to her desk. "Why don't you go eat lunch or something?"

You're not going to be the boss of me, BK thought, even though she was hungry.

"Aren't you going?" Bitsy asked.

"I'm on a diet."

"Oh, great. Not only a neat freak but a skinny calorie-counter to boot."

BK glanced at herself in the mirror. *Skinny*. She stared at her heavy thighs for a moment before getting back to work.

Stepping out of the library, BK looked up at the full moon and inhaled the crisp winter air. She checked her watch. Ten minutes until curfew. She had studied through dinner again.

Inside her dorm, groups of girls were gathered in the lounge, talking and laughing. No one looked up at her or invited her to join them as she moved through the room. The buttery smell of popcorn made her mouth water.

At the top of the stairs, incense and laughter drifted out of her room.

"She's so weird. She never eats. At night when I'm trying to fall asleep, all I can hear is her stomach rumbling." As Bitsy made the appropriate sound effects, the other girl in the room couldn't stop giggling.

BK froze outside the door.

"You should have seen the junk she moved in here." BK heard the closet door slide open. "This is the suitcase she had."

One of the other girls made the sound of a phone ringing. "Goodwill is calling. They're looking for their missing luggage."

"I don't know where she got the money to come here. Her family obviously can't afford to buy her a decent suitcase. She must be one of the Beechies," Bitsy said, using a derogatory nickname for students on an Albert Beecham Memorial Scholarship. "And she's Miss Neat and Clean. She makes her bed as soon as she climbs out of it in the morning and when she moved in, she washed everything in the room."

BK turned and ran blindly down the hall. She threw open the door to the stairs and ran squarely into the back of a girl, knocking books out of her arms.

"Hey, watch where you're going. I could've fallen down the stairs you know." The angry girl gathered her books from the floor and turned to face BK. "Don't you have anything to say for yourself?"

"Sorry." BK kept her eyes down, hoping the girl wouldn't notice she was crying.

"BK? Is that you?"

BK looked up, shocked to see a familiar mass of jet-black hair. "Shelby!" She threw her arms around her old friend, a lifeline just when she hit a new low. "What are you doing here? I haven't seen you in ages."

They stepped back from each other. "I go to school here. I live on the fourth floor."

"I can't believe this. I moved in about a week ago. I'm on the second floor."

"It's a small world." Shelby stopped smiling. "What's the matter? You look upset."

"Roommate problems."

Shelby rolled her eyes. "I've had my share of those. I was just headed downstairs to do a little homework. Come along and tell me all about it."

The study lounge was empty except for the two of them, apparently the only ones not interested in watching the new episode of the Gilmore Girls.

Shelby popped open a warm soda, took a sip and held it out to BK. "I gave up asking your mother if you were ever coming back to Seaside. She used to say, 'Maybe next week' but you never showed."

"I was living with my great-aunt until they sent me here." BK took a gulp of the soda.

"I'm glad they did. Who's this roommate that made you so upset tonight?"

"Bitsy Vanderburg."

Shelby's mouth fell open. "I can't believe it. You don't remember who she is, do you?"

BK shook her head.

"She's the one I used the old laxative switcheroo on before we did it to Heather and Evangelina. Remember I told you about that girl at school I couldn't stand?"

"Her? Now I understand why you did it. She's having a grand time bad-mouthing me to all the girls on our floor. I overheard her just before I ran you down tonight. It's no wonder they all look at me like I'm weird."

"Don't let it bother you. She's an idiot and if they believe her, they're idiots too."

They were still talking at eleven when the dorm director blinked the lights to signal that it was time for bed.

"I can't send you back there after she made fun of you. My roommate moved so I have an empty bed in my room. Want to sleep over? We can stop by and pick up your toothbrush and some clothes on the way."

"I can't wait to see the look on Bitsy's face when we walk into the room together. She'll think she's having a nightmare."

When Shelby flicked on the overhead light in BK's room, Bitsy rolled over and squinted in their direction. "What's going on?" She sat up. "What are you two doing together?"

BK quickly gathered up the things she'd need. "Don't worry, Bitsy, we're getting as far away from you as possible." They giggled as they went out the door, leaving the light on behind them.

"I have nothing to wear," BK said as she flipped through the meager selection of dresses hanging in her closet.

"You've been saying the same thing for the entire four years we've been roommates," Shelby said, rolling her eyes.

BK slammed the door and flopped down on her bed. "I don't want to go to the stupid dance anyway."

"You have to go. It's our last homecoming dance," Shelby said. She walked over to her closet, plucked out a dress and tossed it on top of her roommate. "I refuse to go alone. You can wear this. It's too tight on me so it should fit you."

BK propped herself up on one elbow. "I don't think this is the right color for a homecoming dance." She laughed as she dodged a flying pillow.

"It'll look fine. If you weren't so darned skinny, you could've had the first pick of my clothes but you'll have to settle for the ones that don't fit me anymore."

"Shut up." She threw the pillow back.

"I don't understand why you're constantly weighing yourself and dieting. And when you do eat, you only pick at the food, pushing it around your plate to make it look like you've eaten more than you have."

BK sat up and adjusted her shirt. She needed to change the subject, fast. "Will you do my hair?"

Shelby sighed and pulled out her chair. "Have a seat, but you haven't heard the last of this."

"I know. You're persistent and pesky. A lethal combination." She smiled but she didn't want to go. Heather had talked about coming back for the dance but she was swamped with work at Mount Holyoke. And it wasn't like anyone was going to ask BK to dance. The night was going to feel like a drawn-out gym class with no one picking her for a team.

"You look great," Shelby said later as they walked into the gymnasium, already packed with students and alumni. "Especially your hair."

BK touched her French braid. "My hairdresser does a great job but she's incredibly pushy."

Shelby elbowed her.

"Do you think we'll come back here in a few years and try to recapture our lost youth? Look at them over there." BK thrust her chin toward a group of alumni gathered together by the refreshment table.

"It's hard to think of us ever being their age. They look so old."

"Watch what you say. We'll be one of them this time next year."

Shelby pointed to the dance floor. "Isn't that Bitsy dancing?"

"Yeah. Who's she with?"

"He looks old enough to be her father."

BK giggled. "She doesn't look like she's having a very good time, but I heard she's having a run of bad luck lately." Even though she had sworn off pranks long ago,

Shelby had convinced her to help with a few tricks at Bitsy's expense. They had done everything from substituting sugar in the saltshaker at her table in the dining hall to sneaking into her room and short-sheeting her bed. Convinced they had been the perpetrators, Bitsy had reported them to the dorm director, but without any proof they hadn't been punished.

"Don't look now but the man of my dreams is walking toward us."

"Who is it this week?" Shelby was always falling in love. BK started to turn and caught a glimpse of navy blue Brooks Brothers.

Shelby pinched her arm. "I told you not to look."

"At least tell me who he is."

"Fred Stillman. He's in my English class."

Fred stopped next to Shelby. His friends kept walking.

BK first noticed Fred's tousled sandy colored hair and ocean green eyes. His striped tie was askew as if he had played catch with his friends on the way to the dance. Shelby introduced them.

"What's the scab from?" BK asked.

"Rugby." Fred rubbed the bumpy patch below his eye. He looked at Shelby. "Want to dance?"

BK caught up with her later in the ladies' room. "How did it feel to dance with Prince Charming?"

"It was a ball."

BK groaned. "That was bad, even for you."

"Are you having a good time?"

"I haven't found my prince yet but I've been asked to dance twice."

"Don't act so surprised. Why wouldn't boys ask you to dance? You're gorgeous." Shelby changed to a nasal tone, mocking her. "I don't have anything to wear. I'm not going."

BK lobbed a balled up tissue at her head.

"You better not have blown your nose in that."

BK grinned. "That's for me to know."

Shelby rummaged through her purse and pulled out a brush. "I've only been able to dance with Fred twice. That guy who was dancing with Bitsy earlier keeps horning in."

BK tucked a few loose hairs back into her braid. "Who is he anyway?"

"Trevor something or other. I didn't pay attention when he introduced himself. He's out of college but not quite as old as I thought."

"He's kind of cute."

Shelby shook her head. "Maybe, but I get a weird vibe from him."

Trevor was hovering outside the bathroom door when they came out.

"Geez," Shelby whispered. "I'll never get to dance with Fred again." Before BK could respond, Trevor grabbed Shelby's hand and led her to the dance floor.

As soon as the song ended, BK pulled Shelby away. "Sorry. We have to go now," she said to Trevor as they walked off.

"Let's get out of here," Shelby said.

BK winked. "I think someone wants to walk you home. Fred's watching us, waiting for his chance."

Bitsy appeared beside them. "Gee, Shelby, I hope you enjoyed dancing with Trevor tonight. I told him how much you liked him but you were just too shy to let him know."

"You said *what*? I should slap that stupid grin off your face right now." The crowd was filing past them toward the doors.

"Remember this the next time you two decide to pull another dirty trick on me." Bitsy turned and walked over to Fred. In a voice loud enough for Shelby to hear, she said, "Will you walk me back to my dorm? I got separated from my friends and I don't think it's safe for me to walk all alone in the dark."

Fred glanced over at Shelby before following Bitsy.

Shelby snorted. "I can't believe the nerve of that witch."

It's called karma, BK thought. *This is the reason I swore off pranks.* But she didn't want to make Shelby feel worse by sharing her thoughts. "At least you know why Trevor wouldn't leave you alone."

The next morning a bouquet of roses were delivered to their dorm. "The envelope has your name on it," BK said as she lifted them from the box.

Shelby tore open the flap and read aloud, "Had a wonderful time dancing with you last night. Wish I could have walked you home. Maybe next time." She flipped the card over. "There's no signature."

"They must be from Prince Charming."

"As long as they're not from that frog, Trevor," Shelby said, sniffing one of the blossoms. "I don't think even a million kisses would turn him into a prince."

Chapter 15
2004

Little Stan held his nose and pretended to fall out of his chair. "BK farted and, boy oh boy, does it stink."

"Did not!"

Jeanne frowned. "Stanny, please. Remember our little talk about manners at the dinner table? You're seven now. You have to act like it."

"BK's the one who needs to learn manners. I just have to learn my a-b-c's." He pounded his chest and burped out the alphabet. He got as far as "q" before he ran out of gas.

"What a pig," BK muttered. She knew little boys could be gross but Little Stan took it to the top layer of disgustingness. Big Stan was the king of auto sales and his son was the king of crude.

"Don't talk about your brother like that," Stanley said.

BK glared at him. "I can't eat when he's acting like this."

"As if you ever eat," Little Stan said.

Heather laughed.

"Shut up, both of you." BK slammed her fork down. Maybe Heather was becoming like her half-brother since she was back living at home for the summer.

Little Stan stuck his tongue out. "Make me."

BK turned to Jeanne. "Are you going to let him get away with that? Are you the same mother who used to be so strict with Heather and me?"

"Boys will be boys," Stanley said.

Jeanne reached over, took Little Stan's napkin off the table and put it in his lap. "Be nice to your sister. Don't spoil the only day she's home. We hardly get to see her anymore." She turned to BK. "We've missed you."

Her mother's words echoed in her head as she waited alone in line for the Piper Island Ferry. Her sturdy red suitcase, a gift from Shelby, sat on the ground next to her. Shelby was coming out on a later ferry after a family picnic.

There wasn't any big send-off for BK. All Jeanne and Heather had done was wave goodbye from the window before having the butler drop her off at the dock. Little Stan must have been too busy to wave to his sister, immersed, no doubt, in one of his important activities such as practicing nose picking or perfecting ways to cheat at whatever video game he was addicted to this week.

After spending yesterday with her family, it was clear that she would never truly fit in with them. Cliffside Manor would never be her home.

We've missed you.

BK doubted it.

She had either been living at school or spending the summers at Shelby's. If Jeanne missed her, she didn't show it.

This summer was going to be different. She wasn't going to be right next door to her family. She was going to be on Piper Island, ten miles offshore, the same island where a lot of her friends from school were working. She and Shelby had been among the first in line to apply for jobs in the island gift shop when a recruiter from the island's hotel came on campus.

"Hanging around the pool all summer is a bore. I'm ready for some action," Shelby had said, watching Fred Stillman fill out a lifeguard application.

"Just what kind of action do you have in mind?" BK asked, earning herself a punch on the arm.

Once on the open water, the temperature dropped at least ten degrees. BK looked at the little patch of land in the distance. Deep green waves collided against rocks along its shore.

Anne, the manager of the Piper Island Hotel, greeted the newcomers as they disembarked and directed them to the employee housing located in a separate building behind the white clapboard hotel. Like her dorm room, BK would just have to make it feel like home.

"Come on in," Tad called. "The water isn't bad."

Fred and his roommate had waited for BK and Shelby to get out of work before coaxing them to go for a swim. The boys were already in knee-deep water, splashing and trying to dunk each other.

The girls remained by the water's edge. "Even after three weeks, I'm still not used to this freezing water. My feet are numb," BK said. "I miss your heated pool."

"Let's just take the plunge."

As they removed their cover-ups, a wave crashed over the guys' heads.

Shelby laughed as she ran past them and dove into a cresting wave. BK started slowly wading in but Tad chased her back to shore, splashing her all the way. As she ran screaming up the beach, she realized he was no longer chasing her. She turned around. "Is anything wrong?"

"I could've sworn I saw someone up there." He motioned toward a clump of bushes.

"I don't see anything." *Maybe he's trying to scare me so he can put his arm around me*, she thought hopefully. He was cute. She wouldn't stop him.

He followed her to their pile of towels. "I think we should head back."

BK turned to call them just as Fred bent forward and kissed Shelby. She quickly pulled away from him, splashed some water in his direction and ran toward shore.

"Come on, let's go," Tad insisted once Fred came out of the water.

Fred threw a sandy towel at him, hitting him on the legs. "What's the rush?"

"I saw someone in the bushes a few minutes ago." He pointed. "Up there."

Fred gave him a playful shove. "Cut it out. You're going to scare the girls."

"I'm not kidding."

"It's getting late for a couple of working girls anyway," Shelby said.

Fred frowned, but picked up his towel. "Come on then. We'll take you home."

The next morning BK found an envelope that had been slipped under their door. "Maybe it's a love note from Fred."

Shelby reached for it.

BK lifted her arm and kept it out of reach.

"Stop teasing! Open it," Shelby said.

BK read it aloud. "You betrayed my trust. You're no longer worthy of my love. I'm watching you." The words made her stomach roll like one of last night's waves. "Is this for real?" BK examined the pale blue envelope but it was blank.

"It's just a lame prank."

They looked at each other. "Bitsy," they said in unison. Shelby grabbed it, crumpled it up, and tossed it in the trash. "She was probably the one spying on us from the bushes last night."

"Ouch." BK struck her finger with the hammer. Trying to nail a board over one of the first floor windows was more difficult than she thought. The wind was picking up and the rain was coming down hard.

"Looks like you could use some help." Anne, the hotel manager, took the hammer from BK's hand and started pounding. "In all my years on this island, we've never been hit by a strong hurricane. I keep hoping this one will change course. The last one lost power and was nothing more than a bad rainstorm by the time it reached us."

"I guess I'm not a very good carpenter," BK said as Anne expertly drove the last nail into the wood.

"That does it. All the windows are boarded up." She shook the board to make sure it was secure. "Let's get back to the hotel."

"I need to grab a few things. I'll be right along." BK hurried off to her room. It hit her once she was alone. A hurricane was headed for Piper Island and she was stranded in the middle of the ocean. Her insides felt like gelatin, quaking and quivering, as she picked up her hairbrush, toothbrush, and a book and threw them into a bag along with a couple of changes of clothes.

"Can you take my things over with you?" Shelby came in and started stuffing items into BK's bag before she could answer.

"Why? Where are you going in such a hurry?"

"I'm meeting Fred. He wants to watch the waves. Doesn't that sound romantic?"

"No. It sounds dangerous and stupid." BK bit her lip. "Promise you won't stay out long."

"Okay." Pulling a piece of paper from her pocket, she tucked it in her intricately carved jewelry box. It was lined with red velvet with a tray that lifted to reveal a compartment below. "A note from Fred. He left it for me at the gift shop. I'm saving it for my scrapbook."

"Why don't you just meet him at the hotel where it's safe?"

"Then we wouldn't be alone." She smiled as she turned toward the door. "Stop worrying. I'll see you later."

BK repacked the bag and ran into Bitsy in the hall as she was leaving. She ducked her head and tried to brush past her.

"Was that Shelby I just saw heading down the beach?" Bitsy said.

BK looked up. "What's it to you?"

"Did she get a note?"

"How'd you know?" BK frowned. "There was one from Fred asking her to meet him."

"Was it in his handwriting?"

"Why all the questions?"

"Just tell me." Bitsy let out a loud breath.

"I don't know. I didn't see it but Shelby left it in our room." BK unlocked the door and let Bitsy in for the first time this summer. She snatched the note from BK as soon as BK took it from the box.

Meet me on the rocks to watch the waves.

Fred

"This looks just like the others except this one is signed," Bitsy said.

What others? BK thought as she took it back. "Do you mean that stupid note you shoved under our door?"

"I told you a million times: I *didn't* write that note."

"Right." BK rolled her eyes. It was time they all grew up and worked out a truce. She was tired of the games.

"Shelby's gotten a couple others."

BK stared. *No she hasn't.* She would've shown them to BK first. Certainly not Bitsy.

"But she never saw them. I kind of took them before she had a chance to find them. The edge of the envelope was sticking out from under the door the first time and the second one was tacked on the message board downstairs." Bitsy's eyes narrowed. "I didn't want to be accused of doing something I didn't do so I hid them in my room. Come on, I'll show you."

The building was empty but not silent with the wind invisibly battering the weathered clapboards as BK followed her. Her stomach lurched when Bitsy pulled two pale blue envelopes from under her mattress.

"The first one is a lot like the one you accused me of sending." She read it aloud. "You *did not* deserve my love. Now you will have to pay. But how?"

BK took the threatening note and stared at it.

"The one I found yesterday really scared me," Bitsy continued. "I didn't know what to do when I read it. If this person's serious, Shelby could be in danger."

BK's clammy hands opened the envelope.

You will die soon, tramp. How do you prefer? A knife? A gun? My bare hands wrapped around your lying neck squeezing tighter and tighter and tighter until your body goes limp and your eyes roll back in your head?

BK sat on the bed, struggling to swallow her panic. *Stay calm*, she thought. *Find Shelby. Bring her to safety.* "How could you read this and not warn her? You should've called the police or at least turned them over to Anne."

"I would've been accused of writing them. You know you would have pointed the finger at me. I don't want to get fired."

BK rubbed her forehead. "Wait a minute. At first I thought these notes were real because the envelopes are all the same. But I almost forgot who I was dealing with."

"What's that supposed to mean?"

"You *did* write them, didn't you?" Relief spread through her muscles, releasing the anxiety knotted and balled inside. "The envelopes would be the same if you wrote them all. Maybe you just didn't have a chance to deliver these two before the hurricane."

She grabbed the envelope and waved it in front of BK. "Look at the hole where it was tacked on the board."

"Anyone can stick a tack through paper."

Bitsy threw it on the floor. "Fine. Don't believe me."

BK stomped out but Bitsy was a few steps behind her all the way. In the kitchen of the hotel, the staff was gathered around a long prep table listening as the radio announcer gave the latest storm update. All the guests had left the island.

Fred walked up next to her holding a clipboard. "Hey, BK, where's your sidekick? Don't tell me the two of you actually spend time apart." He smiled. "She's the last staffer unaccounted for."

"What are you doing here?" BK's heart pounded. "Shelby's waiting for you at the rocks."

"See?" Bitsy said.

"The rocks? I don't know what you're talking about."

BK glared at Bitsy. "Did you send her on a wild goose chase in this storm?"

"I did *not* write those notes." Bitsy raised her right hand. "Swear."

"Then I've got to find her." BK ran out the back door, her feet barely touching the steps, fueled by adrenaline and panic. Wind whipped across the island, blasting sand against her legs. The hurricane was getting closer by the minute. She put her hand up to shield her eyes. Stumbling forward, she tripped on driftwood as she made her way to the jetty.

Shelby, where are you?

When she reached the line of rocks that thrust out into the tumultuous sea, she called her friend's name over and over. Movement on the last rock caught her eye but she couldn't see clearly.

That could be you out there. Hold on, Shelby, I'm coming to get you.

BK carefully stepped onto the first rock. She looked out to the reflective sign that was mounted at the end of the jetty to warn boaters. She was one of the few not brave enough to scratch her initials on the back.

Further beyond, between two of the rocks, loomed a large split and the only way to pass was to take a running jump.

I'll have to do it.

She placed one foot tentatively on the next rock. Taking a deep breath she continued, ignoring the storm raging around her. Her muscles tense, she moved slowly, careful to keep her footing. Her wet hair stuck to her face. She wiped it away with the back of her hand.

It seemed to take hours to get to the point at which, on a normal day, she would have turned around and headed for shore. She had reached the split between the rocks.

BK stood rooted to the spot.

Be brave. Do it for Shelby.

"Here goes." She closed her eyes, took a few steps back, ran forward and jumped.

I did it.

She looked ahead after she landed on solid rock.

Now I have to make it all the way to the end.

Waves splashed up on the rocks, soaking her. She heard an indistinguishable noise and she looked to where she thought she had seen movement. She couldn't see anything but the ocean battering the long line of rocks ahead. Suddenly she slipped and fell between two rocks, wedging her foot in a crevice.

Twisting and pulling frantically, it wouldn't budge. The tide was coming in and the surf was getting rougher. It wouldn't be long until it engulfed the jetty. She had to free herself.

I'm going to drown.

She took a deep breath.

Don't panic.

She grit her teeth and twisted her leg, trying to get loose. She tried bouncing up and down and still her foot wouldn't move.

Please, God, help me. I'm too young to die. I've got to get myself free.

Reaching down into the dark fissure, she felt a smaller rock next to her ankle and tried to wiggle it. As her knuckles became raw, she felt some movement. With one last pull, her foot came loose. Blood ran from her ankle as she sat panting on the rock.

Taking a deep breath, she looked to the end of the jetty. The rocks at the end were now completely covered in water. Shelby was gone.

It must have been my imagination. She probably wasn't even there.

She managed to stand and began to hobble back. The split in the jetty stood between her and the shore.

I did it before and I'm going to have to do it again.

She tried to avoid landing on her injured foot and ended up falling forward onto her hands. Pain shot from her wrists to her elbows.

I'll cry later. Right now I have to concentrate on Shelby. Where is she?

BK looked back to where she had been stuck. She would be under water by now if she hadn't gotten loose.

Limping down the beach, she screamed Shelby's name but like everything else that wasn't nailed down, her voice was whisked away, blown across the island.

Fred, Tad, and Bitsy caught up with her. "Any sign of her?"

She shook her head. "No."

"You're hurt. You should go back to the hotel," Fred said.

"I'm fine. I'll take care of myself after I find Shelby." Her voice cracked. "She's my best friend."

"We'll help," Tad said, joined by most of the hotel staff. He divided them into search teams and assigned each a section of the beach.

BK ran lopsided through the sand. The wind pushed her from behind, propelling her forward. The storm was getting stronger. Soon, it wouldn't be safe to search.

Chapter 16

Anne caught up to BK, waving a torn sweatshirt. "We found this on the beach. Is it Shelby's?"

BK touched the gray fleece material with navy blue stripes sewn in a ring around the wrist and nodded. "She was wearing this when she left our room."

Tad pulled on Anne's arm. "I see something bobbing in the water."

Anne grabbed her binoculars. "I do, too. It looks like a capsized boat."

"Can you see Shelby?" BK asked.

Anne handed her the binoculars and said, "It looks like someone may be clinging to it but I can't tell if it's her. The waves are bringing it closer to the jetty."

Everyone raced to the edge of the water. "I'm going in," BK yelled.

Anne grabbed her arm. "Don't be ridiculous. You won't be able to help her. You're not a strong swimmer as it is."

"I have to."

"Leave it to the lifeguards. They know what they're doing."

BK paced, her ankle throbbing. She watched four lifeguards with Fred and Tad in the lead as they ventured onto the jetty, linked together by rope. Waves crashed, the wind howled, and the sea grass on the dunes was blown flat.

Anne put her arm around BK's shoulders. "They're doing their best to save her."

"I should be helping."

"She'll need you as soon as they rescue her." Anne continued to look through the binoculars. "I think they've got her." BK hobbled over as fast as she could.

"It isn't Shelby," Fred said as he helped carry the person to shore. The team was as drenched as their rescued victim.

"She wasn't with the boat?"

"No. Just this guy. Stand back, BK. Give him some room."

She stared at the man's face as he coughed up water and fought to catch his breath. He looked familiar. "Trevor?"

"I recognize him. He's been a guest here a couple of different times this summer," Anne yelled over the wind.

BK grabbed Anne's arm. "He was at our homecoming dance last fall. He wouldn't leave Shelby alone." It all made sense now. A chill passed through her despite the balmy temperature outside. The notes were from Trevor.

Fred's face hardened. "I remember him."

BK pounced, grabbing Trevor by the shoulders. Shaking him violently, she screamed, "What have you done to Shelby, you bastard?"

His head flopped around like a bobble-head. Someone grabbed her from behind and pulled her away from his limp body.

He wheezed. "Who?"

Like a tornado, BK whirled from the arms that restrained her and landed on Trevor's chest. Arms pounding, nails digging, teeth biting, she attacked, only dimly aware of the hands that tried to pry her away. Trevor covered his face but didn't seem to have the strength to fight back as she wrapped her fingers around his neck. "What happened to her?"

Three people pulled her off him.

Fred kneeled next to Trevor and growled, "Tell us what happened to Shelby or we'll let her loose on you again."

Trevor rubbed his neck. "I don't know what you're talking about."

BK looked toward the heaving water.

Shelby is still out there.

Before anyone could stop her, she turned and waded into the surf. The undertow sucked the sand from under her feet and the water stung her raw flesh. Directly ahead, a wall of water mounted.

The next thing she knew she was laying on her back in the sand gasping for air, the briny taste of the ocean in her mouth.

Where is Shelby?

Trevor wasn't talking. They helped him back to the hotel, much too gently in BK's opinion, and questioned him.

"We've got to go back out there," BK said, limping back and forth outside the guest room where they had Trevor detained.

Anne was firm. "It's too dangerous now. We have to wait until the storm passes."

"It'll be too late by then. She'll be dead."

"We don't even know if Trevor had her on the boat with him." Anne touched BK's arm. "And if she was, I'm afraid it's probably too late anyway. No one could survive in that rough water this long."

Tears rolled down BK's cheeks. "I should have stopped her. It's all my fault."

"Don't blame yourself. You've done everything you possibly could to find her."

Fred put his arm around her. "Come on. Let me wrap your ankle so you'll be ready to go back out and start searching again when the storm calms down."

The search resumed at first light. They split up to cover the entire island, including all the rooms in the employee dorm. BK and Fred were assigned an old World War II bunker.

"I didn't know this was here," BK yelled over the sound of the rough surf. They walked off the main path to a narrow walkway. They approached the concrete bunker which was set into the side of a hill. The door had been removed so they passed through the opening which was flanked by poison ivy and walked down the steps.

"That's the whole idea of a bunker. The enemy's not supposed to see it," Fred said. "Shelby and I stumbled upon it when we were out walking a few nights ago."

Once inside, it took a moment for her eyes to adjust to the dim light coming from two narrow rectangular windows. Colorful graffiti was spray painted on the walls. Mustiness stung her nostrils as she looked around the room. There was something on the floor in the far corner and it wasn't moving.

"Shelby!" BK ran to her and started to take the tape off her mouth. "I don't think she's breathing."

Fred took Shelby's wrist and checked for a pulse. "She's alive."

As he slapped her face gently and called her name, Shelby's eyes opened slowly. "Fred," she murmured.

BK was in the hospital, waiting for her mother to pick her up. In her typical fashion, she had tripped helping Shelby back to the hotel and broken her ankle. They kept her overnight for observation but she could've told them she was fine. She stared at the bouquet of flowers from the Fultons that had been delivered to her hospital room.

She reached out and touched the envelope, remembering the flowers that were delivered to Shelby the morning after the homecoming dance. That had just been the beginning of all the gifts that had followed. Candy, stuffed animals, perfume, candles, and even a chocolate chip cookie so big that it was in a pizza box had arrived with unsigned love notes.

She shivered. "These flowers are not from Trevor," she said aloud in the empty room. A nurse with particularly kind brown eyes allayed BK's fears last night by wheeling her down the hall to Trevor's room. A police officer was posted outside the door.

BK hoisted herself up on her crutches and headed back to Trevor's room.

The shift must have changed because there was a different officer outside the door. She introduced herself then asked, "When is he going to jail?"

"The doctor said he'll be ready by tomorrow."

"Good." She turned and tried to maneuver around a cart of medical supplies. "I want him locked up as soon as possible. Preferably in a small, rat infested cell without a key."

The officer chuckled.

Trevor's door burst open. "BK!"

She swung around, almost toppling over.

Blood was dripping from the back of his hand where he had ripped out his IV tube. "Dead, dead, dead, dead, dead," he repeated loudly as he stared at her. "Dead, dead, dead..."

"Nurse," the officer called as he blocked Trevor from reaching BK.

Three nurses, moving so fast that they looked like white streaks, pulled him back into his room and pushed the door closed behind them. A doctor soon followed.

BK leaned on her crutches as a tear rolled down her cheek.

The officer steadied her. "Should I get a nurse to help you back to your room?"

"I'll be fine in a minute." She shook her head. "He's really nuts."

"Don't let his lawyer hear you say that. They'll probably try to get him off with an insanity plea. They try it all the time."

"He can't get away with what he's done. It was too horrible."

One of the nurses came out of Trevor's room, smoothing out her uniform. "He insists the girl is dead. We had to restrain him. He won't be causing any more trouble."

BK made her way up the hallway and stopped to rest on a sun-warmed chair. She stared out the large windows, watching people walking in the parking lot, seemingly unaware of the evil in the world, or the evil right here in this building. She wondered if the darkness of the hurricane would ever be gone from inside her.

BK sat on the edge of Shelby's hospital bed.

Shelby grinned. "Did Fred do CPR on me?"

"Are you kidding? This is what you're concerned about?" BK rolled her eyes. "No. All he did was slap you around a little."

Shelby's voice was soft, almost a whisper. "Trevor did enough of that."

"I'm sorry. That was my feeble attempt at humor. It was a stupid thing to say." BK touched her arm lightly. "Are you ready to talk about it yet?"

She looked away, staring out the window. "It all happened so fast. I was looking for Fred at the jetty when Trevor grabbed me from behind. He came out of nowhere and overpowered me. I didn't even have a chance to run. I was able to wiggle out of my sweatshirt but he caught me again before dragging me to the bunker. I screamed as loud as I could but the wind was blowing so hard, it would've been a miracle if anyone heard me."

"I should have followed you."

Shelby shook her head. "You didn't want me to go. I should have listened."

"Did he…" BK searched Shelby's face. "Did he… do anything to you in the bunker?"

Shelby looked down. "Not in that way. He hit me. He told me he loved me. I don't know which was worse. And when I didn't respond the way he wanted, he turned into a lunatic. He called me horrible names and said I was disloyal."

"Disloyal?"

"He raved on and on about how I had kissed Fred when we were swimming that night." She shook her head. "And I didn't even really kiss him. I splashed water in his face."

"I remember."

"He even knew I had taken a walk with Fred. He must have followed us."

"It gives me the creeps to think he was following you, watching you. Though that is what that first note had said. 'I'm watching you.' And we blamed Bitsy."

"I wish it *had* been her."

BK nodded and listened to the rubber-soled footsteps of a nurse as she passed the room.

Shelby twisted the edge of her pillowcase. "He tried to strangle me." She tugged at the neck of her green hospital gown. The marks were visible. "I can still feel him squeezing tighter and tighter. I couldn't breathe." Tears filled her eyes. "He said we were going to spend eternity in each other's arms so I pretended I was dead."

BK hugged her.

"The coward. He didn't even end up killing himself. I heard him running out of the bunker."

"He must have gone to his boat and tried to escape. If it's any consolation, I tried to strangle him after they pulled him out of the ocean."

Shelby's mouth smiled but her eyes were dull. "Too bad you didn't finish the job."

"If you like that, you should've seen me when I thought you were out on the jetty. You would've been amazed when I jumped over the split. Just like a mountain goat."

"Oh, yeah. I see." Shelby pointed at BK's crutches.

"Be nice. I wouldn't even be on crutches if I hadn't gone traipsing all over the island after I hurt it."

"Okay. Just like a goat. I believe you."

"A *mountain* goat."

"Right." Shelby's stomach growled.

BK pulled the bedside tray closer. "Why don't you try to eat a little more? It will help you get your strength back."

Shelby bit her lip but didn't say anything. BK could almost hear the words her friend was holding back. She'd heard them a hundred times before. *You're getting boney. Boys like some curves. You need to eat.* Sometimes Shelby's eyes would well with tears, forcing BK to look away.

She lifted a spoonful of soup and held it out. "What? You don't like delicious hospital cuisine?"

Shelby pushed further back into the pillow. "I can't. It smells like B.O."

BK sniffed what appeared to be chicken noodle and made a face before dropping the spoon back into the bowl. "You're right."

"I'd die for a nice greasy cheeseburger. With fries. And a chocolate shake."

"Don't even joke about dying." *Or about eating that garbage*, she thought. Even though she used to enjoy junk food when she was young, the thought of eating anything heavier than fruit or vegetables now repulsed her.

Shelby got serious again. "I thought I was going to die."

BK squeezed her hand. "You're safe."

CHAPTER 17

Sweat beaded on the back of her neck as BK looked at the flowers in front of her, the fragrance drifting up to her nose. As beautiful as they were, bouquets of flowers were forever linked to Trevor. Now, nearly four years later, the mere thought of him made her want to run to Shelby and make sure she was all right.

Before she could pull the card from its envelope, there was a knock on her dorm room door.

Jeanne and Stanley entered single file, followed by Heather and Little Stan who was tugging on his underwear.

"You're early," BK said as her mother gave her a kiss on the cheek and a stiff hug. She checked her watch. "The ceremony doesn't begin for three hours." Then she backed away to let them pass and bumped the vase, nearly knocking it over.

"I see you got our flowers," Jeanne said.

"And I see that graduating from college hasn't changed you from being a klutz," Heather said.

BK ignored her and thanked her mother. "They're beautiful." *But if you knew me at all, you wouldn't have sent flowers. You would've known better.*

Heather turned in a complete circle. BK had already stripped the room. All the boxes were piled in the corner. "You shared this tiny room with Shelby? How did you fit all your stuff in here? It's like a shoe box. Where is Shelby, anyway?"

"She's giving her parents the grand tour of our new apartment."

"I hope it's bigger than this place."

BK wasn't about to pick a fight but her tongue itched to give Heather a dig about living back at home because she couldn't get into law school. For now Heather was answering phones at Stanley's car dealership to pay her expenses. No way was Stanley going to let her mooch off him.

Little Stan, who was jumping on the bed, reached his hand up and touched the ceiling with each bounce.

Stanley coughed. "Nice day for a graduation. No rain in sight."

"We better get going. I want good seats," Jeanne said.

"Go on without me. I need to talk to BK," Stanley said. "Alone."

Jeanne looked puzzled but pulled Little Stan's arm, yanking him off the bed. "Come on, Stanny."

Little Stan grinned as they left.

BK pinched her nose as she ran to open a window. "Little Stan strikes again."

Stanley sat on the bare mattress. "You know what I always say."

"I know. 'Boys will be boys.'"

Stanley looked serious. "I got your note. You do realize that what you're doing is blackmail, right?"

BK snorted. "Blackmail? Don't be ridiculous, Stanley. Did you bring the keys?"

Stanley pulled out a cigar and chewed on the end. "I don't negotiate with blackmailers."

"In all these years, I've never threatened to tell your secret, not once, even after you sent us away to live with Aunt Beatrice. So how can you call this blackmail?"

"It's implied."

"I never said give me a car or I'll spill the beans. I don't even think your secret is a big deal."

Stanley averted his eyes. A breeze blew in, freshening the air.

"You don't have to be uncomfortable. So what if you prefer men? It's not like we're living in the dark ages."

"Then you expect me to believe that you think I'll hand over a car to you just because I'm a nice guy?"

I'd never think that. "It's not like I asked for a flashy sports model. I left that up to you. I just need a little car to get me around. New, used, whatever."

"If this isn't blackmail, then why'd you think I'd *give* you a car? You're not really my kid."

"You've made that perfectly clear." BK licked her lips. "I feel like you owe me for all the years you sent me away just so I wouldn't tell that I walked in on you and the butler. I missed out on spending my childhood with my family. You took away my chance to get to know my brother. Do you realize he's now older than I was when you sent me away? Do you think he's ready, even now, to be without his parents' love and protection?"

Stanley was silent.

"Plus, I'd never hurt my mother by outing you. I couldn't do that to her."

"She knows. She's always known."

BK put her hands out, palms up. "Then why live a lie?"

He shrugged. "It's the business. I can't risk all the years of hard work I put into it."

BK quoted him from his TV ad. "The king of car sales. Come in and get treated royally at Georgopolous Auto Kingdom." She always cringed when it came on with him dressed in a crown and velvet robe.

"Can't you just hear the assholes calling me the *queen* of car sales?"

"That would be their problem, not yours."

"Decreased sales *are* my problem. But what do you know about business at your age? You'll learn fast enough when you start working at the Lindlay Group. PR is all about image."

BK nodded. She hadn't thought about it that way but it made perfect sense. Stanley put business first. Of course he'd be concerned about the bottom line above all else.

"So why do you need a car so bad? Your apartment is close to your job. You can take the T. It would be more of a pain to try to park the thing than it's worth."

"I'll have a space in the parking garage at work so that's half the battle. We wouldn't want it to go to waste, right?"

Stanley popped the cigar in his mouth. It bobbed as he talked. "A nice perk but not reason enough to use extortion to get a car, especially for a girl like you. Now your sister is another matter. She does anything to get what she wants but I know what kind of kid you are. So tell me, what's the real story?"

She sat next to him and took a deep breath. "It's because of Trevor. I'm still scared even though I know he's locked up. I feel like he's still around watching Shelby. Watching me."

"I see." Stanley chuckled. "No pun intended."

BK grinned. "I'd feel a lot safer if I had my own car and didn't have to rely on public transportation."

Stanley went over to the jacket he had slung over the rod in her empty closet, pulled out a set of keys but didn't hand them to her. "I was going to give you a clunker just to get you off my back but now that I know your real reason, I'll pick out a new car with an alarm system for you." He took the Auto Kingdom key chain off and tossed it to her. "You can pick up the keys Tuesday."

As she wrapped her fingers around the cold metal crown, her heart filled with a warmth for Stanley she'd never felt before.

"Thank you," she said.

"Hello." He extended his hand. He didn't have the manicured office worker type hand; instead, his callused hand clasped hers gently, despite the obvious strength. Even his cologne was manly, with no hit of floral undertones. "I'm Max Emerson." He was over six feet tall with thick, dark hair.

"BK Hartshaw," she replied with a nervous smile. "It's a pleasure to meet you, Mr. Emerson. Please have a seat." She gestured to one of the leather chairs in her new office. Her office was the smallest at the public relations firm but it was quite a step up from her former cramped cubicle. She had personalized the bland beige walls with framed photographs taken by Shelby. A bright orange sunset over the marsh was her favorite.

"Senior account representative," Max read the line under her name as he fingered one of her business cards that sat in an ornate brass holder on top of her desk. "How can someone as young as you have an office like this?"

"Hard work, long hours, and absolutely no personal life."

He nodded as if he could identify with that. "Your boss tells me you're the one to see for fresh ideas."

"I'll do my best," she said before launching into her carefully planned presentation. By the end of the meeting, she had felt as though they were already friends.

BK circled the block one more time hoping to find a spot closer to her apartment. She noticed the silver car again. "Wasn't that parked on the opposite side of the street yesterday?"

Shelby shrugged. "I don't know."

"Now that I think about it, I've seen that car a few times this week."

"How can you tell? It's a pretty ordinary car. There must be hundreds that look just like it in the city."

"It has a bent antenna."

"Maybe one of our neighbors got a new car," Shelby said.

BK shook her head. "It's not new."

"People do buy used cars. Not everybody has a stepfather who sets them up with a new car every two years."

A parking space opened up directly in front of their building but BK drove past it.

"Hey! What are you doing?"

"I want to take a closer look." When she rounded the corner, the silver car was gone. She pulled into the space it had occupied.

Shelby checked the glove compartment for a notepad and pen. "Next time, write down the license plate number, Sherlock. Then we'll have something to go on."

The musty smell in the entry hall of their apartment building was stronger than usual. The loose basement door combined with a wet spring had made the problem worse. "Now that I got my promotion and we're both earning decent salaries, maybe we should start looking for a new place. New being the operative word," BK said as she unlocked their door and went inside.

"Our lease is up in a few months, so why not?" Shelby tossed her purse and coat on the couch. "I'm going to hop in the shower. I hope you're still coming with us to the movies tonight."

BK didn't answer. How was she going to get out of it this time? She opened her closet door and pulled out her favorite sweats. Maybe Shelby would get the hint when she saw what BK was wearing. Not exactly clothes to wear out on the town. Before she could hang up her work dress, the phone rang. She pulled her robe on as she ran into the kitchen and checked the caller ID. Unknown. "Hello?"

Silence.

"Hello," she repeated. "Is anyone there?"

Her ear was assaulted by the windy sound of an obscene caller.

"Drop dead, idiot," she blurted, jabbing the end button forcefully with her index finger and slamming the phone back on its base.

She had one leg in the sweatpants when the phone rang again. She answered in her most stern librarian tone.

The dial tone hummed in her ear.

Before she got back to her room the phone was ringing again. She clicked talk immediately followed by end, unclipped the phone line and left it dangling.

A few minutes later Shelby came out of the bathroom wrapped in a towel. "Who called?"

"No one. Just a crank caller."

She frowned. "I thought it might be Fred. He's supposed to call tonight."

BK reattached the phone cord. "We wouldn't want to miss a call from Dr. Stillman." Fred was an intern in Chicago.

When the phone rang, Shelby grabbed it and headed for her room. Before she got there, she turned and grabbed BK's arm. "Listen," she mouthed as she tipped the phone so BK could hear.

"You thought you heard the last of me but I'm in your life. Accept it."

BK clutched her stomach. She recognized the voice as Trevor's.

"I don't have to accept anything, Trevor." Shelby's voice was rising. "I'm going to call your doctor and he'll put a stop to this."

"I'll be watching you for the rest of your life."

Shelby dropped the phone, her eyes fixed on it as though it was alive. "He's crazy."

"That's why he's locked up." BK hung up the phone.

Shelby chewed on her fingernail. "Do you think he could be out? What if he was the one in the silver car?"

"Call your lawyer and have him find out if Trevor was released."

She glanced at the clock as she moved on to her next fingernail. "It's after hours."

"Try anyway."

"I had to leave a message," Shelby said, shivering in her damp towel after she made the call. "I can't deal with this. I thought the whole nightmare with Trevor was over. I can't go through it again."

BK put her arm around Shelby's shoulder. "We're not sure where he was calling from. We're probably jumping to conclusions about that silver car. I doubt it was him. It was probably the friendly neighborhood burglar waiting for a chance to get at our treasures." She pointed to the old, out-of-style furniture that came with the apartment. "Or maybe our priceless jewels." She held out her hand to model the small birthstone ring Jeanne and Stanley had given her on her twenty-first birthday.

Shelby took a deep breath. "I hope you're right."

"There's no use getting upset until we know if he's out. Now go get dressed before you catch pneumonia."

As she waited for the lawyer to call, BK started dinner. Neither of them liked to cook and they usually had cold cereal or Chinese take-out from the place down the street. BK practically lived on their steamed vegetables over white rice. The single serving was enough for dinner and lunch the next day.

"Are my eyes playing tricks on me or am I actually seeing BK Hartshaw bent over the stove?" Shelby said, returning in her pajamas. "I get it. You're going to try to poison me before Trevor gets his chance."

BK threw a potholder, hitting the side of Shelby's head. "Don't give me any ideas." She stirred the bubbling pot of ziti.

"Obviously, I'm going to skip the movies tonight so you're off the hook. You can be a TV-watching hermit for another night."

"Don't say that. I like going out with your friends from *City Scene*." BK pitted an avocado and put the halves in the food processor. She added lemon juice, olive oil and spices before blending. It was her kind of sauce: no cooking, low calorie.

"But it must get boring for you when we talk about deadlines, photography, and office gossip."

BK drained the pasta and tossed it with the avocado cream sauce. "I find that all quite interesting, especially the office gossip. What bothers me is the way you're always trying to push Rick and me together. You're not a matchmaker, you know."

"He's handsome. He's a successful writer. And better than that, he's nice. Maybe I should be a matchmaker." Shelby stuck her index finger in the sauce. "Mmm."

"I know Rick's a great catch but I don't feel like going through the whole dating ritual again unless I'm really into the guy. It's too exhausting."

Shelby sighed. "Oh, I get it. He's actually able to support himself. I forgot that's one of your turnoffs. Here's how your personal ad would read: Professional SWF seeking emotionally unavailable male between twenty-five and thirty-five. Must have means to pick up own unemployment check."

BK smiled as she thought of "BK's Deadbeats," the poem Shelby had written as a joke on BK's last birthday. "Okay, I'll admit I haven't had the best track record but today might be the turning point. You'll never guess who I ran into at the gym."

Shelby set the plates of food on the table. "I don't know but judging from the look on your face, it must be somebody good."

"Max Emerson."

"The rich, handsome client?" Shelby chewed her first bite. "Tastes good."

BK smiled. "He asked me out! I gave him my number."

"I haven't seen you this excited about a date in a long time. I hope the stress of this whole Trevor thing doesn't ruin it for you."

"What do you mean?" She took a few bites of her dinner before absently pushing the rest around on her plate.

"Whenever your life gets stressful, you seem to slip back into your old habits."

BK didn't say anything.

Shelby frowned. "This is the only thing that ever comes between us. Other friendships get strained over men or clothes or money but not ours." Shelby pushed her plate into the center of the table.

"I thought you liked it."

"Your cooking isn't the problem."

BK struggled to swallow the gummy wad of pasta that had formed in her mouth.

"I know you don't like me to talk about this but I'm going to anyway," Shelby said.

BK's eyes darted to the door but, like a fly buzzing at a closed window, there was no escape.

"You know where this is going. Don't even think of trying to run away."

They had been friends too long. Shelby could almost read BK's mind. "This isn't a good time to talk about it. Why don't we wait until this thing with Trevor is resolved?"

"Nice try, but you're not going to get off that easy. I'm worried about you. This has nothing to do with me or Trevor."

BK folded her arms across her chest. This wasn't fair. She tried to swallow her resentment but it was stuck in her throat like the pasta.

"I keep thinking you're making progress but then you slip. I noticed it from the day you got your promotion a few weeks ago and now I'm afraid these calls from Trevor will push you over the edge. You already eat next to nothing all day and exercise like mad. I don't get it. You seem to have more energy than ever." She threw her hands up. "But I know that it can't go on like this forever. Eventually, you're going to damage your body. I'm scared for you."

BK looked away. None of her co-workers criticized her. In fact, she was praised for her discipline and self-control. "Exercise is good for me and you said it yourself, I have plenty of energy. So what's the problem?" She didn't give Shelby the opportunity to respond. "There isn't one."

"You hide it well in your baggy old sweats but you can't fool me. I know you're nothing but skin and bones."

BK fought back her tears. She was much more than skin and bones. She was a reasonably intelligent person, hard working, a good friend. When the phone rang, she shoved her chair back so fast that it toppled over. "I'll get it in case it's Trevor."

The caller ID read unknown again. She picked it up but he spoke before she had a chance to say hello.

"I want to talk to Shelby."

"I know it's you, Trevor."

There was no response.

"You really picked the wrong time to be pulling this with me. Talk to me, you coward." BK felt ready for battle, heart pounding, muscles tense. She may have to listen to Shelby but she wasn't about to take any crap from Trevor.

"I want to talk to Shelby. I know she's sitting at the table. Go get her."

"You're not going to do this to us again." She hung up.

Shelby put her hand out when the phone rang again. "Let me get it this time. Maybe I can reason with him." She tipped the phone sideways so BK could hear. "What do you want, Trevor?"

"I knew you'd talk to me."

"I want you to leave me alone."

"No can do. We're meant to spend our lives together. We're going to get married."

Shelby's posture was rigid. "You don't even know me. How can you say that?"

"Don't use that tone with me. It's disrespectful to speak to your future husband that way."

"Just get out of my life. I don't want to marry you. I don't even want to know you. Got it?" She disconnected and threw the phone on the table.

When Trevor's words registered in BK's mind, she inhaled sharply. "He knew you were sitting at the table." They switched the lights off and ran to the front window.

"Oh my God," Shelby cried. "The silver car."

BK ran around and pulled down all the shades in the apartment. The phone rang before she finished.

"What?" Shelby yelled.

BK ran over to listen.

"Blocking my view wasn't very nice, Shelby. I enjoy watching you. Especially when you were wrapped in that little bitty towel."

"You're sick."

"Not anymore. I've made a complete recovery. Ask my doctor."

"After he hears what I have to say, you'll be back in your padded cell before tomorrow night."

"Don't say that," he shouted. "We have to be together. Nothing else matters, can't you see? You're meant for me."

"No!"

"Don't try to deny our destiny."

"I want nothing to do with you. You need help."

This time, he hung up on her.

"He's completely deranged, BK," Shelby said, collapsing into a nearby chair, tears flowing as she gripped her face.

BK peered out through a crack between the shade and the curtain. "We'd better call the police before he makes his next move."

Chapter 18

There were no secrets from the upstairs neighbor, a widow alone in the world except for her cats. Mrs. Harvey heard everything. Lack of privacy. Another reason to move.

The sharp rap on the door didn't precede a complaint about the TV volume for a change. "Take this," Mrs. Harvey said, handing BK a dusty answering machine. "As soon as the police finished talking to me, I dug it out of my stuff in the basement. It's old but it still works. If that guy leaves any messages, you can take the cassette to the police." She pressed a button and a cassette popped out. "It will make it easier for you."

Now BK's stomach clenched at the sight of the blinking message light. She set her grocery bag on the chair and stared at it. As she ran her finger over the play button, she thought about how long it had taken the police to arrive at their apartment. By then, Trevor had retreated back into the darkness.

"There's no sign of him, ma'am," the officer had reported after searching in and around the building. "No silver car either."

She reached for a pen and a piece of scrap paper before pressing the play button. *Beep.*

"Shelby, this is John Weintraub. You can't get the common type of restraining order because Trevor isn't a relative or someone you've dated. We're going to have to go for a harassment prevention order in court. And I'm still trying to reach the administrator at Willowbrook Hospital to find out why they failed to notify you that Trevor had been released. I'll let you know when I find out."

She pressed pause and jotted down the message from Shelby's lawyer.

Beep. "Why, Shelby?" As the voice faded to a whisper, the hair on her arms stood on end. "How could you do that to me? Why call the police? All I wanted was to talk to you, to tell you that I love you."

Beep.

"Shelby. I don't think you understand. The past is over. I've changed. I'm not the same as before." Trevor's voice was stronger, more confident this time. "Now that I'm free, there's nothing to stop us from being together."

Beep.

"Look, Shelby, in the past I tried to win you over the old-fashioned way. I sent flowers, candy, gifts. I gave you my heart. And how did you repay me? You betrayed me with that boy." His voice began to sound agitated. "I've tried talking to you nicely. What's left for me to do?"

Beep.

BK braced herself for the next one but, instead, she heard a deep, soothing voice.

"Hi, BK. This is Max. I was wondering if you would like to go to dinner with me tomorrow night. Call me at my office. Bye."

BK pressed the rewind button and listened to him again before going on to the next message.

Beep.

"Why won't you talk to me, Shelby? When a man puts himself on the line like I have, a decent woman would at least acknowledge what's been said. But no. *You just ignore me. It is your duty to respond.*"

The beep-beep-beep noise signaled that there were no more messages. After popping out the tape, BK grabbed her purse and headed out the door. Maybe this would convince the police that Trevor should be arrested.

BK felt like she and Max had been together for two years instead of two months. Max kicked his shoes off, loosened his Gucci tie, and sighed as he collapsed on the sofa. "I'm exhausted. Let's stay in, eat junk food all night, and watch TV."

"Sounds like a plan to me." BK wasn't so sure about the junk food but he could have whatever he wanted. She'd make herself a salad after she checked the answering machine. "No messages."

"Trevor caught on fast," Max said. "One tape to the police and he backed off."

BK hung up their coats. "I know he's still keeping tabs on Shelby. He wouldn't give up that easily."

"It gives me the creeps to think this guy is free to do whatever he wants."

"Tell that to the doctors at Willowbrook." Trevor's doctor had been less than cooperative. Even with Shelby's father calling in favors, Trevor was still on the streets.

"Why haven't the police arrested him?"

BK rolled her eyes and plopped down next to Max. The salad could wait. "I'm sure they'd love to but they have to catch him breaking the law. Shelby's lawyer wants us to document everything he does so we can show a pattern of behavior. But he's onto us. He's not giving us anything concrete to use against him."

Max massaged her shoulders. "Has she considered moving back to her parents' house?"

"She doesn't want to." BK had overheard Shelby talking to her parents in a firm voice on the phone. *I'm not going to move out of my home and change my life because of him. I can handle this.* She was on the verge of yelling and in all her years around Shelby and her parents, she had never once heard any of them raise their voices other than to call someone in for dinner. *Are you crazy? A gun? Never!*

"She needs to think of her safety... and yours," Max said.

"You haven't gotten to know Shelby very well yet. You don't know how stubborn she can be. When the police said stalkers get off on the feeling of power they get by scaring their victim, that's all Shelby had to hear. She's not budging. She refuses to give him any satisfaction."

Max got up and checked the locks on the windows, then inspected the new locks on the doors. "I don't like the idea of you living in this apartment. There's not enough security." When he sat back down, he resumed the massage.

"Our lease is up soon and then we're out of here." The muscles in BK's neck began to relax. "You're magic. Have you ever considered a career change? You can change Max-Maids to Max's Magical Hands."

Max laughed. "That has a whole different connotation."

BK winked and got up to close the curtains. "Fine. I'll keep your powers all to myself. Let the rest of the world suffer."

Max grabbed her hand and pulled her back down. She nuzzled into the curve of his body, feeling his muscles through his white dress shirt. "Aren't you scared of this guy?" Max said.

"I was but now I'm just pissed. Trevor dictates our lives, forcing us to live like hermits with the shades drawn and locked inside by multiple deadbolts. It's like a prison lockdown every night. But enough about him. I'm sick to death of Trevor." She looked at Max's strong jaw line and the way his hair curled around the back of his ear. "I've got better things to think about."

Max's stomach growled.

"Want some salad? Or popcorn? It's my specialty," BK said.

"I'll get it," Max said. "You look wrung out. The purple circles under your eyes match your shirt."

BK looked down at her purple silk blouse. "Gee, thanks. I go to great lengths to coordinate my outfits. It's nice to know it doesn't go unnoticed."

He kissed her cheek before heading for the kitchen. "I'm glad Trevor didn't get obsessed with you."

"I wish he hadn't gotten obsessed with anyone."

Max returned carrying a bag of steaming popcorn and two diet sodas and set them on the coffee table. "I don't even know what this guy looks like. Do you have any pictures of him?"

"No." She shook her head. "Why are we back to him again?"

Max picked up a handful of popcorn and stuffed it in his mouth. A piece fell on his pants, leaving a grease spot next to the crease. He rubbed the spot to no avail. "Okay. Tell me what you're doing for Christmas."

"I guess I'll go to my mother's on Christmas day. They always spend the holidays in Seaside." She wrinkled her nose. "I don't suppose you'd like to join me?" As soon as the words were out of BK's mouth she wanted to suck them back in and swallow them. How would Max receive her family? Worse, how would her family treat Max? No doubt Little Stan would fart and burp at him. Heather would rudely ignore him. Her mother would probe a million different ways trying to figure out how much money he makes. At least Stanley would talk business with him. Max would like that.

"You're not going to drag me to another soup kitchen like on Thanksgiving? I was beginning to think you were ashamed of me." His eyes twinkled.

"Hey, I was only trying to spare you from a day with my family. But it was good to see another side of you, joking around with the other volunteers. You were enjoying yourself and you treated the people we were serving with respect. I liked that."

Max's cheeks flushed slightly as he gathered up another handful of popcorn. "They're no different from you or me."

"When you first came to the Lindlay Group, I assumed your motive for sponsoring the charity ball was just to bolster your company's image." She kissed him. "But now I know the truth."

"You don't think your family would mind if I crashed their holiday?"

She shook her head. "Not at all. They'd love to give you the third degree and tell you all kinds of embarrassing stories about me." She started indexing stories starting with the worst-case scenario on down. It could be a long day. Her mother would undoubtedly go into great detail on how BK ruined her engagement party, *the* event of the season, by getting stuck in an elevator. Jeanne had gotten a lot of mileage out of that one over the years.

"They can't be that bad."

She grimaced. "You'll see." She picked through the bowl and put a partially popped kernel in her mouth. "There is an added benefit if you come. They might forget about me and concentrate their efforts on you."

"So you're going to sacrifice me to save yourself?"

"You bet." She laughed as he lobbed a piece of popcorn off her head. "What about your family? I know you didn't see them at Thanksgiving, so..." She let the sentence hang, hoping he would jump in and fill in the blanks.

He took a gulp of soda. "I don't have any family that I care to see."

"Oh." She waited in silence, again hoping that he would say more.

"What do you want to watch?" He picked up the newspaper and flipped to the television listings.

"Not so fast, mister." She crumpled the paper down. "Is that it?" The words from the fake personal ad Shelby had made up popped into her head. *Emotionally unavailable.* Did his refusal to share the details of his life qualify? Maybe she really did sabotage herself by picking men who would never last for the long haul.

He leaned over and kissed her hard as if that would seal her lips.

Shelby held the theater door open for Max and BK. "I'm starved. Want to go for a pizza?" She looked at BK. "Or a Greek salad?"

"Sure," Max said. "The movie made me hungry. They were eating in every other scene."

"Want to walk? Vito's is just a few blocks away." BK tried to calculate the number of calories she would have to burn if she skipped the salad and ate a slice of her favorite onion and mushroom instead. This was progress despite the calculation. There was a time when she wouldn't even consider putting a piece of pizza near her mouth. Someday she'd be like Shelby and eat whatever she wanted, worrying about calories only when her clothes started to feel a little snug.

Shelby looked up at the sky dotted with stars. "I never go out after dark anymore and it's such a beautiful night, why not? I feel safe with two protectors by my side."

Max grabbed BK's hand as they strolled down the sidewalk. "Out on the town with two beauties. I wish the guys at the gym could see me now."

Turning onto a cross street, Shelby glanced over her shoulder. BK could see her stiffen as Shelby pulled her coat tighter around her. "Don't look now but I just spotted the Red Sox jacket. I think Trevor might be following us."

Shelby had been noticing a guy in a Red Sox jacket trailing her for at least a week but since he always wore a hat and kept his distance, she wasn't positive it was him. BK told her to call the police but she wanted to be sure it was him before calling.

"It's got to be him. Who else would it be?" BK said.

"This is Boston," Max said. "At least half the population wears Red Sox hats and jackets." He pointed to the logo on his own jacket.

Shelby nodded. "But on this guy's jacket, the 'd' in Red is loose. The stem of the 'd' flaps as he walks."

Max turned to look. The man quickly ducked in back of a group of women walking about ten yards behind them.

"I said not to look," Shelby cried as jacket man took off running. "Now he knows I've spotted him."

Max bolted after him, nearly colliding with a woman. "Excuse me," he called as she steadied herself.

"Watch it," she shouted before stopping to observe the action.

Max closed in on him. "Stop," he yelled. "I want to talk to you."

He didn't slow down.

Max caught the back of the jacket and grabbed a handful of material. "Gotcha!"

Trying to wriggle free from his garment, the man's round belly heaved. "Let go of me! I've done nothing wrong."

Chapter 19

When Shelby and BK caught up, Max had the man wearing the Red Sox jacket by the arm. "You've been following Shelby and it's going to stop right here, right now." He turned to Shelby and thrust the man forward. "Is this Trevor?"

BK was relieved. She'd never seen this guy before but her relief quickly changed to anger. Why was he following Shelby?

The man tried to shake his arm free. "Let me go, man."

"That isn't Trevor." Shelby squinted her eyes. "But why have you been following me?"

"I wasn't. You're crazy, lady."

"Yes, you were." She flipped the stem of the "d" on his jacket. "I've seen you. Just because I thought you were someone else doesn't change the fact that you've been trailing me."

The man's eyes were on Shelby's trembling hands. He turned to Max. "It's not what you think."

Max loosened his grip but would not release him. "Tell her the truth or I'm calling the cops and you can tell it to them."

"Okay, okay. I can see she's upset. She wasn't supposed to see me." He started to reach into his jacket.

Max grabbed his other arm, catching his wrist.

"Easy there, buddy. I'm getting a business card out of my pocket."

"I'm not your buddy." Max released his wrist, reached into the jacket, and pulled one out. He read from the cheaply printed card, "Harvey Waxman, Private Investigator."

BK's hand flew to her breastbone. "I can't believe this! Trevor hired you to follow Shelby? Don't you know you're working for a maniac?"

Waxman snarled. "You've got it all wrong. I don't work for the stalker."

BK exchanged a look with Shelby.

"You know I'm being stalked." Shelby put her hand on her hip. "Then who are you working for?"

Waxman looked at the sidewalk, seemingly studying each crack and dried wad of gum.

BK noticed the woman Max had bumped was standing to the side, listening. "Do you mind?"

The woman stayed put. "I want to know who hired him. This is better than the soaps."

Max shook Waxman's arm. "We all want to know."

Waxman looked up and snorted. "Tom Fulton."

By the look on Shelby's face it was obvious that she wasn't happy with his answer. BK could understand Mr. Fulton's desire to protect his daughter and wished her own family would care as deeply about her.

"I'm going to kill him," Shelby said. "I told him to stay out of this."

"Who's this Tom?" the woman said. "A current beau or an ex?"

BK glared. "Her father. Now will you move along?"

The woman frowned and started walking away slowly. "Last I knew, this was a *public* sidewalk."

Max pulled out his cell phone. "I'm sure you won't mind if we confirm your story with Mr. Fulton."

"You don't have to do that."

"Why? Got something to hide?"

Waxman squirmed. "No. I'm telling the truth. But if Mr. Fulton knows you spotted me, I might not be able to collect the rest of my fee."

"Tough." Max kept his grip on Waxman and tossed the phone to Shelby. "You dial."

Shelby walked to an empty part of the sidewalk. Waxman never took his eyes from her. When she returned, her face was still flushed. "It's true. He was working for my father." She looked at Waxman. "I hope you noticed I said *was*."

Max released his arm and tossed the business card back at him. It hit his chest and fell to the ground. "You can go now."

"My father wants to talk to you first thing tomorrow morning," Shelby said.

Waxman swore under his breath as he walked away.

Shadows from the fire danced on the walls of Max's penthouse. Like a photo in a decorating magazine, the décor was sleek, modern, and manly. BK snuggled under a Sherpa throw, her cold feet pointed in the direction of the gas fireplace. Light from a torchiere reflected rings on the ceiling.

"I made some hot chocolate to warm us up." Max set two Max-Maid mugs on the glass and metal coffee table. "Topped with miniature marshmallows, of course."

BK wrapped her fingers around a mug and breathed in the steamy chocolate as she watched Max standing by the fireplace rubbing his hands together. She wondered if she could inconspicuously flick the marshmallows off without him noticing. "I had a wonderful time today. I haven't been skating in years."

Max turned around and grinned. "I needed an excuse to hold your hand all afternoon."

BK put the mug down without taking a sip and went to retrieve her tote bag. "Guess what I have?" She pulled out three boxes wrapped with red and green foil paper topped with elaborate ribbons that had taken her an hour to perfect.

Max picked them up one by one. "Are those all for me? I've never gotten so many gifts at once."

BK tilted her head. *He's never gotten three gifts at once before? Even from Santa when he was young?* She really didn't know this man she'd fallen in love with. He looked excited enough to clap his hands.

He stood. "I feel bad. I only have one for you."

"Don't be silly. I wouldn't care if you didn't have any for me. Decorating your tree and going ice skating has made this the nicest Christmas ever." *So much better than if we'd gone to Seaside,* she thought. At first she felt hurt that her mother booked a cruise for Christmas, leaving her behind, but now she was glad she wouldn't have to be on guard all day, wondering what her family was going to say or do to embarrass her.

"Hurry up and finish your hot chocolate so I can open these."

Or not, she thought, calculating the calories that would be wasted on a *drink.* "Go ahead. I'll have it later."

Max bit his lip and hesitated for a moment before getting her gift from the other room. She was sitting cross-legged in front of the tree, the blanket draped over her shoulders when he came back.

"Open yours first," he said, handing her a small box.

She held it by her ear and shook it. "I wonder what it is."

"Watch out. It's *very* fragile."

She froze. "I hope I didn't break it."

"You'd better open it and see."

She ripped off the paper and flipped back the hinged top of a gray velvet box. She took a slow deep breath to prevent herself from hyperventilating as she removed a dazzling diamond necklace and placed it around her neck. "It's beautiful."

"You like it?"

She leaned forward and threw her arms around him. "Of course I do! How does it look?"

Before he could answer, she got up and ran to the mirror by the front door to admire it. "I can't believe this. Thank you so much."

His whole face smiled. "I'm glad you like it."

She stopped, her eyebrows raised. "Wait a minute. This wasn't breakable."

Max laughed. "I couldn't wait another minute for you to open it. I've been dying to give it to you all day."

She pushed his boxes closer to him. "Your turn."

He ripped into the largest box like a child. "Big Papi," he said, holding up an Ortiz jersey. The Red Sox were as necessary as air to Max. He'd already booked a flight to Fort Myers to catch some spring training games, too impatient to wait for the regular season. His eyes sparkled brighter than her diamonds as he ran his hand over the embroidered lettering.

"Open the others," she said, smiling.

He tore open the baseball autographed by Ortiz and a baseball card packaged with a splinter of wood from a bat used by Big Papi. He threw his arms around her. "Best presents ever."

Later, Max brought out a platter with broccoli florets, celery sticks, and slices of Muenster cheese and Granny Smith apple along with a bottle of her favorite Pinot Grigio. Relieved that she skipped the hot chocolate, she added up the calorie count of a glass of wine and a piece of cheese. She'd fill up on the fruit and vegetables but she wanted to savor the wine and delicious orange-edged Muenster.

Curled up together on the sofa sipping wine while listening to Christmas carols, Max squeezed her tight and whispered, "I love you, BK."

BK looked in his eyes and felt like she had finally found her way home after a lifetime of searching. "You've never said that to me before. And I thought the necklace was the best gift I could possibly get today."

"I don't say it often but when I do, I mean it."

"I love you, too." She kissed him. "I want to remember this moment forever."

BK sat up straight in bed; her head cocked as she strained to hear whatever had woken her. She heard the familiar hum of the refrigerator before she heard the strange noise again, a soft rustling out by the trash cans. *More skunks in the trash*, she thought as she focused on the clock radio's green numbers glowing like the eyes of an alien. She slid down in bed and pulled her puffy comforter up around her neck.

Less than a half-hour later, she woke again to the sound of Shelby's voice. "BK. Are you asleep?"

She groaned and tried to bury her head deeper in the pillow. "Just five minutes more. I found this great jacket for sixty percent off."

"You're dreaming." She felt a sharp jab to her arm. "Wake up. I think someone's outside."

BK's unwilling eyes opened. Shelby was standing over her. "I heard something earlier. I think a skunk was in the garbage."

"Did you see it?" Shelby asked.

"Of course not. Do you think I went outside in the middle of the night to introduce myself? 'Hello Mr. Skunk. I'm BK. Oh! Thanks for that spritz of perfume!'" She struggled to sit up. "I didn't actually see him but you know the problem we've been having with them."

Shelby didn't smile. "I think someone's trying to break in. It could be Trevor."

"Call 911." BK swung her legs out of bed and grabbed her robe, now fully awake thanks to a shot of Trevor-induced adrenaline.

"Let's go see first." Shelby bit her nail. "I don't want any innocent skunks arrested."

"That would really stink for them."

Shelby groaned. "Save your attempts at comedy for the daytime when you're more coherent."

Together they started checking the locks on the kitchen and bathroom windows, looking out each one but seeing nothing. The knob of their front door wiggled one way and then back, rattling so slightly that if BK hadn't been headed for the living room, she never would have heard it. Dropping the robe on the floor, she whispered, "Someone's out there."

Shelby's voice quivered. "Trevor."

BK noticed the dead silence in the apartment. "I don't hear the refrigerator running anymore." She flipped a switch. Nothing happened. She frantically flipped it up and down before trying a lamp. The room remained dark. "There's no electricity." She raced to the front window and pulled back the heavy drapes. "But the street lights are still on."

Panic stained the edge of Shelby's words. "The circuit breakers are in the basement. We can't get to them if someone's out there."

"Go call the police."

Shelby didn't move, standing like an Italian statue over the robe.

BK crept back to the kitchen. In every shadow she saw Trevor. She was sure he crouched around every corner. She felt as though a boa constrictor had somehow slithered its way down her throat while she was sleeping and was now squeezing her internal organs as she picked up the phone.

The line was dead.

She got her purse and started rummaging through it on her way back to the living room. Shelby was sitting on the floor hugging her knees. "The line is dead and I can't find my cell phone. I must have left it at work."

"I should have listened to my parents." Shelby rocked back and forth. "They've been trying to get me to move into that horrible high-tech high rise with security twenty-four-seven but I didn't want to lose my normal life." Her eyes bulged. "He's come to get me. Tonight's the night. He's finally going to kill me."

"Snap out of it. We'll be fine." BK grabbed her under the arms and stood her up. "Ha, ha? Remember when we were stuck in the elevator? That's what you said to me."

"You're joking? With Trevor outside our door?"

"I'm trying to calm you down. If it is Trevor, we have to keep our wits about us so we can outsmart him. Where's your cell phone?"

Shelby closed her eyes and took a deep breath before grabbing her purse from the end of the couch and dumping the contents on the floor. "It's not here."

BK's words clung to her dry tongue. "Both phones lost on the same day?" She shook her head. "Too much of a coincidence."

"What are we going to do?" Shelby rubbed her forehead. "I can't think straight."

"He wants us to panic but I refuse to." BK paced. "We can't go upstairs for help; he still might be in the hallway. If we go out the back door, he might be waiting for us there." She went to the broom closet. "I've got it. Take this." She tossed a sponge mop at Shelby. "Start banging on the ceiling." She grabbed the broom for herself.

"Mrs. Harvey," they screamed. "Help!"

Someone pounded on the door. "It won't do you any good," Trevor yelled.

Shelby and BK froze, holding the broom and mop midair.

"Your neighbor isn't home. I watched her drive off toward the airport with her kitty carriers and luggage this morning. Seems she and her fancy cats won an all-expense paid trip to the purebred cat show in Orlando from the Trevor Clearinghouse Sweepstakes."

BK's stomach dropped as she tossed her broom aside. She put her finger to her lips and pulled Shelby into the kitchen.

"I know exactly where you're going," Trevor yelled. "A friend from upstate has his gun aimed at the back door and has instructions to shoot to kill. And you know what I mean by upstate, don't you? The hospital. Where everyone is crazy enough to kill."

BK cracked the mini-blinds and peeked out. "I don't see anyone," she whispered. "He's bluffing."

"Let's try," Shelby said as Trevor rattled the knob, obviously trying to pick the lock.

"Get down." BK timidly turned the first deadbolt, then the second and opened the door a crack.

Immediately, a shot rang out.

She slammed it and flipped the locks with shaking hands as Shelby sobbed on the floor.

"You must feel invincible tonight," Trevor yelled. "But no one will get hurt if you do what I ask."

BK grabbed two knives, giving one to Shelby before returning to the living room. Only a slab of wood separated them from Trevor. She was grateful for the three deadbolts and the chain lock, but wished they had upgraded to an impenetrable steel door. "What do you want?" she yelled.

"Certainly not to talk to you, BK. You're always in the way. I want to talk to my Shelby. Open the door and let me in."

"Go away. We already called the police. They'll be here any minute and you know they'll arrest you."

"Don't lie to me, bitch! You know damn well I cut the phone line. You didn't call anyone."

"I used my cell phone."

"*Liar*! Your phone is missing. I paid a pickpocket to get it. Shelby's too. I have them. *I hate when people lie.*"

His body hit the door with a chilling thud. Shelby's scream was deafening. Over and over he tried to knock down the door.

BK held a lamp over her head, ready to crack it over the top of his skull. Then the thumps stopped. The wind whistled outside.

BK pressed her ear to the wall, her nose near the crack of the door. She could smell the familiar mustiness of the cellar.

"What's he doing?"

"He went downstairs. This is our chance." She ran to one of the living room windows and unlatched it. "Follow me."

"No." Shelby moved from one foot to the other. "I can't go out there. What if he has another friend out front? He'll catch me." She shook her head. "I can't."

BK opened the window. "I don't see anyone."

"You didn't see the nut out back, either."

BK hesitated until she heard a creak on the stairs. "Lock this behind me. I'm going for help." She knocked out the screen and jumped out the window. Her flannel nightgown caught on the branch of a shrub. She tugged at it, looking from the front door to the shrub and back. The nightgown ripped free and she ran into the chilly night with nothing on her feet but an old pair of tube socks with a hole in the left heel.

Chapter 20

The rhythmic thud of running feet echoed behind her as BK sprinted across the street. Her lungs ached from the cold but she kept going, heading for the twenty-four-hour coffee shop five blocks away. Stealing a look behind her, she saw that Trevor was too far back to catch her. All the hours spent at the gym were paying off.

He stopped and threw a hammer in her direction. It hit a metal trash can, toppling it over with a clang. "Damn you, BK! Just keep running. Don't ever come back." His voice echoed in the empty street.

BK slowed, her breath puffing out in white clouds. A light had flicked on inside the building where Trevor stood.

"Go ahead. Call 911!" He looked up at the window, shaking his fist. "The cops can't stop me." He turned and went back toward BK's building.

I can't leave Shelby alone with him.

She ran back and picked up the hammer, stopping long enough to scan the windows hoping for confirmation that a call had been made to the police. All the curtains were drawn although light seeped out around the edges.

When she reached her front steps, the lights in her apartment came on in a burst. *Trevor must be in the basement at the electrical panel.*

Slipping in, she hid on the stairs leading to the other apartment to wait for him to come back. Her hand was wrapped around the shaft of the hammer, ready to strike.

"BK made a terrible mistake," he shouted as he climbed the stairs. "I just wanted to see you, Shelby, but your stupid friend messed everything up. Now I might not have enough time. I really *hate* her. I always have."

He was holding a reciprocating saw, the jagged blade exposed. The landlord's tool belt hung on his waist, the spot for the hammer empty.

Surprisingly, Trevor didn't have the face of a madman. With his smooth, unblemished skin and neatly trimmed mustache, he could have passed as a mild-mannered accountant or other white-collar professional. Except for the crazed look in his eyes. That gave him away.

"I'm coming in, Shelby." He waved the tool through the air. "No locks will stop me."

"Go away," she screamed.

"I've *always* loved you but you broke my heart. Not just once, but over and over and over again. We had something special, something magical together."

"You've got it all wrong. We never had anything together. It was all in your imagination."

In the distance a police siren wailed. BK tightened her grip on the hammer. Spending time in Willowbrook hadn't helped Trevor. He *believed* everything he was saying. She could hear the certainty in his voice that he and Shelby had a relationship. To him, it was reality.

"You're lying to me again. Anything to save your precious skin. All that comes out of your mouth are lies, lies, lies." He plugged in the saw. "But I still want us to be together, if not in this lifetime, at least in the next."

He slid the blade between the door and the jamb, just above the first deadbolt. As he switched it on, BK rushed out and swung the hammer at his head. The blow missed, hitting his shoulder with a crack.

Trevor spun around, letting go of the saw that was wedged in the door.

She lifted the hammer over her head again but someone caught it from behind.

"Freeze," a voice commanded. "Police."

Max picked up a box and walked to Shelby's car, illegally parked outside the apartment door with its four-way flashers blinking to ward off any tickets.

"What about the accomplice? The one who shot at you," he said.

BK rearranged a couple of boxes in the trunk. "There wasn't anyone else. The back door was rigged so when I opened it, a recording of a gun shooting played. The sound was so real, it scared us back into the house."

Max shook his head. "He thought of everything." He turned to Shelby. "What do you have packed in here? Rocks?"

Shelby reached into the box and pulled out two green marble bookends. "Sorry. I'm not a good packer like BK. Is that better?"

Max chuckled. "I thought I was kidding about the rocks."

Shelby set the bookends on the floor behind the front seat of her car. "I guess that does it."

BK thought of all the moving around her family did when she was young. Her mother kept a stash of flattened boxes she saved from move to move crammed under the beds and in the back of every closet. She threw her arms around Shelby. "It's going to be so lonely here without you. I vowed I wouldn't cry." She bit her lip. "I know you have to move but it doesn't make it any easier."

Shelby stepped back. "A security building is a must before they decide to release Trevor on bail or something. He'll never leave me alone. At least I'll still have my job with *City Scene* to keep me busy. I can do most of my work from home. Tonight's going to be tough, though, without you around."

Max walked up behind BK and slid his arm around her waist, giving her a little squeeze.

"The offer still stands," Shelby said. "You're welcome to join me in my new high-rent prison. My cell has three bedrooms. There's no shortage of space."

"It would feel small once Fred moves in. You guys have been apart long enough. I don't want to be the third wheel." *And maybe Max will invite me to move in with him*, she thought. They hadn't been together long but there was something special between them.

"You know he's not finished his internship in Chicago yet. He won't be here for weeks. Plus, you'd never be a third wheel."

"Fred may think differently."

"We'd better get going if we want to unload before dark." Max ushered them into their respective cars. "I'm going to double-check the door."

"I locked it already," BK called after him.

"Better safe than sorry." Once in the car, Max shook his head. "I'd feel better if you were moving too."

BK smiled, waiting. *Go on. Ask me. You know you want to.*

"They should never let him out again but we both know what *should* happen isn't necessarily what *will* happen."

Her smile dissolved. "Trevor's not after me. He's obsessed with Shelby. The police found a detailed log when they searched his apartment. He documented her every move. It's clear that he's been following her for weeks, recording her daily routine from the time she gets up in the morning to the kind of cereal she eats."

"So they've got enough evidence to put him away?"

"That's up to the judge. It looks good though. They even found an envelope he had full of Shelby's junk mail. He was picking through our trash. I guess our skunk problem isn't as bad as I thought."

"You had a skunk—a great big human skunk."

"You can say that again. He also had a shrine to Shelby in his living room with all kinds of pictures of her on a bulletin board and a candle burning under them."

"Creepy."

They stopped behind Shelby's car at the imposing black security gate while she signed them in as her guests. Inside the building, a guard was posted around the clock.

Her apartment was on the fourth floor and as she put the key in the lock, they could hear Clyde, her new watchdog, barking ferociously.

"I hope he doesn't bite," BK said, taking a few steps back from the door. She'd never been afraid of dogs but this one sounded fierce.

"He better or all that money I paid for him will have been wasted. But I'll teach him that you're not very tasty, BK. Not enough meat on your bones."

BK hit her on the arm. "Don't badmouth your mover." The forced lightness in her tone covered the heaviness in her heart. Too many conversations included some reference to her weight. *And Shelby thinks I'm obsessed with my weight. Maybe she's the one who's obsessed.*

Shelby swung the door open. "Good boy." She stooped to give Clyde a welcoming scratch on the side of his head. Clyde eyed BK and Max suspiciously as they hauled in box after box of Shelby's belongings.

"I'm glad you don't own any furniture," Max said as he set down the last box.

"Me too." Shelby flopped down on her new sofa. "I wouldn't have been able to move myself. Having the furniture store deliver was easier."

"Move *yourself*?" Max teased.

"You know what I mean. You guys are the best."

"Your new furniture is beautiful," BK said, running her hand over the expensive material. "I hope Clyde doesn't mess it up."

Shelby patted the drooling bullmastiff's head and talked as though he was a baby. "You wouldn't be a bad boy, would you, Clyde? No, no. Clyde's a good boy."

"Uh-oh, Max. Trevor has finally pushed her over the edge."

"This isn't called a throw pillow for nothing," Shelby said, launching one in BK's direction.

Max chuckled as BK went after Shelby with one of the sofa cushions. "I can just imagine what you two were like when you were younger."

"Okay, Clyde, don't get upset," BK said, backing off as the dog began to growl low in his throat. "See? She's fine."

Shelby patted his head. "Good boy, Clyde. You'll keep me safe, won't you?"

"I can't believe the ball is just three weeks away," BK said into the phone. "It sounds like we're in a fairytale." She affected a British accent. "Have you decided if you're coming to the ball, Cinderella?"

There was a short, awkward silence. "I don't know yet."

BK was sprawled upside down. Her head hung off the edge of the sofa with her legs folded over the back cushions. "Come on, you have to. It wouldn't be the same without you."

She heard Shelby draw a deep breath. "With Trevor being out on bail until the trial, I'm not sure I dare go out in public."

"You're right. I wasn't thinking about Trevor although how he slipped my mind, I'll never know. I was being selfish."

"Let's go out after the ball, okay? Once Fred gets here, we'll be like teenagers on a double date."

"If I'm still seeing Max, then." Just saying the words made her feel like crying. She thought he was *the one.*

"Things aren't getting any better between you two?"

"Not really. Our relationship was fine until Valentine's Day. He brought me a huge box of chocolates." When she untied the golden ribbon, she had heard her mother's voice in the back of her head. *You're not eating candy again are you, BK?* And her sister's singsong taunting. *You're going to get fat. Fatty, fatty, Beatrice Karen is a fatty.* "When I didn't dig into them right away, he got upset. We never even left the apartment that night. Instead, we spent our first romantic Valentine's Day together arguing about dieting. He's like you. He doesn't understand."

"He's only saying these things because he loves you and wants you healthy and strong. You've heard it all from me for years."

BK was silent. Oh, she'd heard it. Ad nauseam.

"I've said it before and I'll say it again. I think you should see a therapist."

BK sat upright on the sofa. "That isn't the only problem coming between us. Ever since Max said he loved me, I've felt him pulling back. He only said it once outright. Now he can't seem to say the words again. And if I try to get him to talk about his feelings, he clams up."

"Isn't this a common complaint about men? Failure to communicate?"

"It goes deeper with him. I can't figure him out. He won't let me get to know the real Max. He won't talk about the future or the past. He says he lives in the moment and the only time that matters is now."

"A therapist could help you deal with those issues."

BK sighed and gazed out the front window at the cars parked along the curb. A tabby cat jumped up on the hood of a black car and settled down for a nap above the warm engine. She was as tired as the cat; tired of the way her life was going. Something had to change. She loved Max too much to let him go without a fight.

Shelby cleared her throat. "Are you still there?"

"Yeah. I was thinking about what you just said. Maybe I'll give it a try."

"I can't tell you how relieved I am to hear those words."

"If a trained professional tells him that I'm perfectly normal then the tension between us will disappear and maybe he'll open up to me."

Shelby sighed. "Right."

Smiling to herself, BK set down her blow dryer, brushed out her hair, and sprayed it. She no longer disliked what she saw in the mirror. For so many years all she saw was a fat girl.

Her stomach was jumpy as she practiced what she was going to say. "Max, I have something big to tell you. I'm in therapy and for the first time I can remember, I feel like I have control over my life."

She made a face. Too abrupt. Not enough detail. She wound the cord around the handle of the dryer. She'd add that the therapist specialized in eating disorders. This was a detail Shelby left out when she provided Dr. Holland's name but it had made a world of difference. She probably would have refused to go if she'd known but there were no judgments. Dr. Holland let BK decide if she had an eating disorder. The doctor said acknowledging the problem is only the first step. There aren't any quick cures but she knew she could beat it.

This revelation would make Max and her close again. She pictured the happiness on his face. He'd pull her close and tell her how proud he was and how much he loved her. Okay, he probably wouldn't say "I love you" but she'd feel it radiating from him.

The aroma of chicken roasting made her mouth water as she put on her makeup. She went to the kitchen and peeked in the oven. Although she was a long way from sitting down and eating one of the hot fudge brownie sundaes she used to love as a child without recriminations and regret, she was beginning to make progress. She was cooking nutritious meals and last week, much to Shelby's surprise, BK had gone to her apartment and fixed her a homemade dinner that was not only edible, but tasty.

The table was set with her best dishes. She straightened the candles and glanced at the clock. It was already after seven.

"Hi. Are you going to be much longer?" she asked when Max finally called.

He coughed, then cleared his throat. "I won't be able to make it tonight."

"But I have a big surprise planned for you. I even cooked." She waited for his comeback. Something smart like that being reason enough not to come but instead he cleared his throat again. "What's the matter, Max?"

"I have to be honest with you. I've tried to tell you this before in person but once I look at you, I can't find the right words."

BK sat down. "You're scaring me."

"I've made a decision about our relationship."

She held her breath as she waited.

"I don't think it's going to work out between us. I think we should take a break and start dating other people."

She chewed the lipstick off her lower lip. *Not yet. He has to come to dinner tonight. Everything will change.*

"This isn't really a big shock to you, is it?"

Her answer came out as a whisper. "Yes."

"You know we've drifted apart."

"I think we can work it out. I still love you, Max." She dabbed her eyes with one of the paper napkins she had folded into a fan.

"Please don't cry."

She sniffed. "I don't want to lose what we have."

"Sometimes love isn't enough to save a relationship." His voice softened. "Don't be sad. This is for the best."

Maybe the best for someone afraid to commit. She could almost hear the relief in his voice. *You say love isn't enough to save a relationship? Fear of the love we have is what killed this one.* She spit out her words in an unexpected flash of anger. "Do you expect me to be happy about this?"

"Not happy, but maybe relieved. You know how our relationship's been going. We were spending more time fighting than having fun and we've hardly seen each other lately. If we weren't working on the ball together, I don't think we would have spent any time with each other. You always have some cockamamie reason why we can't be together."

"That's exactly what I wanted to talk to you about tonight. You see, I've been having appointments with—"

"Appointments! Please. No more explanations. For all I know, you're seeing someone else."

"No. That's not true!" He *knew* it wasn't true. He grasped for an excuse, any excuse, to blame her and this is all he could come up with. He'd say anything to get out of this relationship no matter how ridiculous he sounded.

"I've heard enough. Actions speak louder than words. If you think I'm gullible enough to believe you, you're crazy. You've certainly made it clear that you put our relationship last and I'm sick of it. I don't know what's going on with you and at this point, I just don't care anymore."

He hung up on her.

Chapter 21

Lenny Mayhew had never worn formal clothes, not even at his wedding. His fingertips snagged the silky lapel of the tuxedo hanging on the back of the door. He was going first class tonight. He even sprang for the black banker's shoes that were sitting next to the motel's mildew-spotted shower curtain. He'd worn them back to the motel to break them in and noted they were already in need of a shine.

He caught a glimpse of himself in the mirror. Medium height with a boxer's wiry build and dirty blond hair even though he should be turning grey. He avoided mirrors thanks to a teen acne problem. *Zit face.* No one else had dared call him that except his father. Lenny resembled his old man. Another reason to avoid mirrors.

Trevor, his only child, was nothing like him. Coming face-to-face tonight for the first time in years was not going to be like looking in a mirror. He hoped he didn't see traces of Gail because that would make it harder to follow through with his plan.

But it wouldn't stop him. His life had changed drastically because of Trevor and he was finally going to thank him properly. As he carefully loaded each chamber of his snub-nosed thirty-eight special, he thought how satisfying it was going to be to watch as Trevor spotted his dear old daddy at the ritzy charity ball. He chuckled as he pictured the recognition, then the disbelief, and finally, the terror on the coward's face.

As he straightened his arm and pretended to aim, the cool handle of the gun felt like a natural extension of his hand. He'd mess with Trevor first, pressing the gun against his temple then dragging it across his cheek before jamming it against his nose as he squirmed and pleaded for Lenny to spare his miserable little life.

Spare his life? No way.

He stashed the gun in the inner pocket of the tuxedo jacket as the phone rang.

"Yeah?" he answered.

"It's Ace."

"Everybody get there?" Lenny fingered the scar on the side of his face.

"Yup."

"All set with the plan? They have to be clear on the timing. Timing is everything."

"I went over it with them."

Lenny sat on the bed. A spring in the mattress complained with a pop. "What about leaks? All it takes is one guy running his mouth in a bar."

"There ain't been time for talking. Till a couple days ago, you and me was the only ones in on it."

"I wish it was still that way. I ain't never pulled a job this big before." Lenny traced a flower on the bedspread. Even the bold floral pattern couldn't hide the built up grime and dried bodily fluids on the sturdy fabric.

"Don't worry," Ace said.

"We meet at three sharp behind the Bubb-L-Lounge."

"I know."

As he hung up, he heard heavy footsteps approaching his room. The paper-thin walls were an advantage if you didn't want anyone to sneak up on you. *Delores.* Her gait resembled that of an overweight truck driver.

A resounding knock at the door confirmed that he had not been mistaken. "Lenny honey, it's me," she hollered over the noise from the heavy traffic on the street.

He slid the dead bolt and unlatched the safety chain.

Lenny stiffened in Delores' steel embrace. She was like an octopus, all arms, grabbing anything human in her path for a hug. Most people would get the message, but her intelligence wasn't the reason he had followed her to the dimly lit bar where they first met.

"I snuck outta work 'cuz the damn cold medicine is making me drowsy. I can't hardly think straight." She wiped her nose on her sleeve. "Besides, I wanna help you get ready for your big job tonight." She smiled, revealing discolored teeth.

He closed the door and locked it. "But you've been so much help already." *If you only knew how much help you've been*, he thought. She had given him a complete tour of the hotel where she worked, the same hotel where the ball was taking place.

"What do..." She closed her eyes and put her finger under her nose to stifle a sneeze. "... you mean?"

Lenny cleared his throat. "You know, helping me pick out the tux and stuff. I ain't never been no magician's assistant before." When Delores spotted the purple cummerbund at the rental store, she had gotten so excited that they made formal clothes in her favorite color, he couldn't disappoint her. He had drawn the line at the purple ruffled shirt though. He didn't want to risk standing out in the crowd.

"What do ya have to do?" she asked.

"Just make sure the old boozer looks like he knows what he's doing on stage with a few tricks of my own behind the scenes."

Lenny watched her walk across the room. His mouth curled in a self-satisfied smirk as he eyed her tight blue jeans. She had curves in all the right places, plus a few extras. Nobody measured up to Gail so he didn't bother being picky. "So you like watching a man get into his fancy duds, do ya?"

"As long as the man I'm watchin' is you, Lenny." Delores tossed her sack-like vinyl purse on the night stand and plopped herself down on the bed. She wriggled out of her quilted jacket and piled pillows behind her head. Her tight purple sweater showed off her best assets but wrinkles creased her forehead and around her eyes. Her face, always puffy from the cigarette smoke and alcohol of the night before, made it hard to guess her age. He knew very little about the woman with whom he had been sharing his life. She was generous to him, not monetarily, but in other ways. Delores gave Lenny whatever he needed freely. If he had met her twenty years ago, maybe his life would have turned out differently.

But she wasn't what he needed now. Only revenge was capable of satisfying him.

Lenny winked. "Too bad there ain't more time." He was quiet for a moment. "I guess I'll have to watch the way I talk tonight. The way I conversate will give me away unless I'm careful. Gotta blend in with the richy-rich guests."

"Why do you have to blend in? You're Vincenti's assistant. You're supposed to be there."

"Any attention is bad attention." He noted Delores's confused expression. "I can't let them know old Vincenti needs help. It would ruin the show."

"Oh, yeah."

"It's not that I can't talk proper English. I've had my share of classes over the years. They love to try to improve you in the joint and I went along with the program 'cuz it made me look good at my parole hearings. Alls I need is to concentrate a little and I'll be able to pull it off."

But concentration and Delores didn't mix. "Be a doll and put a first class shine on my shoes before you go home, babe." He pointed to the bathroom. "They're in there." He smiled, thinking how easy it was for him to manipulate broads. He'd get rid of her and get his shoes spiffed up at the same time.

The sound of Delores' gasp startled him. She appeared in the doorway with the gun dangling from two of her fingers.

"What dis for, Len honey?" She lapsed into her annoying habit of baby talk. It usually drove Lenny up the wall but this time he barely noticed.

He growled as he lunged at her. "Put that down."

Her childish pout changed to fear as his arm rose to hit her. "Don't!" She cringed and let go of the gun. It landed on the matted carpet with a thud. "I... I'm sorry."

"You should know enough to mind your own business." He scowled but his fury had already begun to die.

She molded her body into the corner.

Lenny scooped up the gun and stomped over to the bed.

The chain danced as Delores struggled with the door. She fled the motel room, her jacket and purse forgotten.

The orchestra was warming up with staccato bursts of music in the main ballroom of the Van Buren Plaza. Purple, lavender, and white lilacs spilled from large vases positioned around the room, perfuming the air like a spring day in the country.

BK chose this venue because it wasn't a typical boxy hotel ballroom. Conversation nooks nestled with couches and a large fireplace at the far end of the room. Chandeliers sent sparkles dancing across the china and silverware.

BK absently swiped some loose hair from her face. Her fluttery stomach had begun to calm down but she wouldn't be able to fully relax until the night was over.

"You've checked everything twice, Miss Hartshaw," the banquet manager said. "Why don't you take a break?"

"In a minute." This was her first big assignment without being part of a team. Everything was her responsibility right down to the linen color. She picked up a napkin and fluffed it. "I have to make sure everything is perfect."

"Everything is."

After all the months of hard work, she supposed it was. The *imperfect* part was still yet to come: seeing Max for the first time since their breakup. She had practiced greeting him with nonchalance like he was just another client instead of the man she still loved but she knew she'd never pull it off.

Clutching a clipboard, BK scanned her list one last time. She clicked her lucky gold pen, a gift from Shelby, and crossed off the last item. "I think you're right. Everything seems to be ready."

BK spotted the news team in the entry hall. She instantly recognized Robyn Prentiss from TV. She was twirling her honey blonde hair around her index finger, looking at BK with a slight frown. When she realized BK was looking back, her lips sprang into a beauty queen smile as she smoothed the skirt of her blue form-fitting gown.

She's probably a size two, BK thought. *Maybe even a zero.* She remembered what Shelby said about manufacturers who produced size zero clothing. "What? They think these women don't exist? They're nothing, null, zeros? Ridiculous!"

When she got close, BK could tell, thanks to years of Shelby's tutelage, that the gown was a knock-off of one worn to last year's Oscars. Shelby loved fashion and you couldn't be around her without it rubbing off. BK couldn't match the dress to the correct movie star but Shelby would be whispering the famous name in her ear with a giggle if she were here.

Robyn waved and greeted BK. "Where would you like me to set up?" Her blue eyes were even more penetrating in person. In her faux-Oscar gown, she looked more like a guest than someone on assignment. In contrast, the cameraman wore a plaid flannel shirt thrown over a T-shirt and tan pants. The rooster's tail on the back of his head stuck out as if he hadn't taken the time to run a comb through it. She waited, giving Robyn a chance to introduce him. When no introduction came, BK stuck her hand out and did it herself.

"Ned Bowen," he said in response, clasping her hand.

"How about setting up outside the front entrance?" BK said to Robyn. "That way you can catch people on their way into the lobby."

Ned frowned and started to object. "I think—"

"That's fine," Robyn purred through her veneers. "I was so sorry to hear about you and Max." She paused, looking at BK's face, obviously waiting for a reaction.

BK cleared her throat. How would Robyn know about her personal life? What do you say to a stranger about something so personal and so painful that you didn't even want to talk about it with your closest friend? She certainly couldn't go with the truth because she would sound pathetic. *Thank you so much for your sympathy, Robyn, because every minute of every day I wish he would call me and take me back. I'm thinking of getting ten cats from the animal shelter and giving up the dream that I'll ever marry and have children.*

She wished she were one of those people that spit fast comebacks like verbal bullets but all she could come up with was, "You know Max?"

"We go way back."

"Oh." Her verbal gun must be jammed. "I'll let you get to work." BK turned abruptly and scooted around the corner to one of the room's many alcoves. As she sank onto a couch to compose herself, she could still hear Robyn and her cameraman talking.

Ned sounded perturbed. "What'd you do that for?"

"I didn't mean to upset the poor girl," Robyn said in the same tone of voice the witch would have used to lure Hansel and Gretel to her house. "She must be one of those overly sensitive types."

"That's—"

"Not any of your business. I'm a reporter. I wanted details. That's what I do. So what? There's nothing wrong with that. Maybe I'll finally get my chance with Max. I've had my eye on him for years. BK's reaction confirms the rumor that they're no longer together. She couldn't get out of here fast enough."

"Who cares?"

"It's easy for you to be judgmental. You have a wife and two kids," Robyn said.

"Three with another on the—"

"Well, *I* care and so do the rest of the single women in Boston. He's a catch: rich, single, rich, handsome—and did I mention, rich?"

"Money isn't every—"

"Max must have dumped her or she wouldn't be taking it so badly."

"How do you know how she's taking it? You talked to the woman for less than three minutes."

"It's right before your eyes. She's pale and drawn. And don't you think she's crossed the line from fashionably thin to too thin? The poor thing looks sickly."

"She looked fine to me."

Robyn snorted.

"Now that you've stopped talking long enough to take a breath, I can say what I was trying to say all along," Ned said. "That's a lousy location you just got us stuck in."

"Huh?"

"You do remember why we're here? Channel Six News? Interviews? Ring a bell?"

"Oh."

Eavesdropping can be an eye-opener, BK thought. Robyn's words had struck a nerve, but Robyn wasn't a friend, so why did she care what this woman thought?

She stood and was starting toward the elevator when Madame Zona stopped her.

"I need to talk to you, BK."

BK only wanted to get upstairs and stand under a stream of hot water. She didn't want to renegotiate Madame Zona's fee or relocate her table. "I'm not psychic but I'll take a guess. You don't like the location of your table?"

Zona glanced over at the table with its deep purple tablecloth. Gauzy white curtains separated the table in a recessed alcove from the ballroom. People would be able to see if Madame Zona was doing a reading while still giving a little privacy. A star-speckled sign announced Psychic Readings By Madame Zona.

"No, that's fine." She fidgeted with her long black dress. "I had a vision. About tonight."

BK sighed. She stopped herself from rolling her eyes. When she interviewed Madame Zona, she thought the woman must have a gift. She knew about Trevor. But then she thought about it later and realized that if Zona read the newspaper, she would have known about Trevor. She was smart enough to do her research. Either way, it didn't matter. She was only hired to entertain the guests and BK was convinced she'd do just that. "I really don't have time right now. I'm running late."

Madame Zona touched BK's arm to stop her. "This vision was a warning. Someone with dark energy is coming tonight. He's going to cause big trouble." She touched her stomach and closed her eyes. "I have an uneasy feeling about this."

BK didn't hesitate to roll her eyes since Zona wasn't looking. "Who is this person? Do you have a name?"

Zona's eyes opened. "That's all I know except the trouble will happen after I've done my last reading."

That wasn't very helpful. BK tried her best to look concerned so Zona would leave her alone. She furled her brow as she spoke. "I'll keep my eyes open."

As the elevator doors opened onto the tenth floor, BK ran into Max. She drew a sharp breath.

"BK." Small lines creased at the corners of his eyes as he smiled.

"Hi." Her eyes darted to the Close Door button inside the elevator but there was no way to hit it without being obvious. This wasn't the right time to see him. She had wanted to be dressed in her gown so when he caught his first glimpse of her, she would be at her best. In her fantasy, she would step into the ballroom and Max would spot her across the crowded room. He'd gasp and all the other people in the room would blur as he walked forward to sweep her off her feet.

Now she knew she logged in too many hours watching princess movies as a kid.

"How's everything? Are we ready for tonight?" he said.

She looked at him in amazement. He stood there dressed in his tux, looking as handsome as she'd ever seen him, without any trace of regret on his face. Didn't he have the hollow feeling in the pit of his stomach that plagued her day after day? Didn't he dread the end of each workday knowing that all that lay ahead was a long, empty night of TV?

"We're ready," she answered, averting her eyes while trying to brush past him.

"Isn't there something you've forgotten?" He put his hand against the elevator door.

"What?" She glanced down at her checklist.

"Your outfit." He chuckled. "Is that what you're planning to wear?"

She looked down at her wrinkled tweed skirt, limp blouse, and pantyhose sagging at the knees. Her jacket had been left somewhere in the hotel. She reached up and felt several strands of hair that had fallen from the bun that had been tightly wound hours ago.

She couldn't help grinning. He could always make her smile.

This man had blanketed her with love, warmed her heart and soul for the first time in her life, and then yanked it away without warning. He acted as though he was joking around with a stranger, talking to her as if nothing had ever happened between them.

"Got to run. I'll see you downstairs." She hurried off to her suite to shower.

"Don't make a sound, buddy," Lenny whispered into the man's hairy ear. He had one hand firmly over the security guard's mouth, the other twisting his arm behind his back. "We're not gonna have no problems, right?"

The guard groaned as Lenny jerked his arm sharply. His eyes watered as he shook his head.

Lenny marched him down to the basement. Hogtied and lined up against the bumpy cement wall was the entire security team hired for the ball, stripped to their underwear. Lenny's team was dressing in their uniforms.

Dripping water echoed in the background as fear flickered in the man's eyes.

Lenny shoved the guard roughly. He made a move toward the stairs when two of Lenny's men started to tape his mouth and tie him up.

Lenny swung his arm and struck the man against the side of his head. Blood trickled from his temple, down a deep wrinkle and onto his cheek. He moved within an inch of the older man's face and could feel hot air coming out of his nose as he labored to breathe. "Just stay calm and quiet and nothing else will happen to you."

Lenny spun around to face one of his men. "Go tell Ace everything's set." He smirked. "It's time to mingle with high society, boys."

Chapter 22

As she finished putting on fresh pantyhose in the suite that had been meant for her and Max, BK realized that it was too big for her. When she had made the reservations months ago, she had no idea that things would change between them. She felt foolish to have such a grand place to sleep in when she was now nothing more than the hired help.

The living room area had a richly upholstered three-cushion couch flanked by chairs, all in tones of brown and beige. They were placed around a coffee table topped with an arrangement of local magazines and a vase of fresh flowers. She opened the drawer of the mahogany desk and pulled out a piece of bond paper with the Van Buren Plaza logo embossed on top. The first thing she and her sister had done whenever they checked into a hotel was search for complimentary stationary. This would have been a prize to them back then. She replaced it carefully in the drawer. She had no one to whom she cared to write.

Suddenly she felt alone. All she really had was Shelby and Max, and after tonight she probably wouldn't see Max very often. He was destined to become just another business associate. They could've had it all, a future with a family of their own, but now he would be on her cheese assortment Christmas list instead of being the one with whom she would share the holiday.

A loud knock at the door made her jump. Adrenaline shot through her body. *Trevor?* "Get a grip," she said to herself, pushing the drawer shut. It couldn't be Trevor. That phony psychic had her on edge, imagining that the bogeyman was on his way to the ball.

The knock sounded again. BK slipped into a robe and went to the door. She sighed as she looked through the peephole and saw the bellman holding her jacket. She opened the door and took it from his outstretched hands. "How did you know it was mine?"

The bellman smiled. "Your business card is in the pocket."

"Of course. Hold on," she said, setting the jacket down on the table and reaching in her purse for a tip. "Thank you."

He nodded and stuffed the folded bills into his pocket. She giggled as a loud growling noise came from her stomach, reminding her that the only thing she had eaten today had been coffee and a few raw carrots. She placed her hand over her flat abdomen. "Guess I should have ordered some room service."

"I can get you something from the kitchen, ma'am."

"No, thanks." She waved her hand casually. "I don't have time now."

He nodded. "Have a nice evening."

As she locked the door, an alarm sounded in the back of her head. She should eat. She *must* eat. She couldn't allow herself to get back into the old habits that had reduced her to an all time low of ninety-one pounds. Her knees, just barely padded with skin, had ground together as she lay on her side in bed at night. She had been doing well in the past few weeks despite all the turmoil with Max and with Trevor being out again. But this lapse made her worry.

No. She shook her head. It was nerves. That's all. No disease. No disorder.

Still, she thought back to the incident earlier in the day. Like fog rolling in, her vision had distorted until her eyes went completely out of focus. Dizziness overcame her and as she reached out to the nearest table she had only been able to grab the tablecloth. China and flowers avalanched to the floor.

The banquet manager, who had been a few steps ahead, spun around in alarm. "Are you all right, Miss Hartshaw?"

"I'm fine. I must have tripped on that chair," she had lied, pointing to a chair leg protruding slightly into the walkway.

While the manager helped her to her feet, the staff started to clean up the mess. She overheard a waitress grumbling under her breath about drunks making messes in her beautiful ballroom.

She shot a dirty look at the woman. Her badge read Delores.

Delores sniffed and stared blankly back at her.

BK had attributed the dizziness to nervous tension and a lack of sleep. After all, last night had been spent tossing and turning in her bed, worrying about last minute details; when she had finally managed to put the ball out of her mind, Max crept in. Now she wasn't so sure. She would definitely eat a full meal tonight, right after she saw that everything was going smoothly.

BK watched from the doorway as Robyn got ready to go live for the six o'clock news. The camera was ready to roll, the lights were in place, and Robyn's hair and makeup were perfect. The camera loved her. When she had reported in the pouring rain at the Boston Marathon, she'd looked fresh and dry under the Channel

Six awning-striped umbrella when most of the other reporters looked like drowned rats. When a child had fallen through thin ice last winter, unlike the rest of the half-frozen reporters, Robyn looked warm and just slightly flushed after standing around for two long hours while they unsuccessfully tried to save the poor little girl. She had been BK's favorite reporter, that is, until she met her in person.

Robyn snapped her compact mirror shut.

"Ready in five, four, three…" Ned pointed to her from behind his camera while he mouthed, "two, one."

"This is Robyn Prentiss, Channel Six News, reporting live from tonight's charity ball at the Van Buren Plaza. Boston's top politicians and business leaders are gathering to raise money to benefit a new shelter for abused women and children. Here with me is the sponsor of the event, Max Emerson, owner of Max-Maids, a statewide chain of cleaning services."

That should please him, BK thought. *That was a nice plug for his business.*

Turning to Max, Robyn continued, "Tell us about the shelter being built."

Robyn looked like she was barely listening as she stared into Max's electrifying blue eyes. If BK were interviewing him, she'd probably do the same. *But I love him*, she thought, *you don't. You just want him for his money. I'd want him even if he lost everything tomorrow and we had to move into a little trailer with a gnome-decorated yard that bordered the highway. I've always liked gnomes.* She shook her head and tuned back into the interview.

Max was still responding to Robyn's question about the shelter. "Haven will house thirty-five to forty women and their children."

"Those are very ambitious goals," Robyn said, clearly flirting with him.

Ned looked out from behind his camera and shot her a puzzled look.

It seemed as if Robyn forgot she was on camera. She cleared her throat. "What can you tell us about the ball tonight?"

"The theme is magic. It's a tribute to all the brave women who have the determination to break away from abusive situations and still manage to keep themselves and their children together, as if by magic. Vincenti the Great will be giving a performance and our guests will be able to bid for a spot to appear on stage with him. But it will take more than magic to complete our center to aid these courageous women. It will take hard work, support of the good people who have volunteered their time to assist the victims of abuse and, most of all, money."

Robyn gave the station's website that had a link for more information and an address for donations. "I'll be here throughout the evening interviewing guests, including Senator Jack Camden. Watch for my update at eleven o'clock. This is Robyn Prentiss, Channel Six News."

"And we're clear." The bright lights snapped off abruptly. Robyn's mechanical smile faded and her face relaxed as she turned once again to Max.

"Thank you for the interview."

"My pleasure." He smiled at her. "I should be the one thanking you. Any publicity we can get for this project is appreciated."

The ball was in full swing by the time Max finished greeting guests in the front lobby. The room looked like a Monet painting in motion, the colors of the ladies' gowns swirling together as they danced. Laughter hung in the air like a light perfume.

The line for Madame Zona was at least ten people deep, all anxious to see into their futures. BK walked past quickly so Zona wouldn't notice her.

"Looks like everyone's enjoying themselves," BK said as she joined Max. The sequins sprinkled on her formfitting white gown caught the light from the chandeliers. Around her slender neck she wore a diamond necklace, the Christmas gift from Max. A borrowed diamond-studded comb caught her hair in a loose twist on the back of her head and little tendrils escaped, forming a soft frame around her face.

Max's eyes sparkled mischievously. "That's a much better choice than the suit you had on earlier."

"I'm glad you approve since it took me over three weeks to find it." She laughed and twirled around. Feeling slightly dizzy again, she reached out and grabbed his arm to steady herself.

"You're such a klutz," he teased, shaking his head. "Right from our first date I knew you were completely and utterly hopeless."

"That's not fair," she said. "It's not my fault I slipped."

"Slipped on what? Ice? It was July."

"You're nasty." She hit him playfully. "Downright mean and nasty."

His expression became serious as he looked deep into her brown eyes. "You look beautiful tonight."

"Thanks," she managed to whisper. Her arms ached to wrap around him and pull him close. She missed him. She missed the smell of his cologne lingering in the air at her apartment; she missed the way he would sneak up behind her and hug her while kissing the back of her neck; she missed their nights cuddled together on the couch eating popcorn and watching old movies; she even missed the way he used to poke her in the sides and yell, "Attack of the killer bees" as she half-screamed and half-laughed. But what could she do? It hadn't been her choice. He made the decision to end their relationship and he had stuck by it.

Robyn Prentiss appeared at his side. "Would you like to dance, Max?"

Max looked away from BK. "Maybe later. It wouldn't be very gentlemanly of me to leave the queen of the ball standing alone."

"Oh, come on." Robyn gave his sleeve a tug. "She doesn't mind."

BK heard herself say, "It's fine." She waved an invisible scepter. "Her majesty the Queen declares it." Her lips formed the words but her heart was screaming, *No! Dance with me!*

Robyn didn't need to be told twice. She pulled Max onto the dance floor.

BK's gaze kept traveling back to them. As if she was seeing Max for the first time, she felt that excited lurch in the pit of her stomach. Right from their initial meeting at the Lindlay Group, she had felt as though they were friends.

That's exactly what we are now, she thought sadly. *Just friends.*

Making their way past the head table, BK saw that Mrs. Camden had tampered with her carefully planned seating arrangement. She had placed herself and her popular senator husband on either side of Max.

Max touched Mrs. Camden on the shoulder. "How nice to see you tonight." As she rose and turned to greet him, he deftly switched his place card with hers. BK stood back and watched with amusement. When Mrs. Camden went to sit down again, Max said, "It looks like you're in my seat." He pulled out the other chair for her.

Her mouth opened as if she was going to protest. She looked at BK and then at Max and sat with a thud.

During the meal Mrs. Camden didn't bother BK, but the man she saw repeatedly poking his head from between the curtains on the stage did. He would look quickly around the room and then would disappear like a rabbit down its hole.

"Max." She poked him. "Look up there." She gestured with her head.

"At what? I don't see anything but a big velvet curtain."

"A guy keeps looking out." She took a roll from the basket and automatically spread some butter on it for Max. "I'm going to see what that's about. He better not be a photographer." She touched the back of her neck. "Robyn Prentiss will raise a stink if she finds out. I gave her exclusive coverage."

"Don't worry. He's probably just a hotel employee trying to get a look at the party."

The man appeared again. She could see a purple cummerbund through the split in the curtains. "Look." She pointed. "There he is again."

Max's head snapped around. "I didn't get a good look at him," he said, swallowing a bite of his filet mignon. "But I didn't see a camera so relax and have something to eat. You've barely touched your food."

BK frowned. "They have cameras so tiny that they can hide them just about anywhere."

"Then he'd be out here, pointing his secret little camera at the guests instead of hiding behind a curtain."

She breathed deep. "Good point."

He pushed her plate closer to her. "So have a bite. It's delicious."

"I guess there's too much going on for me to be able to eat." She pushed the plate back.

Max sighed. "You haven't even tried. You've only taken seven bites."

"You're counting the number of bites I take?" She shook her head. "You're unbelievable."

He put his fork down on the table with a clang. "I want to see you after dessert."

"It always comes back to this. You can't leave it alone." BK looked at the other guests at their table, all of whom seemed to be absorbed in their own conversations. "And I don't care for your tone." She stood. "I'm going to see what that man is up to."

Max grabbed her wrist. "We need to talk. You can't avoid this forever."

She leaned down and spoke firmly in his ear. "If there's something wrong with the party, that's one thing. But if you're just going to lecture me, you can forget about it. We're not going out anymore, remember?"

"I need to get this off my chest. Just hear me out."

"Not tonight."

His eyes were wide as he looked up at her.

BK was silent. If she wanted him back, she'd have to come clean about everything eventually.

His head tilted. He looked like a little boy. "Please…"

She sighed. "It'll have to be before Vincenti goes on."

"Meet me in your suite in ten minutes." Max glanced at Mrs. Camden who was doing her best to eavesdrop. "I don't want anyone else listening."

Mrs. Camden put her napkin to her lips and feigned a coughing jag.

Shelby slammed the phone down. "Where are you, BK? I haven't been able to reach you all day."

Clyde nuzzled his wet nose on her arm. "I don't know what to do, boy." She stuck the tip of her index finger in her mouth but realized there wasn't enough left of her nail to bite.

Opening her closet, she fingered the gown she bought yesterday. "What do I do, boy? Since Max broke up with BK, she's been a mess. And just when she'd begun to make some progress..." She let go of the gown. "She's going to need me tonight when she sees Max again."

Clyde looked at her as if he was really listening. A thin line of drool connected like a dot-to-dot from his mouth to the carpet.

"I'm torn. I want to help BK."

Clyde tilted his head.

"But at the same time, I have this tiny voice in the back of my head telling me to stay home and protect myself from Trevor."

Clyde blinked.

"He might not be anywhere near the ball, but if he is I might not live to regret my decision." She scratched Clyde's furry face. "Why can't you talk?"

Pacing in front of the window, Clyde followed on her heels. "Trevor's been keeping his distance from me so far but this might be the chance he's been waiting for. But how can he get to me? The place will be packed with people. There's safety in numbers." She stopped and looked out at the tree covered with buds. "BK stuck by me throughout this whole ordeal with Trevor and now she needs me."

Turning sharply, almost stepping on Clyde, she marched into the bathroom and turned on the shower. "I'm going. I can't be a hermit for the rest of my life. Look at me, Clyde, I'm actually having a conversation with a dog. It's a good thing I'm going to have human contact for a change."

Within an hour she was ready. Standing by the front door, she pulled a black shawl around her shoulders.

"Yes, boy." She patted Clyde's head. "I'm going out. I'm going to live my life like a normal person. If there isn't too much traffic, I'll be able to get to the ball even before the fashionably late crowd arrives."

She took a dog cookie from the jar that she kept by the door and set it on his nose. He balanced it and waited patiently for the signal.

"Eat the cookie."

Clyde knocked the bone-shaped biscuit from his nose with a jerk of his head and caught it before it hit the floor.

"Be a good boy. Eat anyone who tries to get in," she said, stepping out the door and locking it securely behind her. Glancing up and down the empty hall, she walked to the elevator. Her pulse was racing and she inhaled deeply, holding her breath for a moment before exhaling.

She walked quickly to her car through the half-empty garage. "It's Saturday night and everyone's out having a good time. I deserve to have a night out once in a while, too." She settled into the driver's seat and smoothed out her gown. "Great. Now I'm talking to myself."

As she put the key in the ignition, the car moved slightly. Looking from side to side, she saw no one.

Then it rocked slightly again.

Pressing the button to lock the doors with one hand, she grabbed her cell phone with the other. The number for security was on speed dial.

One ring. Her eyes scanned the parking garage.

Two rings.

"Front gate."

Shelby dropped the phone on the leather seat. An arm was around her throat, crushing her windpipe.

Chapter 23

In the suite, Max stuck his hands in his pockets and looked at everything but BK. He seemed particularly interested in examining a print of Boston Common. He took a deep breath. "You *know* why we're not together anymore."

He said it as a statement, but it was still a question in her mind. "Not really." She shook her head as she moved her dirty clothes off the sofa. "I knew we had some problems but they weren't that serious, nothing we couldn't have worked through. I do have a theory though."

She sat down, grabbed a throw pillow edged in fringe, and set it on her lap. She could be direct at work but in her personal life, she had always stuck with avoidance. Her mother and Stanley taught her to keep her mouth shut and not make waves or she could be sent somewhere else to live. The only waves they liked were the ones crashing against the rocks outside Stanley's seaside mansion.

"Let's hear your theory," Max said. He took a seat at the other end of the sofa and leaned back.

She inhaled. "I think that you don't allow yourself to get close to anyone. You're afraid of commitment."

Max glanced at his watch.

BK continued, fidgeting with the pillow. "I don't know anything about the *real* Max. All I know are a few inane details that could apply to a hundred different people. Not your inner emotions, not your dreams and desires, nothing like that. I know all about Max-Maids but nothing about you."

Max sat up straight. "That's not true."

"Oh, really?" BK's voice got bolder. "I can think of ten examples without even taxing my brain. Like when we went skating on Christmas Eve. I told you my mother wouldn't buy me skates even after she married Stanley and could afford to so I obviously stunk. There I was teetering on those skinny metal blades at the edge of the ice, gripping the wall, when you whoosh past me, turn fast, and come to a stop facing me like an NFL player."

Max almost smiled. "NHL is hockey. NFL is football. You don't see many football players skating down the field."

BK rolled her eyes. "That doesn't really matter, does it? You just don't like talking about yourself."

He wiped away the traces of his smile. "Classic BK, but go on."

"Okay. I asked you how you learned to skate like that and you started to tell me you played hockey with your friends when you were younger. When I asked where you played, I saw that face. I can always tell by the look on your face when I'd gone as far as you'd let me. You put up an invisible barrier around yourself that prevents me from probing any deeper." She shook her head. "You're an expert at changing the subject when things get too close, too personal, for your taste. You don't want to let me in. Am I right?" She looked him straight in the eye.

After a moment's hesitation Max replied, "I guess you're right… to a point. You don't understand."

"That's because you won't talk to me. You're a typical man. Just like Stanley. I don't think he and my mother have had a real conversation in years." She crossed her arms and waited.

"You're comparing *me* to Stanley? I'm not as bad as that." He got up and began to pace. "I guess I find it hard to open up to everyone who enters my life."

Disappointment crashed over her. "*Everyone?* I thought I meant more to you than that."

"That didn't come out right."

BK jumped up. "I don't want to hear it. I thought you loved me. I was ready to move in with you. I thought we might even get married someday but I guess you don't trust me."

"No!" He pounded his thigh in frustration. "I didn't break up with you because I didn't trust you and you know it."

She took a step back. She was not going to let him turn this around on her. *He has issues but won't admit to them. End of story.* "There's no point to this discussion. Apparently we can't communicate." She threw her hands up. "I'm sick of running in circles. I've got to get back downstairs."

"Wait." Max put his hand on her shoulder as she walked toward the door. She tried to shrug it off but he spun her around.

"Let go of me," she said through clenched teeth.

"You can't go until you hear this." His voice was gentle. "I realized tonight that I still have strong feelings for you."

BK paused for a moment to give him a chance. *Say it. Tell me you love me straight out.*

He didn't take his chance.

"So?" She was through playing games. "What are you saying? *Strong feelings?* What the heck does that mean? Do you want to get back together?"

He dropped his hand from her shoulder. "We can't have a relationship unless you face up to your problem and take care of it."

His words clanged in her ears like incessant wind chimes. "This again. This is all you ever want to talk about."

"It's important."

"And your issues aren't, apparently."

"Not like yours. I watched you eat tonight." He began to speak faster. "I'm worried about you, BK. You have to deal with your anorexia."

She opened her mouth to explain.

"No." He put his hand up. "No more excuses. No more denial." He stepped into the hall, leaving the door ajar. "You're right. We don't communicate and it's not because I'm a typical man. How can you communicate when you're in denial?" He pressed the elevator button. The doors opened and he stepped inside. "I'm done."

"Max, come back," she said, following him. The doors were closing behind him. She saw him look at her but he made no move to stop them.

Gasping for breath, Shelby clawed harmlessly at Trevor's arm. For once she wished she had listened to her mother about not biting her nails. She should have grown long, sharp nails so she could paint them red with Trevor's blood.

"Don't make so much as a peep," Trevor hissed in Shelby's ear. He grabbed her phone and cut off the call to the front gate before grabbing her keys from the ignition.

If only I had been paying attention when I climbed in the car, I would have seen him hiding in the back seat, she thought.

He stuffed a rag in her mouth before letting up on his chokehold. Catching her arms as she pulled the gag out, he pushed her head forward, banging it against the steering wheel. He bound her arms together hastily with duct tape and then jerked her back upright. "Now you'll finally pay attention to me." Trevor pressed a gun against the back of her head. "Make any noise, any sudden movements, and you're dead."

She spoke softly not to rile him. "You're out on bail. If you leave now, I won't tell anyone you were here. You've done so well staying away from me, which must have been hard. I know they'll take that into consideration when the trial starts but if they find out you came here tonight it won't look good for you."

"I didn't stay away from you because of any stupid bail or trial. That's all meaningless compared to our destiny." He ground the gun into the back of her head. She bit her lip, determined not to show any fear. "I waited until the time was right to see you in person."

Facing the garage wall, Shelby couldn't tell if anyone was around to help her. He caught her stealing a glance in the rearview mirror and knocked it with his hand, twisting it sideways. "You're not getting rescued this time."

She needed to keep him talking so he wouldn't take her somewhere else. If they stayed here, maybe someone would come along. "How did you find me? I got a new car, put everything in the name of a dummy corporation, got a private mailbox, shredded every piece of mail…and yet, here you are."

"Technology, baby. They make devices to track wandering dogs. You clip it on the pooch's collar and, voilà, you can track her on your cell phone. I stuck one in your wheel well. Didn't think you'd appreciate wearing it around your neck." He chuckled. "I named you Princess when I registered you as my precious but naughty little doggy."

She could feel his breath on the side of her neck as he leaned forward to talk.

"When I got out, I figured you'd have a different car. I'm not stupid, you know. Your pitiful little maneuvers were just little bumps on my road to you." He moved closer. "I staked out City Scene and waited. At first I thought you'd quit but when I checked the latest issue, your mark was all over it. You can use a pen name but you can't change your writing style. So I waited for you to show up. A little sticky tape and my GPS tracker and I could monitor you without leaving my apartment. Very convenient." He moved back. "But then I would have missed the pleasure of seeing your beautiful face."

He seemed to be getting off on telling her all the details. She had to keep him talking. "How did you get past security? The guards have your picture and a copy of the restraining order."

"This so-called security building is a joke. You wasted your parent's money moving here. I figured out how to get to you in less time than it takes for a pizza to be delivered." He snorted. "It's easy to get a job delivering pizza. There's a high turnover rate and they're happy to hire just about anyone who can drive. A little hole in the wall in the theater district sells fake mustaches and bald comb-over wigs. People can't take their eyes off a bad comb-over so they don't focus on the face. Once the security guards got to know the disguised me, I could come and go anytime, especially if I had an extra order of breadsticks with me. I'd park, change the batteries on the GPS, deliver a pizza, and be out of here in less than ten minutes."

Shelby closed her eyes. She hadn't thought about the different ways he could circumvent security. "How did you get into my car? You didn't break a window and you didn't set off the alarm."

One corner of his mouth went up. "I copied your car's VIN off the dashboard, made a fake title on my computer and took them to the dealership looking really upset and annoyed. You see, I stupidly locked the keys in my car and I needed them to make me a key." He dangled the replacement in front of her wide eyes. "They were so helpful. They didn't even charge me." He stroked her hair.

Her muscles tensed under the touch of his repulsive hands. She pulled back.

"My only problem was that you hardly ever left your damn apartment. But I can be patient. While you stayed holed up day after day, night after night, it gave me time to formulate the perfect plan. All I had to do was wait a few weeks for the big charity ball. It was advertised everywhere. I knew you wouldn't miss BK's big night."

"I almost didn't go."

Yanking roughly on her hair, he twisted her head toward him. She looked into his vacant eyes. "I was beginning to think you were losing it. You even had your groceries delivered. That's not normal. You wouldn't want people to think you're *crazy*. I know. I've been on the inside. Spend one day committed and you're labeled for life. Whatever they call it: loony bin, nut house, bug house, mental in-sti-tu-tion. It doesn't matter. Your old life is over. Forever." He pulled her hair again. "All because of you, Shelby."

A whimper escaped from her lips.

"You drove me to this. If you had cooperated with me, none of this would have happened. I wouldn't have gotten arrested. They're going to send me back to Willowbrook. I can't go back there. Those people are crazy. I'm just in love. I don't belong with them."

She tried to listen for any sounds in the garage as he ranted.

"Maybe we should go there together. You were getting pretty paranoid even before I visited your old apartment. The way you had BK's boyfriend accost that P.I. was shameful."

Her eyes narrowed. "I knew you were following me."

He knocked her on the side of the head with the gun. "Did not! If you'd known, you would've gone to the police, waving your little log book." He leaned over the seat and got in her face. "I *hate* when you lie. Why do you always lie?"

She knew it was no use trying to reason with him. Closing her eyes, she said a quick prayer, sure that this was going to be the end of her life.

She had to try something, anything. Slamming her head into his, she tried to swing her legs up to kick the window out but her gown trapped her legs in a sequined cocoon.

"You bitch!" He rubbed his head.

"Help! Help me!"

"Shut up! No one's here." He hit her on the head again before stuffing the gag back in her mouth. She struggled, twisting back and forth.

"Stupid, stupid girl." He shook his head and clucked his tongue. "But you always were. All I wanted was for you to pay some attention to me. You were too snotty. Never gave me a second look. I should've known from the first time we danced. Even then you were making eyes at that boy. Disgusting."

A warm stream of blood ran down Shelby's neck onto the collar of her gown.

"Now look what you've done. You've gone and ruined your beautiful new dress. I personally would've picked the black one that you tried on first but you never do what I want."

Shelby shuddered. He was at the store.

With the gun pressed to her temple, he deftly maneuvered his body into the passenger seat. Popping open the glove compartment with one hand, he removed a length of rope. "See how perfect my plan is? I even thought to stash what I'd need ahead of time."

Shelby closed her eyes for a moment and thought of Clyde, her loyal companion. She knew her big, brown-eyed, drooling dog would miss her. She couldn't bear to think of her parents or BK. A tear rolled down her cheek. *This is it. It's over*, she thought. *If I try to get away, he'll shoot me. If I don't try, he'll rape me, then shoot me.*

Pushing her body over, she tried to knock the gun out of his hand.

"Give up already," he said. They stared at each other for a moment before the gun hit her head with a thwack. The car began to spin.

He set the gun down on the seat and bent forward as he wound the scratchy rope around her legs, making pulls in her pantyhose.

She brought her knees up and caught his head between her legs and the steering wheel trying her best to crack his skull. He jammed his fingers into the flesh on her legs and pushed her back down. Pulling his head out, he grabbed the gun and pointed it between her eyes. "I'm going to have to use this if you don't stop."

She sat still and concentrated on focusing her eyes.

"I'm glad you have enough sense to calm down. I don't want you dead before tonight." A sick grin spread across his face.

She fought to suppress a wave of nausea. *I can't get sick now with this gag in my mouth*, she thought. *I could choke to death on my own vomit.*

He pulled her down on the seat, stuck the gun in the waist of his pants and sat on her as he finished tying the knot. Outlining her face with his index finger, he gazed into her eyes.

She jerked her head away.

"Look at me." He grabbed her on either side of her face. "I've been waiting for this for years. Tonight is our wedding night."

She shook her head. She wanted to scream, *No!*

"Don't do that, Miss High and Mighty Fulton, shaking your head as if we're not meant to be together. You'll behave differently when you're my wife." He slapped her, but softened his voice as he caressed her cheek. "You'll see. It will be a dream come true. We won't be married in a church but I have a private ceremony planned and a beautiful wedding dress for you. You're going to look exquisite. It will be just you, me, and BK."

Shelby tried to speak. "Not BK! Leave her out of this," but her words were too distorted by the gag to be understood.

"You don't have to thank me, my beloved. I'm willing to put my personal feelings about BK aside because I knew you'd want her there. I want you to be as happy as I am. I'm going to pick her up at the ball. I have my ticket right here." He patted his pocket. "Till death do us all part."

Shelby fought back as he stuffed her onto the floor on the passenger side. As she bucked and writhed, he covered her with a blanket grabbed from the back seat. A strong odor of mothballs made her queasy stomach swirl.

"Stop moving. I mean it, Shelby. This is your last warning."

She continued to fight. *I'd rather die than marry you*, she thought.

A final blow to the back of her head ended the struggle.

Chapter 24

Backstage, BK walked up the steps and asked if Vincenti needed anything before his show started. Vincenti drank from a half-empty bottle of vodka. He tried to hide the bottle from her, placing it on a stool behind him as he spoke.

"I need nothing right now, my dear, but maybe something after the show." Vincenti's magical hand appeared out of nowhere and descended onto her behind. BK shook him off and took a few steps back. She decided to ignore his advance. It wouldn't be smart to offend the highlight of the evening's entertainment before he went on.

She could hear Max on the other side of the curtain conducting the charity auction. She was numb to the sound of his voice now but knew she would pay tonight. Sleep was not in the near future for her.

"The bidding is almost over," she said. Just as she finished her sentence, the man with the purple cummerbund appeared. Her eyes narrowed. "Who are you?" She hadn't been able to locate this peeping Tom when she checked backstage earlier. Then the talk with Max had put him out of her mind completely.

"This is Lenny Mayhew, my offstage assistant." Vincenti's nervous laugh released noxious alcohol fumes into BK's face. "Not that my magic requires help behind the scenes."

BK ignored him and looked at Lenny. "Why were you peeking around the curtain during dinner?"

Lenny shifted on his feet. "Just doing my job, ma'am, getting to know the layout of the room."

BK didn't know why but she didn't believe him. But there wasn't time to get into it further. "You better get ready. You're on in less than five."

"And now, the man you've all been waiting for, Vincenti the Great." Max's hand was raised as Vincenti ran across the stage, a black cape embroidered with silver stars and moons trailing behind him.

Lights flashed and music blared as Max slipped down the side stairs. BK was waiting for him.

"Putting our personal issues aside, this has been a magical night. You've really outdone yourself, BK."

She didn't acknowledge his compliment or his attempt at humor. "Trevor's here." Just saying his name made acid ooze in her stomach. Maybe Madame Zona was legit after all. Trevor was sure to cause trouble. "I haven't been able to find any security guards to throw him out. There isn't a blue uniform in sight."

"He's not going to try anything. Too many people around."

"At least Shelby's not here." BK pictured Trevor grabbing Shelby as she arrived at the hotel. He was capable of it. "But I thought she was coming. She bought a dress and wanted to be here to support me." Her voice softened. "She knew seeing you again was going to be hard for me."

Max averted his eyes. "So call her. Find out one way or the other."

BK chewed her bottom lip. "I haven't been able to reach her."

"Okay, don't panic. You know she hasn't ventured out much since Trevor came back." He put his hand on his chin and rubbed it. "Try her again. Maybe her phone is buried at the bottom of her huge purse and she didn't hear it."

"I tried her at least five times since you and I… uhh… talked upstairs." The first thing she did was call her lifeline. No one understood her like Shelby. Heather was blood but BK had a bond with Shelby.

Max swallowed hard. "Did you try her parents' house?"

"They're out of town."

"Is it possible she went somewhere else? Maybe out with friends from work?"

"Come on, Max. This is Shelby. My best friend. You know she'd be here with us if she went out at all."

"You're right." Max's jaw tensed. "If he hurt her…" His head swiveled as he scanned the room. "Where is the s.o.b.? I'll kill him before he has a chance to touch either one of you again."

"He's over there." She pointed with a shaking hand. "Standing next to Senator Camden."

Lenny's head was poking out of the trapdoor of a supposedly solid box. Vincenti cut the power to his microphone as he bent down to whisper, "What are you doing? You're going to ruin my act."

Lenny was out of view of the audience, shielded by the sides of the box. He pointed his gun in the direction of the magician's head and hissed, "I ain't planning to use this on you but I will if I have to. Just keep doing the damn trick."

Vincenti tapped the box with his wand.

"Get the old broad over here. Now," Lenny commanded.

"But it's not time yet," Vincenti croaked, a bead of sweat trickling down his forehead.

Lenny cocked the gun. "Do it."

The magician's multiple chins quivered as he gestured toward the side of the stage. "The high bidder who won the chance to take part in my next trick was Senator Jack Camden with the high bid of ten thousand dollars. One hundred percent of the money benefits Haven." The audience burst into applause.

No, Lenny thought. *One hundred percent of tonight's money is going to Lenny Mayhew and associates.*

"Taking the senator's place is his lovely wife, Claudia." More applause erupted.

Lenny waited while Mrs. Camden made her way across the stage. He could hear her high heels click, click, clicking toward him. Vincenti reached out and took her bejeweled hand. She took a bow as Lenny started to inch out of the small compartment at the bottom of the box.

BK's stomach lurched as she watched Max storm over to Trevor. She quickened her step to catch up with him.

The senator was talking. "…and because of it, I was able to get the teacher's union endorsement."

"That's very impressive, Senator." Trevor was nodding as Max grabbed his arm from behind and pulled him aside.

"Please excuse us, Senator," Max said.

"Is there some kind of a problem?" the senator asked hesitantly.

"Believe me, Senator, you don't want to get involved. It's between me and Trevor."

The senator muttered something and hurried away.

Max led Trevor to a less crowded area outside the ballroom. BK followed. They stopped beyond the restrooms where they were unlikely to be noticed unless someone stepped out from one of the nearby elevators.

Max growled at Trevor. "What have you done with Shelby?"

Trevor blinked rapidly. "I…I don't know what you're talking about." He wrenched his arm from Max's grasp. "Keep your hands off me."

Max sneered. "You're not such a big man when you're up against someone your own size, are you?"

"It sickens me that you're out and free to do as you please while Shelby lives like she's a prisoner," BK said. "She never did anything wrong."

"If you've done anything to her, you're going to regret it," Max said.

"I already told you. I don't know anything about Shelby."

"You're pushing your luck, Trevor," BK said. "Coming here was a stupid idea."

Max jerked his thumb in the direction of the door. "Time for you to leave. You're coming with me."

"I have every right to be here." Trevor patted his pockets and pulled out a ticket.

Max grabbed Trevor by his lapel and drew him in close. "I'll give you a refund. We don't need your money. Haven shouldn't be tainted with money from a stalker."

BK glanced around and spoke in a hushed tone. "This isn't the place to get physical."

Max looked at her. "Don't try to stop me. He's got this coming."

"Believe me, I'd love nothing more than to watch you beat him to a pulp." She glared at Trevor. "I'd even like to help." She didn't have a hammer but she'd figure a way to inflict damage. "But beating him up at an event you're sponsoring won't help either Shelby or the women who are depending on the services of Haven. If he's done something to her, we need to find out where she is. Let's take him outside and make him talk." Max released Trevor's lapels with a little shove. Trevor stumbled backwards, landing against the wall.

Just as Max started to escort him out, what sounded like a gunshot pierced the air.

BK and Max rushed back into the ballroom. Trevor followed.

Lenny dragged Mrs. Camden around the stage as he paced back and forth, aiming his gun at various people in the audience. "No one move," he yelled. "Drop all your phones and Black Cherries, or whatever them things are called, on the floor."

Lenny saw Mrs. Camden look to Vincenti for help but the magician was still, facedown on the stage. His arm was angled unnaturally, splayed awkwardly against the oak planks. Blood pooled around him, leaking from an unseen gunshot wound.

Mrs. Camden yanked Lenny's arm, trying to loosen it.

"You're probably used to boas around your throat but this one ain't made of no feathers, it's a snake," Lenny hissed in her ear. He tightened his grip then pressed the gun against her temple. He scanned the room. "Nobody wants to see the old bag get it through the brain."

The senator gasped and dropped his phone at his feet. Security guards swarmed the crowd, scooping up phones and rounding people into a tight circle.

Searching for an escape, BK inched back toward the big ballroom doors. Armed men blocked each exit. Although they were dressed in the security company's uniforms, it was clear from the scowls on their faces that they were not part of the detail she hired. She looked around for other possible escape routes.

"Don't move, BK." Max's strong, controlled voice should have calmed her but she was having trouble catching her breath. A searing pain shot through her temple and jaw.

"I want everybody to take off your jewelry—all of it—and put it in one of the bags," Lenny instructed as the guards passed large burlap bags from person to person. "Put all your wallets in there, too."

The room was eerily silent except for Mrs. Camden's sobs as she was used as a human shield.

BK's fingers ran over her diamond necklace. *It's all I have left of Max*, she thought, as she fumbled with the catch. She couldn't get it open.

Lenny yelled into the microphone. "Move it! Move it!"

"Max," BK whispered. "Can you help me?"

"I'll help." A security guard stepped over and yanked it from her neck.

Her eyes flashed as she rubbed the dent it left in her flesh.

The guard smirked.

Max made a move toward him. When the guard pointed his rifle at BK, Max put his hands up and stepped back.

BK's whole body trembled as she stood in the line of fire. She tried to breathe but the air was thick with the stench of fear and desperation.

When the gunman moved to the next person, she closed her eyes, exhaled, and reached out for Max.

He wasn't there.

She opened her eyes. He had stepped away from her. *I keep forgetting*, she thought. *Why should he be here for me? We're not together anymore.*

Pain shot down BK's arm and a cold sweat clung to the back of her neck. *I think I'm having a panic attack.*

She closed her eyes again, tried to breathe evenly, and prayed. She ended with a plea for Shelby's well-being.

Finally the bags were set on the floor of the stage near Lenny. Sirens could be heard in the distance.

Lenny tightened his grip around Mrs. Camden's throat again as he began to talk. "You didn't think you could hide from me, did you? Going off to them fancy schools didn't fool nobody. You must have known, deep down in your lily-livered heart, that someday I'd come and find you, Trevor."

A murmur rippled through the crowd. Heads swiveled, searching for the madman's target.

BK followed Lenny's piercing gaze. Trevor's eyes were wide.

Madame Zona's words sounded in BK's head like an alarm. *Heed my warning. Stay as far away from Trevor as possible.*

BK called in a low voice, "Max, move. Trevor's behind you."

Max didn't budge. His eyes were fixed on the maniac on the stage. *He's so busy figuring out how to save the day that he doesn't realize he's standing right in front of the target.* She called his name again, slightly louder this time.

Mrs. Camden's face was contorted in pain. Her manicured fingernails scratched her captor's arm, drawing lines of blood. Lenny didn't seem to notice.

BK felt as though a circus elephant had climbed on her chest as she continued to try to get Max's attention. She wanted to yell for him to move but she couldn't catch her breath.

"You can't hide from me anymore, you coward." Lenny continued with his tirade as Mrs. Camden passed out and hung limply from his arm. Lenny either didn't care or didn't notice.

When the senator rushed toward the stage to help his wife, a shot rang out. High-pitched screams ricocheted around the room. The senator fell to the floor, clutching his arm, blood pouring from between his fingers. "I've been hit!"

The crowd shifted and shoved like penned sheep with nowhere to run, desperate to escape the sharp teeth of an approaching wolf. The guards moved in closer and contained the crowd, pointing their guns at anyone who stepped out of the circle.

"Shut up or I'll shoot you again." With a defiant smirk Lenny waved the gun. "Anybody else want to be a hero?" He looked down at the subdued crowd. "I didn't think so."

His attention turned to Trevor again. "Not you, eh? You never had it in you to be a hero. You always gave in to me. Never could take it. If you really had been my kid, you would've had guts instead of being the wimp that you are." He raised his pitch. "No, Daddy, no. Don't hurt me."

BK tried again. "Max. Come here!" He didn't seem to hear her. She realized that her voice was barely a whisper.

"I can tell by the look on your face. You didn't know, did you?" Lenny continued. "That's right. I ain't your real daddy. Believe me, ain't nobody happier than me. You can take that piece of truth with you to your grave." He leveled the gun and squeezed the trigger.

Max dropped to the floor. So did Trevor.

BK couldn't tell who was shot. *Did the bullet go through both of them?*

The guards backed out of the room. Lenny dropped Mrs. Camden and grabbed the bags of stolen property.

The crowd scattered, pushing and shoving. A woman fell facedown, while Pradas and Blahniks and Louboutins trampled her.

"Max…" BK reached out as her voice completely faded. She couldn't see straight as she clutched her burning chest. She, too, collapsed on the floor as blackness enveloped her.

Chapter 25

When her eyes opened, BK was looking into the face of a stranger. "Where am I?" she asked.

"In an ambulance heading for Boston Memorial. I'm an EMT," he said, checking her blood pressure.

BK thrashed around.

"Hold still, ma'am. You're going to be all right."

"Max..." she muttered.

"Quiet now. We're pulling into the hos-pit-al," the EMT said slowly into her ear.

The ambulance doors opened and BK was wheeled to a massive brick building. The red lights of the ambulance reflected in the glass doors and windows. Once in a small curtained area, people in scrubs swarmed around her. A nurse cut her expensive designer gown down the front and attached monitor wires to her chest. "Can you hear me?" she asked.

BK nodded, then moaned. The fluorescent lights made her squint.

"That's right. Stay awake." The nurse peeled off the paper backing and stuck one more electrode on BK's skin. "What's your name?"

"Stop...Mayhew..."

"Good, Miss Mayhew," the nurse said, misunderstanding BK's words. "Keep talking to me."

"Not Mayhew..." BK's heart monitor bleeped irregularly.

The nurse spoke loudly. "What?"

"Should have known," BK mumbled. "Something...wrong."

"Yes. Something's wrong but you're at the hospital now and we're taking care of you."

An orderly parted the curtains. "A doctor will be in soon."

BK tried to tell them about Lenny Mayhew. "Saw him..."

"No, honey. The doctor hasn't come in yet." She kept an eye on the monitor.

The orderly said, "One will be along as soon as possible. It's crazy in here tonight."

"That must have been some ball," the nurse said.

"Wait till you hear this." The orderly poked his head further inside and lowered his voice. "They found someone stuffed in the trunk of a car in the parking lot."

"Dead or alive?"

"I don't know."

BK murmured. "All my fault… all my fault…"

"She's not making sense," the nurse said.

The last thing BK heard was the monitor sounding an alarm.

"This is Robyn Prentiss reporting live from the parking lot of the Van Buren Plaza where tonight, an unidentified gunman opened fire at a charity ball held to benefit the city's newest shelter for battered women."

For the first time in her career, Robyn looked disheveled. The wind had picked up and was blowing her hair across her face.

"As you can see, I was among those wounded," she said, pausing while the camera zoomed in on the bloody bandage tightly wrapped around her arm, "in tonight's carnage that has left an unconfirmed two dead and eleven wounded. Among the wounded are Senator Jack Camden and his wife, prominent socialite Claudia Camden. Both were taken out of the ballroom by stretcher. The unidentified ringleader, who reportedly used Claudia Camden as a human shield during tonight's botched robbery attempt, is still at large. Police have taken nine suspects into custody."

Robyn held a composite drawing up to the camera. "This is the man the police are looking for. He is armed and considered dangerous. If you should see him, notify the police immediately and do not, I repeat, *do not* approach him."

After listing the color of his hair and eyes and his approximate height and weight, Robyn flashed the prearranged signal to the cameraman to indicate that she needed to sit down. As they had planned, the camera panned the scene of police cars, ambulances and guests in formal attire being questioned in the background as Robyn read from an impromptu script written on the back of her grocery list. Once she was settled in a folding canvas chair, the camera returned to her and she continued.

"Many are saying that tonight's debacle could have been avoided if proper security measures had been taken. Seated next to me is Delores Digby, assistant to the banquet coordinator here at the Van Buren Plaza. Miss Digby," she said, shoving the microphone in Delores's face, "when did you first suspect that something was wrong?"

Delores bared her yellow teeth to the camera. "It started out bad, you see. I've got this terrible cold." She gave a full-bodied sniff that sounded like it started from the bottom of her feet and thundered up throughout her body, culminating in a chunky swallow.

Robyn cringed. On camera.

"And then some clumsy lady knocked down a whole table full of dishes." She lowered her voice as if confiding to the thousands of viewers watching the report on live TV. "I think she already had a touch of the grape, if you know what I mean."

Robyn redirected her rambling story. "We're interested in when you found out about the gunmen."

"Oh, that would be when I went downstairs to the supply closet to get some extra napkins and there were all the security guards laying on the floor, trussed up like turkeys on Thanksgiving morning. They had tape stuck over their mouths. I ran back up to the ballroom to tell my boss and that's when the big one with the gun grabbed me from behind."

Robyn frowned. She'd hoped this debacle could be blamed on her rival, BK Hartshaw. Max was obviously still hung up on her. "So you're telling us that there *were* security guards on the premises?"

"Yup. A bunch of them. The rest were found locked down in the... ahhh... ahhh... choo..." Delores sneezed without fully covering her mouth, allowing her germ-ridden saliva to spray all over Robyn. She swiped her nose with the back of her hand before finishing her thought. "They were locked in the basement."

"Bless you." Always professional, Robyn continued calmly with the interview. "Were you in the ballroom at the time of the shootings?"

Delores nodded vigorously. "I seen it all. It's going to take me hours to get the place cleaned up right again. My boss will have to pay me time and a half, at least. Blood and guts were splashed everywhere, splattered innards dripping off the walls and furniture. A terrible mess."

Robyn cringed and ended the interview.

"That was a short interview," said the cameraman after Delores walked away.

"You told me that Digby woman would say there were an inadequate number of security guards," Robyn said.

"That's not what I said. I told you she knew something about the security guards and you jumped to your own conclusion. You're bent on trying to make that woman look bad in front of her ex-boyfriend."

"What woman?"

The cameraman was banging equipment around. "You know exactly who I mean. The one who organized this whole thing, the one you were bad-mouthing earlier."

"I was just trying to get a story, nothing else," Robyn protested. "Besides, the Digby woman's description was making me sick to my stomach. I know I might've gotten more details out of her but I couldn't stand to listen a minute longer."

"I think she had more to tell."

"Why?"

"Before this all came down, I think I saw her talking to the gunman. It must have been her because the woman I saw kept sniffing and wiping her nose on the back of her hand. They looked pretty cozy, if you ask me."

Robyn's voice got loud. "Why didn't you tell me about this before the interview?"

"It didn't click until she sneezed on camera."

"I've never shortchanged an interview before and I'm not going to start now. Get her back over here."

"Listen, I'm not your lackey," he said. "Don't use that tone when you're talking to me."

"I thought you might want to help me out," she said, popping up from her chair. "Reporting live about a multiple shooting while being wounded myself and then getting an exclusive with a person who knows the ringleader will win me an award for sure. Goodbye fluff pieces, hello hard news. I might even get the chance to be an anchor." Her voice went higher as she got more excited. "This might even be big enough to launch me into network news!"

"Hey! Are you all right? You look like you're ready to pass out." The cameraman helped her back into the chair. "Sit down. I thought the EMT told you that the bullet just grazed you."

"I just got up too fast."

"I'm calling the station to have them send someone out to replace you. You're in no condition to continue interviewing. One of the ambulances can take you to the hospital."

"I'm fine," Robyn snarled. "You don't have to do that, Ed. Just get that woman back here so I can talk to her again."

"My name is Ned," he said before starting to walk away. He stopped at a nearby car.

Robyn got up, slower this time, and joined him. "What on earth are you doing, *Ned*?"

"I heard knocking. Look at that," he said, pulling on a small piece of sequined material sticking out above the license plate. Putting his ear on the trunk, he knocked on it and called, "Hello?"

Robyn huffed. "You made me get up because someone slammed the trunk on their dry cleaning?" She yanked on the material. It was saturated with blood.

Ned shouted to one of the police officers questioning a witness nearby. "We need help over here."

Robyn snapped her fingers. "Quick. Set up for a report. This is too good to pass up."

"Doctor Holland's answering service."

Trevor gave his name. "I need to see Doctor Holland. Right away."

He glanced at the clock. It was after midnight. "It's an emergency. Tell her it has to do with the shooting that took place at the Van Buren Plaza tonight."

Chapter 26

Trevor got a call back from Dr. Holland in ten minutes. Within the hour he was in her office, sitting in an overstuffed leather chair outlined with upholstery tacks. Next to the framed diplomas, a copy of Vermeer's *Girl With A Pearl Earring* hung on the dark green wall.

"You know I've been avoiding the topic of my childhood," Trevor began.

"Yes." During normal office hours, Doctor Holland's shoulder length hair hung straight around her face but tonight, the grey-streaked brown strands were pulled back in a ponytail. Her customary suit was replaced with designer slacks and a jersey. She was still dressed better than most of the women he'd seen at church last Sunday.

"Tonight the past caught up with me." He picked at one of the tacks with his fingernail. "I saw my father for the first time in years."

She nodded and waited for him to continue. Doctor Holland was not one to push. She would interject a well-placed prompt here and there but she kept it to a minimum. This was why he felt comfortable with her. He could go at his own pace, which so far had been turtle-fast.

"He tried to kill me."

Doctor Holland, who usually didn't betray any emotion, opened her eyes wide. Still, she remained silent.

"And this isn't the first time he's tried."

"Perhaps," she said, "it would help to tell me your first childhood memories." She had her pen poised, ready to record what Trevor was sure was going to be one of the most dysfunctional childhoods she'd ever heard about.

"1985 was the year my mother died. I don't have many memories from before her death, but I sure remember that day..."

When Lenny and Ace neared the cabin, it was well after midnight. No lights guided them through the glorified paths that passed as streets around Drake Pond but they had been to the cabin after dark before and found their way fairly easily.

Ace maneuvered the stolen pickup around the side of his cousin's cabin and parked between two of the pines that hugged the rustic structure. The brightness from the headlights flooded the yard, startling a skunk into the bushes.

As Lenny stepped into the leaf-carpeted yard, he inhaled. After a lifetime split between the joint and the city, he was always surprised by the crispness of the air here, even if it was faintly laced with the scent of skunk.

Ace reached his hand into a large planter filled with gardening tools. The key was at the bottom, not that it would take more than two minutes to gain entry into the place without it. The cabin was old and rickety; it looked like a window could be popped out without much effort.

Inside was colder than out, the chill of the winter still trapped within the walls. Still, Lenny didn't want to fire up the woodstove because it would send a smoke signal alerting the police of their presence. Plenty of moth-nibbled blankets were available once the heated rush of the night's events wore off.

The décor looked like it hadn't changed much since the cabin was built sometime in the 1950s. A Formica table surrounded by chrome and vinyl chairs filled the kitchen area, a couch and chair made up the living room area, and two twin beds built into nooks in the wall marked the bedroom area. It was really one room divided by purpose, plus a tiny lean-to bathroom addition on the back.

Lenny had lived in smaller quarters courtesy of the overcrowded state penitentiary. At least this was temporary and there were only two of them staying here. The rest of the boys were at separate motels. Experience had taught Lenny that it was best to keep everyone apart for a few days. One guy quietly checking into a motel created very little suspicion. Plus, it gave him time to tally the loot and divide the shares.

After pulling all the shades and lighting a lantern, Ace carried in the bags of wallets and jewelry from the car and set them on the table. He dumped the first one like a kid would a plastic pumpkin after a night of trick-or-treating. He picked up a diamond necklace, pulling a loupe out of his pocket, but the flickering flame was not adequate to make a proper appraisal. In a few days he would take care of fencing the jewelry. That was his specialty.

Lenny sat back and didn't touch anything. Usually he wouldn't even let Ace near the bounty until he finished his inventory. When Lenny didn't yell or slug Ace, he looked at Lenny with curiosity. "What's up with you? You ain't acting like yourself tonight."

Lenny shrugged.

Ace set the diamonds down gently and leaned his back against the cracked vinyl that covered the thin padding of the chair. The flower pattern was still vivid, a testament to the dyes used before people became concerned about toxins and the effects on the environment. "This whole job was about your kid, wasn't it? It had nothin' to do with money this time."

He leaned forward. "Don't get no ideas about takin' my share."

Lenny saw Ace run his tongue over the chip in his front tooth before he spoke. "I know better than to do somethin' as stupid as that. You taught me that lesson when we was ten."

Lenny looked at his old friend. "You're right. The job was all about Trevor." He plucked a bulging wallet off the table and flipped it open. "And just a little bit about the money."

Ace lit the gas stove and fixed an ancient percolator to go on the burner. "We got a long night ahead of us if you want to talk."

"I ain't some woman, all sensitive, needin' to rehash my feelings." He spoke in a nasal tone. "I don't need to express my *inner thoughts*."

Ace put his hands up. "That's not what I meant. Believe me, no one would *ever* think you're sensitive. Not in a million years."

"As long as that's clear." Lenny got up and paced for several minutes. Then he turned and looked at Ace, still standing by the stove. "Seeing Trevor's face was a shock after all these years. He looked like his mother. A lot. You know how I felt about her. Gail was, and still is, the only girl I ever loved. I almost couldn't go through with it." He sat down while Ace poured their syrupy coffee. He wrapped his hands around the mug and blew the rising steam. "But then I remembered the last time I saw him and it didn't matter who he looked like. I wanted him dead."

Trevor had stopped talking to Doctor Holland. The clock read almost four in the morning. His hands were shaking.

The doctor waited a few minutes before saying anything. "Have you had enough for now?" She stood. "Let's take a break and then we can come back to this at our next session. I'll have my receptionist call you with a time."

"No," Trevor said. "I need to finish this once and for all."

He agreed to a short break, and had taken a walk to the corner convenience store to pick up snacks. Packaged powdered doughnuts, honey buns that exceeded the maximum daily-recommended grams of fat, and two lattes topped with whipped cream sat on Doctor Holland's coffee table. "My trainer would have a heart attack if he saw this," Trevor said. "I was craving junk food."

Doctor Holland laughed. "I think you should indulge if it makes you feel better."

She looked like she had taken their short break to freshen up. Her hair was smoother and her face looked freshly scrubbed. "You said you wanted to finish the story," she said, taking her seat and one of the fat-laden honey buns. "Go ahead."

He set his doughnut on a napkin, the powdered sugar sprinkling onto the recycled paper like snow. He swallowed. "I want to tell you about the last time I saw my father before tonight. I was in eighth grade, hungry as usual, looking for a snack. My grandmother was late getting home from work."

Even though it was the biggest cliché, Trevor laid down on the couch. He closed his eyes. It was if he was reliving the worst nightmare of his life.

Trevor was thirteen again, standing in front of the open refrigerator, staring at a package of hamburger. Gram was supposed to cook her special meatloaf surprise and his mouth watered at the thought. He closed the refrigerator door and reached for the cookie jar. "A couple more cookies won't spoil my appetite tonight," he mumbled.

As the lid touched the top of the jar, he thought he heard a noise outside. Tilting his head, he listened but the rain was too loud. He went to the window and pushed the curtains aside. Peering out into the darkness, he could barely see the staircase, let alone anything on the street below. Shrugging, he went to watch TV.

Moments later he heard his grandmother yelling, "Stop! Stop! Stop!"

Trevor moaned. *Great, another stupid drill. I'm too hungry to do this tonight.* He shook his head but snapped off the lights anyway. *I passed just a couple of weeks ago so why is she making me do it again?*

He ran to the kitchen, stubbing his toe on a chair in the dark. He hobbled over and grabbed another cookie before heading for his hiding place. He was trying to lock the door but he couldn't feed the hook through the eye. He stepped from his hiding place. The hook had twisted around and was stuck pointing up. As he tried to straighten it, the doorknob turned.

He jumped back into the broom closet just as the kitchen door opened. *That was close. If she catches me out in plain sight, she'll make me have a drill every day.* He shifted around trying to get comfortable.

The lights went on and then he heard a strange noise.

Shhht, shhht, shhht.

It sounded as if his grandmother was dragging something in through the door. Maybe a surprise for winning the spelling bee. It was most likely a big bag of clothes from the thrift shop. Gram loved to find designer cast-offs so she could make Trevor look as trendy as possible. She probably got him to climb into the closet so she could bring it in without him seeing. She knew he'd just tell her for the hundredth time that he didn't care about fancy labels.

Shhht, shhht, shhht.

He banged his head on the shelf as he tried to peek through the knothole. He couldn't see anything. She wasn't in his line of vision.

The back of a man's head came into view. "Come on out, Trevor. I heard you make a noise," the man called as he turned around. "I know you're in here somewhere."

Trevor immediately recognized his father's pitted face from his nightmares. He had an unfamiliar scar down his left cheek but it was definitely Lenny. Holding his breath, Trevor wondered if it was possible for Lenny to feel his shock or to smell his fear.

Oh my God, where's Gram?

Lenny's face disappeared from Trevor's tunnel vision. Afraid to make noise, he remained perfectly still. He listened to the sound of glass breaking and furniture overturning as Lenny ransacked the apartment.

He's looking for me. Sweat covered Trevor's body, turning the closet into a sauna.

Lenny returned to the kitchen and bent down. He was out of Trevor's sight but he could hear him talking in a low voice. A sickening lump rose in his throat. Was his grandmother the thing being dragged through the door?

Please, God, don't let him hurt her. It's me he's after.

"Where's the kid? Do you hear me, old woman?"

Trevor heard the crack of Lenny's hand hitting his grandmother's skin.

"I said, where's the kid? Wake up, damn you." He stood up and continued muttering as he walked away. "Useless old broad."

Trevor heard the lid hit the tank of the toilet. He cracked the closet door open and gasped. His grandmother was on the floor, and she was covered in blood and mud.

His muscles tensed. He was ready to burst from the closet, shove Lenny headfirst down the toilet, and then go to Gram and hold her tight until help arrived.

He ignored his first instinct. *Think. I can't end up in the same condition as Gram or I won't be able to help her. Lenny will be coming back in a matter of seconds. I need to take him by surprise.*

Stepping from his safety zone, he grabbed a butcher knife from the top drawer. He darted back into the closet, leaving the door slightly ajar so he could see. He tested the sharpness of the blade by rubbing it across his finger. A small stream of blood trickled down his hand and he absently wiped it on his pants thinking of how many times his grandmother had warned, "Careful, honey, that's a sharp knife."

He took a deep breath.

This is it, life or death.

I want life. For myself and for Gram.

"You awake yet, you old bag?" Lenny yelled from Trevor's room. Drawers were slamming, the contents of his life being invaded.

"I know he's here. The little pansy's probably peeing his pants right now, just like he used to."

Trevor didn't allow the old feeling of shame to take over. He just wanted Lenny to keep yelling so he could tell where he was in the apartment.

"Come on out, Trevor," he coaxed in a singsong voice. "Come on. Daddy wants to see you."

Over my dead body.

"What's this? A widdle teddy bear?"

Trevor heard Benny's glass eyes clink against the wall as Lenny threw his bear. Gram had spent part of her first paycheck to buy Benny so he'd have something to hold onto at night when he was afraid. Now the embodiment of his nightmares was in his bedroom.

"I knew you was a loser from the day you were born. A mama's boy, Grandmaw's lit-tle man."

A slight movement diverted Trevor's attention. His grandmother's eyes fluttered open as she slowly tried to prop herself up on her elbow. Staring at the door that stood between her grandson and death, she collapsed.

Hold on, Gram. I'm going to help you.

Her eyes closed again.

"Ain't you conscious yet?" Lenny limped back to the kitchen and gave Beverly a sharp kick in the ribs. She didn't stir.

I want to kill him with my bare hands.

Common sense held Trevor back. *I have to wait until his back is turned and I have to be accurate. I can't risk losing the knife in a struggle before I have a chance to do some major damage.*

Lenny shook her violently. "Wake up, *Gram!*"

She groaned and drew a labored breath. "Don't you dare... call me Gram... you scum."

"I'll call you whatever I want to, old lady." Lenny slapped the back of her head then poised his hand to do it again. "Where is he?"

"He's not home." She paused to gasp some air. "At a friend's house." She was silent for a moment. "Won't be home tonight."

Hitting her again, he yelled, "I want the truth. Where is he? The lights were on before. I seen 'em. I know he's here."

"It's... the truth."

Trevor knew the fear in her voice was for him, not for herself.

"I don't believe you." He raised his hand to hit her again.

"Lights are… on a timer."

Lenny removed his blood stained knife from its sheath and growled, "You sure you ain't lying?"

Trevor tightened his grip on the handle of the butcher knife. He couldn't wait a moment longer. Bursting from the cabinet, he plunged the knife into Lenny's back.

Stunned, Lenny dropped his weapon and twisted around to face his son.

"That was for you, *Daddy*."

"You bastard." His hands reached out toward Trevor's throat.

Trevor lifted the knife high and stabbed his father again. "That was for my mother." And again. "That was for Gram."

Lenny blinked.

"And this one is for me."

Lenny pushed his coffee cup to the center of the table. The contents had gone cold while he spilled his guts to Ace. "It's like all the old-timers say. Time flies. It seems like yesterday but it was at least twenty years ago."

Ace whistled. "How'd we get so damn old?"

Lenny stared at the codfish print curtains hanging in the window over the sink. "It's his fault I ended up in jail."

"You got the last laugh tonight." Ace scooped up a handful of jewelry, letting an emerald necklace dangle from his finger. He made it sway like a pendulum.

"But I didn't finish what I set out to do." Lenny stood up. "I'm going back."

He got his notebook and made a quick log of the jewelry before handing it over to Ace. He put the wallets into a bag to take with him back to Boston.

Back to Trevor.

Chapter 27

As Lenny left the cabin, Ace called to him, "You gotta be back here by two or you'll miss your ride." Lenny had arranged a ride to Canada. He knew his face would be too well known to stay in the country. He'd have to go away and start over. The ride wouldn't be comfortable but it would get him away from the heat. He expected to be hidden in the back of an eighteen-wheeler as a man wanted for armed robbery and murder.

He thought Trevor would be dead.

He hadn't finished the job.

Canada was too cold for him anyway.

As he retraced the route he and Ace had taken to the cabin last night, he thought about what Trevor had done to him. It was unforgivable.

The drive back to Boston went fast as he listened to reports of the robbery at the charity ball on talk radio. Traffic was light until Lenny got closer to the city. He was careful to obey the speed limit to avoid being stopped with a bagful of strangers' wallets hidden in the spare tire of a stolen truck.

Lenny had studied the maps he'd gotten off the Internet for so long that he navigated the streets like a native Bostonian. He had done his surveillance homework too. He knew where Trevor worked. He knew where Trevor parked.

Passing a tall, shiny office building, he shook his head. His boy, the dirty little dipshit that used to pee his pants, had become a businessman.

He parked and checked his gun and adjusted the car mirrors so he could see behind him. It was only a matter of time until Trevor showed up. Right now, time was all Lenny Mayhew had.

When BK Hartshaw had a lucid moment, she knew she was dying. She always thought that if someone were going to kill her, it would be Trevor.

Surprise, surprise. It was Trevor's father instead.

She knew the end was near because her life replayed like a movie projected on the back of her closed eyelids. The soundtrack was the beeps and blips of the machinery in the intensive care unit.

BK had always imagined that a review of her life would happen *after* she passed through a golden tunnel of light and had a last stop before being admitted into Heaven. There, she thought, all her deeds would be judged, from birth until death.

That's not what was happening. There hadn't been any glimmer of a tunnel, not one golden ray, not even a split-second flash. No one was showing up to judge her.

Where is the light? What if I haven't been a good enough person?

The machine sped up its tempo.

Her last panicked thought before losing consciousness again was that maybe she wasn't going to Heaven after all.

Still wearing his tuxedo, Max drove to his leased parking spot in the garage across the street from the corporate headquarters of Max-Maids. All he wanted to do was to sit behind his desk, stare out the window at his view of the city and think. He almost didn't believe what happened last night was real until he looked down at the dried blood splatters on his shirt.

He locked his car and waited for the elevator that would take him back to ground level. Just as he pressed the button he heard footsteps echoing on the concrete and a man with a strange voice calling for him to hold the door. The man moved fast, holding onto his baseball cap as if it was going to blow off.

"Thanks," the man mumbled, his head down as he made his way through the elevator door. He was carrying a gym bag and wearing jeans and a hooded sweatshirt.

Max checked the time but his wrist was bare, his watch stolen at the ball. He figured it was about six o'clock. Luckily, as the man was standing with his back to him, he didn't have to make small talk. He closed his eyes until the man punched a button, stopping the elevator abruptly.

Max gasped as the man pulled a gun from his bag.

A slow smile crept across the man's pitted face as he watched Max. "We're finally face-to-face," he said, each word dripping off his tongue like melted chocolate.

Max looked into the eyes of the bastard who had shot up the charity ball and put BK into intensive care.

Lenny Mayhew licked his thin lips. "Surprised to see me again so soon?"

Max straightened to his full height and stared down at Lenny. "I thought you'd have crawled back to the depths of Hell by now. Isn't that where you're from? Or is that where you're headed?"

Lenny shook the gun at him but seemed at a loss for words.

"You look shocked that I'm not afraid of you. You're the one who should be afraid. The police are looking for you. You don't stand a chance of escaping now. You should've gotten as far away from Boston as you could."

As Lenny took a step closer to Max, the enjoyment had been wiped from his face. "You know I have some unfinished business with you, *Trevor*."

Max recoiled at the closeness of this madman. "Trevor's dead. You killed him."

Lenny's eyes narrowed. "I killed a Trevor Hayes at that fancy ball of yours, I know that. It was all over the news. But you know damn well he wasn't the one I was after. I wanted the Trevor who's standing in front of me right now. My boy. The one who's been hiding from me all these years."

"Trevor Mayhew doesn't exist anymore. He's been gone for years. You killed him when you stabbed his grandmother. From that day on, Max Emerson took his place. I became another person. I survived."

"You shoulda disappeared years earlier. It woulda made all our lives better." Lenny's grip on the gun was so tight that his fingers were white.

"Why didn't you send me to live with my *real* father if you hated me so much?"

Lenny smirked. "He never wanted you. You shoulda heard how relieved he was that I was gonna claim you as mine."

"Give me his name."

"Never." Lenny sneered. "Bein' my son don't look like it hurt you much. In fact, you look like you done damn well for yourself, *Maxy-boy*. Rich businessman driving around in his fancy car, throwing parties to help out them so-called abused women and kiddies who were probably just getting what was coming to 'em."

"Is that the kind of thinking that helps you justify what you did to my mother and me? Does it help you sleep better at night to tell yourself that we had it coming to us or does the memory of my mother still haunt you?"

A look crossed over Lenny's face that Max was shocked to see. He took a step back. "You still love her, don't you? In your own sick, demented way, you still love my mother."

"I always will." Lenny averted his eyes for a split second. "But we ain't talking about Gail."

Max grabbed the gun.

As he twisted it from Lenny's grip, it went off.

Chapter 28

When BK was wheeled from the intensive care unit into her new room, Shelby was there holding a balloon and a stuffed teddy. "Welcome, roomie!" she said. She made the teddy's arm wave.

Faux wood-grain cabinets covered one wall of the small tan room. A chair and small table were next to the bed. Shelby tied the Get Well Soon balloon to the arm of the chair and tucked the bear in next to BK.

"Did you say roomie? Are you being readmitted or are you moving back into the apartment with me?"

"Neither," Shelby said, sitting in the chair. The helium balloon bobbed. "I got permission to spend the night here with you." She smiled. "It doesn't hurt that my dad is on the hospital's board of directors."

BK picked up the bear, dressed in green scrubs, complete with a surgical mask. "I'm going to name him Doctor Fred."

At the mention of her longtime love's name, Shelby's smile spread from her lips to her whole face. "I'm glad they were able to move you today. I've been so worried about you."

BK adjusted the wires that still attached her to a heart monitor that was wheeled in alongside her. "I honestly thought I was going to die." Looking into her friend's eyes, BK saw tears.

"I did, too. Miraculously, both of us are still here."

BK hadn't found out Shelby's fate until she regained consciousness. "When I couldn't reach you the night of the ball, I was worried beyond belief."

"We're tougher than we look."

"Funny you say that. It all started for me when I couldn't reach you," Shelby said. Settling back in the chair, she told her story.

BK sat up straight in the hospital bed when Shelby was finished. "Trevor's dead?" She knew it was bad to be grateful but that's how she felt.

"Lenny Mayhew shot him," Shelby said.

"You're free. Just like Madame Zona predicted! She said you'd be released from your prison the night of the ball."

"Free from Trevor, thanks to Lenny Mayhew. Free from the trunk Trevor stuffed me in, thanks to Robyn Prentiss and her cameraman."

"You were freed by a news team?" BK grinned. "What'd you do, call a press conference?"

"Robyn was broadcasting live from the parking lot, near my car. I had to wait until she stopped yammering long enough so they'd hear me knocking."

"What a nightmare," BK said, crooking her finger. She couldn't imagine being confined to a small space. She'd panicked when she was trapped in the elevator all those years ago and it was roomy in comparison. "Come here so I can give you a hug."

"Hold off. There's more you should know about Trevor." Shelby winked. "That is, if Madame Zona hasn't already informed you."

"I wasn't a believer either but there's no need to be sarcastic. What else do I need to know?"

"Trevor Mayhew shot his father the morning after the ball."

"Trevor Mayhew?" The last name of Shelby's stalker was Hayes. Did Shelby misspeak?

"Two Trevors. Trevor Hayes and Trevor Mayhew."

BK shook her head, trying to process the information. It didn't make sense. "There weren't two Trevors on the guest list." She'd gone over the list so many times she could probably recite most of the names by heart.

"We didn't tell you this while you were in intensive care because we didn't want to upset you." Shelby looked at BK's monitor. "Trevor Mayhew changed his name. He's known now as Max Emerson."

BK's jaw dropped.

The sun was shining through the hospital window. BK watched Shelby as she unfolded herself out of the chair and rubbed her neck. "I didn't think you'd ever wake up, sleepyhead," BK said. "I've been awake for hours thinking about Max, Lenny, and Trevor, trying to wrap my mind around it."

"I hope I wasn't drooling in my sleep like Clyde."

"I'll never tell."

Shelby reached in her bag and pulled out her laptop. "I have something that will help make everything clear for you. Lindlay Associates got Channel Six to make a copy of all the news stories for you. Your boss dropped it off after you fell asleep yesterday afternoon. He thought it would help with the PR in the aftermath of the charity ball."

"He brought me *work* to do in the hospital?"

Shelby pointed to an arrangement on the windowsill. "He brought a plant too, if that makes it any better."

"At least he didn't bring flowers. You know how I feel about floral arrangements." BK snorted as Shelby played the disc.

Robyn Prentiss's face filled the small screen.

"We're interrupting programming for breaking news. Police have just confirmed that the alleged ringleader of the shootout at the Max-Maids charity ball was pronounced dead at Boston Memorial Hospital. The suspect has been identified as Leonard Earl Mayhew of Philadelphia, Pennsylvania. He was shot early this morning after a confrontation with Max-Maids founder and CEO, Max Emerson. We'll update you as more details become available."

Now BK understood why Max was so evasive about his past. All the times he dodged her questions made sense. Suddenly Stanley didn't seem so bad.

Robyn was still talking. "That brings the death toll related to the charity ball to two. It has been confirmed that Trevor J. Hayes, a local Boston resident attending the ball, was pronounced dead at the scene. Eleven others were wounded."

Robyn paused briefly. She looked like she was trying to stifle a sneeze.

"Another suspect, Delores P. Digby of Boston, seen here in an exclusive Channel Six interview immediately following the robbery, has been taken in for questioning after police searched Mayhew's motel room and found personal items belonging to Digby. The connection between Digby, a Van Buren Plaza employee, and Mayhew is not yet known." Robyn flipped a page on the desk in front of her.

"In a related story, Shelby Fulton, daughter of A & F Industries president and founder, Thomas Fulton, was found locked inside the trunk of her car in the parking lot of the Van Buren Plaza minutes after the shooting ended."

Shelby cringed as it showed the close-up of her taken as she was rescued from the trunk. They had zoomed in on the tears that filled her eyes as the police ripped duct tape off her mouth.

BK gasped. "That looked like it hurt."

Onscreen, Robyn shoved the microphone in Shelby's direction while bombarding her with questions.

"No details are being released pending a full investigation by the police but Channel Six has learned that Trevor J. Hayes, one of the shooting victims, had recently been arrested for allegedly stalking Fulton. Hayes was out on bail awaiting trial. We'll expand this report on the six o'clock news. Now we'll return you to your regularly scheduled programming."

Max arrived holding a cactus. He thought it was appropriate since he had been as easy to get close to as the thorny plant. "Is she feeling up to visitors?" He set it on the windowsill.

"She's sleeping," Shelby said before giving him an update on BK's condition.

BK opened her eyes. "Max!"

She sounded happy to see him. He searched her face for clues. She should be angry, any other woman would be. He had lied to her, the only person who deserved to know the whole truth. Max kissed her cheek and sat in the chair by her bed. "You gave me quite a scare. When I saw you collapse on the floor, I thought you'd been shot. It never crossed my mind that something was wrong with your heart."

"I'm getting better. They unhooked the heart monitor this morning."

"The years of living with anorexia took a toll on you," Shelby said.

BK's lips pressed together in a thin line.

Max understood that she didn't want to talk about it but it was time to get her problem out in the open. "We need to talk about the elephant in the room."

"Hey! No need to call names. This elephant will be back later. You two need to be alone." Shelby grabbed her bag and left.

Max rubbed his hands together "I was afraid I was going to lose you without being able to say what's on my mind and in my heart. Do you feel up to talking?"

After a moment she answered, "I guess so."

Before they had a chance to get started, Doctor Holland stuck her head in through the open door. "Have a minute?"

BK waved her in and introduced Max.

"I already know her. I've been seeing her since our breakup." Max stood and shook her hand. He looked at BK expectantly, waiting for her to explain her connection to the doctor.

"She's my therapist too. She's been treating me for my elephantiasis."

Doctor Holland looked puzzled. "You can explain that one to me later. I'm available to see you this afternoon if you want."

"Yes, I'd like that," BK said. "We have a lot to talk about."

Max waited until she was gone. He knew what BK had meant. "You've been getting treatment for your anorexia?"

"I was going to tell you the night you broke up with me. It was going to be a big surprise."

Max touched the side of his face. *I refused to listen,* he thought. *What an idiot. All the time spent apart was my fault.* "I remember you said something about appointments." He moved to the edge of the bed and took her hand in his. "You know it was a lie when I said that I didn't care anymore. I want to work things out between us, BK. I can't live without you."

She put her hand on her chest. "It's a good thing I'm free of the monitor or the nurses would be racing in here thinking something is wrong."

"The only thing wrong around here is my thick-headedness."

An elderly man with a walker paused at the doorway and looked at them before continuing on his way.

"And a troubled past."

Max gazed out at the parking lot. An ambulance with lights flashing and siren wailing drove toward the emergency room entrance. Where could he begin? His life in a few words: abused, kidnapped, loved, transformed. He looked back at her. "All those times you accused me of holding back, not telling you about my past, you were right. I was scared by our relationship so I backed off and tried to push you away. But I never felt like we broke up."

"Me either. The words said we did but my heart said we didn't." She smiled and the sun hit a part of his soul that had been dark for years.

"I shut off my emotions for a long time, until I met you. I've never gotten serious about anyone else. You're special."

She leaned forward and hugged him.

He pulled away, walked over to the window and leaned his head against the glass. "When you hear the whole story you might not want to be involved with someone like me. My past is..." He searched for the right word. "Complicated. And because of it, I didn't dare love anyone as much as I loved you."

Max took a deep breath and looked at her. "Until the night of the ball, I believed Lenny Mayhew was my biological father. I don't care who my real father is as long as he isn't Lenny. All these years I tried not to be like him and it turns out I had no reason to worry after all. It's always been in the back of my mind that I could be like him."

"Never," BK said. "You're one of the kindest people I know. You couldn't be cruel."

He sat back down and revealed his entire past. He thought he'd feel naked but instead he felt weightless, floating on a cloud of relief.

When he finally stopped talking, BK had concern etched on her face. "What happened to your grandmother? Was she.... killed?"

"Lenny could never get the best of her. She had a slow recovery but she was tough and bounced back. She spent her final years in a retirement village in Florida fighting off advances from old men in the winter and the rest of the year up here with me. She lived long enough to see me succeed but her true joy came from seeing me happy rather than anything I could buy for her. She passed away two years ago." BK touched his hand. He missed Gram every day. "She would have loved you."

"She sounds like a special lady."

"She was but I'll tell you all about her another day." He let go of her and stood. "I want you to get back to your nap. You look exhausted."

She settled back in the bed. "Answer one last question before you go. Why were you so scared by our relationship?"

"I saw the anorexia consuming you and I couldn't face losing another person that I loved."

Tears filled her eyes. "You'll never lose me."

Chapter 29

She couldn't believe it, but BK was driving to Madame Zona's house. She'd never tell Shelby or she wouldn't hear the end of it.

Zona lived in a small cape in the suburbs. Inside, the living room was strung with plastic ivy intertwined with twinkling white lights. Angels were everywhere—pictures on the walls, dusty figurines on shelves and tables, and one was painted on the ceiling.

"Sit," Madame Zona said, moving an angel blanket to make room on the couch cluttered with pillows.

BK waited while Zona closed her eyes.

"Congratulations are in order," she said so loudly and suddenly that BK jumped. "You're getting married by the end of the summer."

BK cringed as Shelby jabbed her scalp with a comb attached to her veil. They were standing in Stanley's library in Seaside. Nothing felt more natural than preparing to spend the rest of her life with Max... until Shelby tried to perform brain surgery with a hair comb instead of a scalpel.

"You've always had such a tender head. I can't remember a time when you haven't fussed when I've done your hair," Shelby said. "If you want it to stay on through the entire ceremony, you'll have to put up with a little pain."

"I don't think Max would be too thrilled to see me walking down the aisle like a zombie with blood dripping from my head." BK put her arms out straight in front of her and groaned.

"Oh, please." Shelby checked her watch. "We better get out there before Max marries someone else. Someone who *doesn't* complain."

"She doesn't exist."

Shelby arranged BK's train. Her strapless gown was tightly fitted down to her thighs where it flared out like a mermaid. The bodice was covered with Alençon lace and tied at the waist with a satin bow. "You look beautiful," Shelby said, her voice breaking.

BK still wasn't completely ready to accept herself as beautiful but she was getting there. Time to deflect. "And you look gorgeous."

Shelby twirled in her sea glass-colored sleeveless dress. The knee-length skirt billowed around her. "Not too bad for a *bridesmaid's* dress."

"Fred's going to propose today for sure."

"One wedding at a time. Let's turn you into Mrs. Max Emerson and then we'll worry about me. Are you ready to hear Max say vows that include the word *love*?"

"I've been ready since the first moment I met him." She hugged her friend. "I'm so lucky. I have the man of my dreams and the best friend anyone could ever imagine."

Shelby rolled her eyes. "Go get married before you gag me with all this sentimental mush." She bent down and straightened the hem of her dress but BK saw her swipe a tear from the corner of her eye.

They stayed out of sight until Shelby signaled the harpist to start playing. "Good luck, kiddo," she whispered.

BK listened to the ocean slapping against the rocks in the distance. A slight sea breeze caught her veil and suspended it in the air behind her as she peeked through the rose covered arch. It was the doorway to her new life, a life she no longer expected to be perfect. It wouldn't be easy but with Max and Shelby by her side, anything was possible, even happiness.

THE END

AMY RAY

Before embarking on a writing career, Amy Ray owned an old fashioned five and dime store where, in addition to regular priced merchandise, she had a display of items that actually retailed for five or ten cents each. Her first novel, *Dangerous Denial,* was published in 2014 by Barking Rain Press. She also has a short story published in *Love Free or Die,* the fourth book in the *New Hampshire Pulp Fiction* anthology series.

Ms. Ray lives near the short but picturesque seacoast in New Hampshire with her husband and daughter. You can find our more about her at her website, on her Writer Amy Ray Facebook page, or on Twitter @WriterAmyRay.

WWW.WRITERAMYRAY.COM

About Barking Rain Press

Did you know that five media conglomerates publish eighty percent of the books in the United States? As the publishing industry continues to contract, opportunities for emerging and mid-career authors are drying up. Who will write the literature of the twenty-first century if just a handful of profit-focused corporations are left to decide who—and what—is worthy of publication?

Barking Rain Press is dedicated to the creation and promotion of thoughtful and imaginative contemporary literature, which we believe is essential to a vital and diverse culture. As a nonprofit organization, Barking Rain Press is an independent publisher that seeks to cultivate relationships with new and mid-career writers over time, to be thorough in the editorial process, and to make the publishing process an experience that will add to an author's development—and ultimately enhance our literary heritage.

In selecting new titles for publication, Barking Rain Press considers authors at all points in their careers. Our goal is to support the development of emerging and mid-career authors—not just single books—as we know from experience that a writer's audience is cultivated over the course of several books.

Support for these efforts comes primarily from the sale of our publications; we also hope to attract grant funding and private donations. Whether you are a reader or a writer, we invite you to take a stand for independent publishing and become more involved with Barking Rain Press. With your support, we can make sure that talented writers thrive, and that their books reach the hands of spirited, curious readers. Find out more at our website.

WWW.BARKINGRAINPRESS.ORG

Also from Barking Rain Press

VIEW OUR COMPLETE CATALOG ONLINE:

WWW.BARKINGRAINPRESS.ORG

Made in the USA
Charleston, SC
11 May 2015